THE STORM PETREL

After young Cressy Latimer is blinded in an accident, which also killed her mother, she returns with her father to the remote Cornish Cove where she had been happy as a child. There, she renews her friendship with her childhood companion, Milo, and tries to come to terms with her blindness. Milo is wonderful with injured animals and extends his care and kindness to Cressy. At last, she dares to return to her specialist in London, hoping for good news about her sight, while Milo waits patiently and devotedly for her return — whether she is sighted or not.

Books by Elizabeth Webster
Published by The House of Ulverscroft:

CHILD OF FIRE
THE FLIGHT OF THE SWAN
SHADOW INTO SUNLIGHT
DOLPHIN SUNRISE
HOME SWEET HOME
THE ACORN WINTER
CLOUD SHADOWS
FOX COURAGE

ELIZABETH WEBSTER

THE STORM PETREL

Complete and Unabridged

ULVERSCROFT
Leicester

First Large Print Edition
published 2001

British Library CIP Data

Webster, Elizabeth
  The storm petrel.—Large print ed.—
  Ulverscroft large print series: general fiction
  1. Love stories
  2. Large type books
  I. Title
  823.9'14 [F]

  ISBN 0–7089–4355–1

Published by
F. A. Thorpe (Publishing)
Anstey, Leicestershire
Set by Words & Graphics Ltd.
Anstey, Leicestershire
Printed and bound in Great Britain by
T. J. International Ltd., Padstow, Cornwall

This book is printed on acid-free paper

Part One

The Coming of the Dark

The bird fell out of the sky at the old man's feet. It landed in a small heap of crumpled feathers on the foredeck of the little inshore crabber — *Kittiwake II* — and lay there panting, too weary, too battered by the wild sea winds to go any further.

The old fisherman bent down to have a look at it. A Storm Petrel, he thought. What was it doing so far inshore? It was a bird of the open seas, following the trawlers as they made their way to and from the far fishing-grounds of the wide Atlantic ocean ... Out there, where he had earned his nickname — Gramp-the-Champ — as he led his little fishing fleet out of Port Quentin and chased the Spanish trawlers every watery sea-mile off his threatened fishing grounds.

'You're a long way from home,' he told the bird. 'I'll put you somewhere warm where you can rest a bit, shall I?' And he picked up the tiny, exhausted body in his calloused fisherman's hands and walked over to a coil of fibrous rope lying alongside the hatch. He could feel the bird's tired heart still beating, still palpitating against his fingers, still struggling not to die. 'You lie there,' he told it, laying it gently down on the rough, warm rope, 'while I get *Kittiwake* home. And maybe Milo will come and have a look at you. He'll know what to do.'

He wasn't far from the shore now — he'd had a good day's crabbing, and there was enough catch to supply the local hotels and restaurants and perhaps leave him something for his tea. It was time to turn for home and slip into Port Quentin harbour with the tide. He would be just in time for Milo's school bus to arrive in the harbour square, and his grandson nearly always stopped by to see if Gramp was in with the little crabber, *Kittiwake*, or out with his crew on the big trawler, *Crystal Rose*.

The sea was like silk this afternoon, calm and still, and with that certain glowing light on it that is not only the reflection of the summer sun in a cloudless blue sky, but yet has an extra silvery radiance of its own. He surveyed it contentedly, and rounded the long, jagged point of tawny rock that sheltered the hidden inlet of Port Quentin's perfect harbour.

Nearly in. The trawlers were in too, but they would be going out tonight, and he would be with them. His buccaneering days might be over — the Spanish trawlers were

too big and powerful to fight any more
— but he still led out his little fleet, daring
all comers. He might be getting old, but he
was not done yet! . . . Just let him get this
small catch in, and he'd be ready for them.

He nosed his tubby crabber into the jetty
and settled her in her safe, familiar berth
along the quay. He had just finished tying
her up when he saw young Milo coming
towards him across the square.

'Got a visitor for you,' said Gramp, smiling
at his tall young grandson. 'Come and see.'

Together they stood looking down at the
bird on the coil of rope. It had not moved,
but its eyes were open, and it watched
them with a kind of defeated resignation,
and no fear.

'A Storm Petrel!' exclaimed Milo. 'What's
it doing here?'

'Blown off course,' said Gramp. He was
used to birds hitching a lift on his trawler
out at sea — they often did it, perching
on the rail or the trawl rigging, or even
the wheelhouse roof, and staying there, safe
and mostly dry in spite of the spray, until
their tired wings were ready for the next
lap of their endless journeyings across the
wild reaches of the ocean swell. But Storm
Petrels didn't often come so close in shore.
They drifted endlessly over the surface of

those distant seas, and only came near land to nest in some far rocky islet.

'Nothing for her to eat round here,' said Milo in a worried tone. 'Deep sea plankton is what she needs.'

'She?' asked Gramp, looking from the crumpled bird to Milo with a certain respect. Milo knew his birds and animals.

'I think so . . . though it's hard to tell — the colouring's the same . . . ' He stooped over the bird and scooped the limp bundle up in his hands, cradling the exhausted creature in gentle fingers.

'You'd better take her home and see what you can do with her,' said Gramp, and began to unload his wicker baskets of crab and lobster, scallops and a few flatfish on to the jetty.

Milo regarded him thoughtfully. 'Are you going out again tonight? Shall I give you a hand?'

'No!' Gramp spoke a bit roughly, and then mitigated it with a roguish grin. 'Not with your mother on the war path! I promised her, remember?' He gave Milo a cheerful pat on his shoulder — noting with surprise that the boy was almost as tall as he was now-a-days. 'You go on home, boy, and get your tea and please your mother. And see to the bird — that's enough for one evening!'

6

Milo laughed. But he looked at his grandfather's weatherworn face and the fine wrinkles round those far-seeing blue seaman's eyes, and thought the old man looked a little tired today. Then he looked down at the bird and said in a considering voice: 'They are supposed to foretell rough weather, aren't they? What's the forecast like?'

'Not bad,' said Gramp. 'Nothing startling.' His wide gaze swept the smooth still-glowing bay, and beyond it to the far horizon. 'Mild as milk,' he said.

Milo's eyes were full of distance like his grandfather's, and they were the same blue, deep and steady and with a curious inner glow of their own which seemed to reflect things that no-one else could reach. 'There's different kinds of storms,' he said, 'and different darks . . . '

Gramp looked at him a little sharply, and gave him a none-too-gentle push. 'Go on with you. Stop talking in riddles. I don't believe in omens.'

Milo grinned at his grandfather's disapproving glare, and sauntered off into the late afternoon sunlight, carrying the tired bird in his hands.

Gramp watched him set off on his long climb up the cliff path to his mother's cottage down in the next little cove, and then turned once more to gaze out at the sea. It seemed to him as he watched the tranquil swell moving gently with the tide in a shimmer of sunlight, that far out near the horizon there was a slow veil of darkness creeping out and quenching the pure, pale light of the sleeping sea.

★ ★ ★

The day Cressy's world went dark began like any other. There was breakfast as usual, and then the school run, with Sally, her cheerful, pretty mother, dropping Cressy off at the school gates on her way to the station for Stephen, Cressy's father, to catch his train to Waterloo, close to the Studio where he worked. Cressy was quite old enough now, at fourteen nearly fifteen, to go to and from school on her own, but their suburban house was at the end of a long road away from the bus route, and there had been rumours of a prowler around the area lately, so Sally preferred to pick up Cressy after school as well, not taking any risks. Cressy didn't mind. She and Sally were pretty close, pretty good friends as mothers and daughters go, and there was a good feeling of warmth and reassurance when Cressy came out of school and saw Sally waiting for her by the car.

Cressy waved, and Sally waved back and smiled a welcome. She was talking to another parent, and looked happy and relaxed in the sunshine. Cressy thought with unexpected appreciation that her mother looked rather beautiful, too, with her long fair hair shining and that warm and loving smile reaching out to her across the pavement.

But then an extraordinary change came over her mother's face, and the smile froze into a look of absolute horror, and she began to run frantically towards Cressy, shouting something unintelligible. It sounded like 'Get back!' or 'Get down!' and Cressy hesitated, looking vaguely round for the trouble her mother had seen. She had just time to recognise the desperate urgency in her mother's eyes, and turn fractionaly to see the gaggle of smaller children pouring out on to the pavement, oblivious of the danger behind them. She had been almost oblivious too, but that flick of white-hot terror in her mother's face had just reached her.

'Look out!' she shouted, shoving wildly at the surging bodies of the children.

'Look out!' shouted Sally, and rushed forward straight into the path of the drunkenly careering wheels and lethal heap of shining metal approaching, just in time to give Cressy an enormous push to the side.

But even so, something lifted Cressy off her feet and flung her forward against the brick wall of the school playground. There was a squealing of brakes, a huge, flat-sounding bang of metal against stone — and then the world went dark.

* * *

Stephen was working from his drawing board to his computer, transferring what he privately considered to be much better and subtler freehand to the brash restrictions of the computerised version of his art-work that the commercial world required, when his desk phone rang and he was informed that the police were asking for him downstairs. He abandoned his work, not without relief, and went down in the lift, puzzled at the summons and trying to recall whether had failed to pay an important bill or forgotten his Council Tax or something, — or parked his car in the wrong place. Then he remembered that he hadn't got his car today, Sally was using it, and he got slightly more worried. But when he saw the grave faces of the two men waiting for him, he knew it was something much worse.

'Mr. Latimer?' asked the older of the two, grey-haired and kindly, and carefully neutral of tone. 'I'm afraid we have some bad news for you.' He glanced round and politely pushed a chair towards Stephen as if he expected him to collapse any minute. Stephen refused and stood still, while his heart did a sudden flip of terror.

'Bad news?'

The police sergeant cleared his throat. 'I'm afraid so. There has been a serious accident — outside your daughter's school.'

'Cressy?' Stephen jerked out, sharp with shock. '*Cressy*? Is she all right?'

'She is in hospital, Mr. Latimer. But we are informed that she *will* be all right.' The quiet voice seemed to hesitate then, as if he had not told quite all the story.

'Oh, thank God!' breathed Stephen. But he had not missed that slight hesitation, and he knew there was more to come.

'But your wife . . . ' went on the inexorable voice, still with exemplory quietude, clearly hating what it had to say and trying to keep the atmosphere calm.

'My wife? Sally?' Stephen, pale with shock already, had gone even whiter, and only just managed to control an insane desire to take the mild-mannered sergeant by the shoulders and shake him out of his careful kindness. '*What's happened to Sally?*'

The kindly policeman blinked, recognising

Stephen's desperation, and went doggedly on. 'It was a car — an ordinary family saloon car — went out of control and mounted the pavement behind your daughter. Your wife saw it coming and rushed forward to push your daughter out of its path . . . '

'She was very brave,' interjected the young policeman helpfully.

'So was your daughter,' agreed the older man, also trying to find something comforting to say. 'She tried to push the younger children away in time, too. And maybe she risked her own life staying a shade too long, — but your wife reached her in time.'

'And — ?' He hardly dared even ask the question. His heart already knew the answer.

'Your daughter was flung clear,' reported the neutral voice tonelessly, 'though the wing of the car caught her a glancing blow, I am told, and hurled her against the school wall . . . But your wife — '

'Yes?' snapped Stephen, forcing it out.

'*She didn't have a chance.*' The quiet voice had changed somehow to helpless pity. 'I am so sorry, — she was killed outright.'

'Oh, my God,' said Stephen dully, and rubbed an incredulous hand over his eyes. 'Oh . . . dear God! *Sally?*' My lovely, darling Sally? *Killed outright?*

'It was a joyrider, in a stolen car,' added the young policeman brightly, offering what helpful information he could.

'A joyrider?' Stephen's voice was bleak. 'A joyrider?' *What joy was there in a young girl injured, a young wife dead?*

'We have come to take you to the hospital,' explained the older man, his voice even gentler now. 'You will be needed.'

'Yes . . . yes, of course,' agreed Stephen, accepting the sudden disintegration of his shattered world with numb acquiescence.

'This way, — ' they said.

And the nightmare journey began.

★ ★ ★

In the hospital everyone was painfully kind, and he was taken first to see Cressy, who was either unconscious or asleep — he didn't know which, and he was afraid to ask. She was lying quietly in a small side-cubicle of the intensive care unit, ('though it's only a precaution really, after a head injury. She'll be out of here tomorrow.') She looked pale and ethereal, fair hair spread out on the pillow under a swathe of bandages. But her breathing seemed even and untroubled, and her expression was one of childish serenity, washed in quiet sleep. And his heart seemed

13

to clench with terror and pity when he thought of the news he would have to break to her when she woke up. *At least she's alive*, he thought, *my precious young daughter . . . But at what expense?*

'She will be all right,' murmured the nurse, smiling encouragement at Stephen's shocked and grief-stricken face. 'When she wakes up, you'll be able to talk to her.'

'Yes,' gulped Stephen. 'Thanks.'

Then they took him down to the hospital chapel where they left him alone with his young wife, Sally: his beautiful, young dead wife, Sally . . .

He was not really aware of how he felt. He didn't think he could feel anything at all yet. But presently he found himself leaning his own head close beside her fair one and weeping helplessly like a child. She looked so young, so lovely and unspoilt — as if she was only sleeping, like her own young daughter in the high hospital bed in the ward above.

'Oh Sally,' he whispered. 'Oh Sally, my dear love, *why*?'

But he knew why — there was an answer to that, albeit an answer of bitter necessity. Sally had died to save her young daughter, Cressy. It had been an instant decision, brave and swift, without hesitation, without counting any cost, that he knew. She had seen the need — she had done what was required of her, what she chose to do. She had known with perfect clarity what the risks were, what the choices were in that split-second moment of decision, and Cressy's future had seemed to her of paramount importance. How could he, Stephen, loving her as he did, *question* that decision? How could he refuse such a sacrifice? . . . And how could he even want to, since he loved his young daughter, too?

But all the same, his heart grieved and ached with irretrievable loss . . . His own, inexpressibly dear, warm-hearted Sally, the focus of his dreams and all his hopes and ambitions, his own dear love, his friend, his ally in all the battles of life, was gone from him . . . And he was left with a daughter to save, a young life to be given room to grow, a future to plan for her, with no looking back, no regrets, no vain longings for a world of unshadowed brightness that could never come back — never be so filled with unthinking happiness again. And Sally, dear brave Sally in her brilliant courageous clarity, had laid this charge on him. There was no way he could refuse this challenge, — nor would he ever want to. But his heart still wept for his loving companion, for the bright days that were gone.

'Oh Sally,' he wept. 'Oh Sally, my heart's love, *where do we go from here?*'

'Mr. Latimer?' said a gentle voice at his side. 'Your daughter is asking for you.'

* * *

'Dad?' said Cressy, not sounding very sure about anything.

'Yes, Cressy, I'm here.' He reached out and took her questing hand in his. Her fingers felt cool and rather slack, but they suddenly gripped his hand hard as she asked the question that no-one yet had dared to answer.

'Where's Mum?'

Stephen swallowed hard. She'll have to know, he told himself. We can't keep her in the dark for ever. But how do I break it gently — with the least shock? 'She's — she can't be with you just now,' he began weakly. 'But she's not far away.'

That was true, at least. Only one floor away — on a different kind of bed . . . But he despised himself for his own weakness — for failing Cressy even now, at the perilous beginning of their new life together . . . their new, lonely life together . . .

'She's dead, isn't she?' said Cressy's voice, clear and cold and hard beside him.

16

Stephen sighed. Trust Cressy to get straight to the point — to sweep away all pretences, all attempts to soften stark facts. Her painful honesty was always difficult to live up to, — and her courage. She takes after Sally, he thought grimly. Not me. I don't have her ruthless clarity. 'Yes, Cressy, I'm afraid she is,' he said at last, and added, echoing the policeman's helpless protest: '*She didn't have a chance.*'

Cressy was silent for a moment. She didn't cry out or weep easy tears. She just lay there under her bandages, trying to put her thoughts in order. 'I don't understand what happened,' she said, her voice so querulous that it was almost cross. 'Why won't anyone tell me?'

'I will tell you,' answered Stephen arduously. 'But you will have to try to see it from Sally's point of view. Not yours. Or mine.'

'Yes?' Cressy was straining at understanding, her open, flower face tense with the effort of concentration, the wide, sea-green eyes dark with thought.

'It was a — a joyrider,' said Stephen, punishing himself all over again with the heartless phrase. 'In a stolen car. It came up behind you on to the pavement, out of control . . . You heard it coming, didn't you?'

Cressy frowned. 'Not till the brakes squealed.'

'No,' agreed Stephen sadly. 'Not until almost too late. But Sally saw it . . . She was looking your way, wasn't she?'

'Yes. She was smiling.' Cressy's voice was small and cold.

'Until she saw what was happening, — the danger to you . . . '

'She looked so beautiful in the sun,' Cressy said, in a strange voice of dream. 'And then — and then her face *changed* . . . and she began to run — ' She stopped abruptly as she remembered the sudden push, the flat, hard sound of the crashing metal behind her, her own wild attempt to push away the other scattering children . . . and the coming of the dark . . .

'She did the only thing possible,' said Stephen, trying to convince himself as well as his young, bewildered daughter. 'She just had time for you.'

'But not for herself?' The small voice was still hard and cold.

'No,' admitted Stephen heavily. 'Not for herself.' Then he rallied, once more trying to put it into terms that Cressy could accept. 'She was very brave,' he began, and meant to go on: 'She gave her life for you . . . ' But somehow he could not say that, could not lay such a burden on Cressy — a lifelong weight of gratitude and obligation — so he said nothing more.

'I don't want her life,' said Cressy, as if he had spoken, and her voice was even flatter and colder. And then, with a sudden surge of inescapable grief, she cried out fiercely: 'I want her *here*! *Now*!'

'I know,' said Stephen. 'I know, Cressy. So do I.'

And then he did the only practical and sensible thing that could possibly help the two of them now, — he put his arms round Cressy in the hospital bed and held her close while she wept away her immediate grief and shock, and if he wept a little too, it did neither of them any harm.

At length she drew back a little from Stephen's warm, protective arms and said rather breathlessly: 'I'm sorry, Dad . . . I didn't mean to make a fuss.'

Stephen almost groaned. He knew how Cressy hated weakness, hated to give way to personal despairs and griefs. She always had been a brave and uncomplaining child (like her mother, again, he thought) and always painfully independent and self-contained.

'I think you are entitled to a bit of fuss,' he said, trying to keep it light. 'We both are — '

She turned her head towards him then, hearing the cadence of grief in her father's voice, and said, almost peevishly: 'I wish you'd come a bit nearer. I can't see you properly.' She pushed impatiently at the bandages on her forehead, and added: 'It's very dark in here.'

Stephen looked round at the brightly-lit ward, and then at Cressy's face beneath her bandages, and felt his own heart grow cold. Her eyes were not obscured by any folds of gauze or lint. They were gazing straight at him in a puzzled way, *trying to see in the dark.*

★ ★ ★

'I didn't take her seriously,' said the little nurse, appalled. 'She asked me if the hospital was on fire, — the ward was full of smoke, she said . . . I thought she was still a bit concussed and confused . . . ' Her voice trailed away as she took in the implications of what Cressy had said. Then crisp decision came back to her professional mind. 'I'll page Doctor Morris. He's still in the hospital somewhere.'

Euan Morris was a kind young man, and he did not want to harass Cressy with too many questions at present. He felt she had suffered enough trauma for one day, so he went very gently. There would be time enough for more detailed and specialist examination later on. 'I gather you are finding it a bit dark in here,' he said carefully. 'Can you tell me, Cressy, how clearly you can see your Dad's face?'

'He's a bit fuzzy at the edges,' she said, still sounding rather querulous. 'And greyish . . . It's so smoky in here.'

Euan Morris looked across at Stephen, but he made no comment on that. Nor did Stephen. 'But you can tell where he is?' the young doctor persisted, still very gently.

'If he comes close enough,' Cressy said, and put out her hand to pull Stephen closer. But her hand collided with Stephen's face leaning over her, and her fingers fitted themselves round the contours of his jawline and chin and held him still. 'Am I going blind?' she asked, as clear and direct as ever.

Euan Morris hesitated. 'You've had a nasty bang on the head,' he explained reasonably. 'All sorts of funny things can happen then, you know. But they are probably only temporary. Shock can take many forms.'

'Can it?' Her voice was still clear and cold. But then she added in a curiously dry and adult tone to me: 'I hope you're right.'

21

Stephen hoped so, too — fervently — but he did not say so.

'We'll sort things out tomorrow,' said Euan kindly. 'The best thing you can do now is rest.' He patted her gently on the arm, mouthed a silent repeat of 'Tomorrow' to Stephen, and went away on quiet feet through the hospital corridors.

Cressy took hold of Stephen's hand again and shut the eyes that could no longer see him clearly. 'All right,' she sighed, making no complaint. 'Tomorrow . . . '

And Stephen sat on beside her, hoping she would sleep.

★ ★ ★

Milo took the steep short-cut over the cliffs to get down to the back of the little cove where his mother's cottage stood, — sturdy and plain, rough stone and slate roof, with its back to the wall of rock. He had a small workshop of his own behind the outhouse, where various of his protegées among the animal population of the Cornish headlands were given shelter and sanctuary, and what help he knew how to give.

The bird lay quiet in his hands, frantic heart still beating, but it was very tired now, and he was afraid it would die before he got it home to somewhere safe and warm.

'Hang on in there, bird,' he told it. 'We'll soon be home . . . ' and he strode on, unconcerned by the sharp edges and slippery flanks of the golden rocks above Crocker's Cove.

There were only two cottages in the Cove now, though long ago there had been a small row of them further up the narrow gap in the hills where the brown-trout stream tumbled into the little bay. Now they were just a fallen pile of stones where the bright lizards and lazy slow-worms sunned themselves on summer days. His mother's cottage stood back, looking across the Cove, but the second one was built further out along the rocky shore-line, with one upstairs window facing straight out to sea. It was known, from the long-distant past, as the Wrecker's Cottage, because of that wicked upstairs window where a light could be put to lure unsuspecting boats on to the fangs of those lethal rocks that enclosed Crocker's Cove in their unrelenting grip. Now, of course, there were no wreckers, but it made a good name to lure holiday-makers and visitors in the summer when his mother could let it for a useful sum. His mother did not own either of the cottages herself, but rented them from an absentee landlord, who in turn had some protective agreement with the National Trust. The whole of that beautiful headland and its hidden, secret coves and little streams and rocky valleys owed its unspoilt tranquillity to that protection (and to the steep, difficult access) and Milo had somehow become the local protector of its innocent wildlife.

'Come on, bird, we're home now,' he said, and slipped in through the old wooden door of his workshop shed. There were several cages round the wall, and his deep blue eyes swept round them, swiftly checking on his charges — the fox cub with the injured paw, the two orphaned baby hedgehogs, the angry squirrel with half a tail, and the hare recovering from a twist of snare wire round its neck. Then, seeing that all was well, he laid the tiny Storm Petrel down in an old colander full of dried grass which he had often used before as a temporary resting-place. 'You lie there and get your breath back,' he said, 'and I'll see if I can find you any food.' He took a long summing-up look at the crumpled feathers and the faintly heaving breast, and decided that she would be all right till he came back.

'A few shrimps?' he said to her, aloud, 'or a bit of chopped-up mussel?' He looked round his workshop shelves, and his gaze settled on a small green glass jar standing on top of a pile of papers. It had been left behind by the people from the seal sanctuary when they had come to collect the sick seal he had rescued the other day. 'A mixture of krill and plankton and vitamins,' they said. 'A liquid feed. You only have to mix it with sea-water. It helps to keep them going when they're too young to eat . . . ' Or too tired, he wondered? But he thought, looking back at the bird, that she would be better left alone for a little while. He might try feeding her when she'd recovered a bit.

He picked up the glass jar and set it down near the bird, to remind himself, but as he did so he dislodged an old photograph lying underneath. It was a faded snapshot of a group of children on the beach at Crocker's Cove — a group that had once been a gang of his childhood friends, and one small girl who was one of his mother's first family visitors at the Wrecker's Cottage . . . He had been very fond of that small girl, he remembered, and she had been fond of him, following after him on her skinny little legs, and climbing the rocks fearlessly wherever he and his friends chose to go . . . Cressy Latimer, he told himself, little golden-haired Cressy . . . He had often thought of her as he went to and fro across that beach, for she seemed to be a part of its pale sands and golden rocks, and the shimmering sea at its edge . . . I wonder where she's got to now? he said, and went out to look for some shellfish for the bird.

He was just crossing the path leading down to the beach, when he almost walked into his mother, who was going in through the door with a pile of washing which had been bleaching in time-honoured fashion on the sunbaked rocks behind the house.

'What have you got there?' said his mother, her voice sharp with suspicion. 'Not another stray?'

Catherine Trevelyan's face was almost as sharp as her voice, though she would have been a pretty woman if she had allowed herself to relax. Her eyes were dark as sloes, not like her son's clear blue ones, and seemed to smoulder with a hidden fire. Her hair was darker than Milo's, and whereas his was a wild, windblown tangle, hers was coiled into two stiff snail-shell braids and clamped tight high on her head, giving her the unbending, regal carriage of one of the ancient Cornish queens. And her figure was as slender and straight as an arrow and just as taut, — a lethal weapon, held back in black anger, waiting to strike.

Milo sighed. He knew — all too well — his

mother's moods of black anger, and he knew, with the anguished understanding of an inarticulate boy, the reason for its cause. It was the sea — the wild and turbulent sea that he loved and feared and sometimes hated and yet still rejoiced in every day of his life — that had put that fierce rage into her soul. The sea that had taken his father, Kitto Trevelyan, in the prime of his young and lusty life, with a wife and son to come home to, — had taken a man who loved the sea and went willingly into its arms to rescue a fisherman friend, and did not stop to count the cost, — a storm-ridden, unforgiving sea that swept him away, and *did not take Gramp-the-Champ*, Kitt's father, the skipper of their boat, who could so much more easily be spared. At least in Catherine's eyes. Yes, Mil knew the cause of that anger, and he always did his best to soothe it down or help to deflect it. One day, perhaps, she would stop hating the sea and hating Gramp-the-Champ for a tragedy that was not his fault, and begin to live again.

'It's only a bird, Mum — a Storm Petrel. Blown off course or something.'

Catherine snorted. 'It *must* have been! They're ocean-flying, aren't they? Where did you find it?'

'I didn't find it,' said Mil unwarily. 'It was on Gramp's boat.'

'On *Crystal Rose*? Have you been out with him again on *Crystal Rose*?' Her voice was growing ominously strident.

'No, of course not. It was on *Kittiwake*. He was only out crabbing.'

'And you went with him, I suppose — in spite of all I've said?

Milo shook his head and spoke patiently. 'No, Mum, I didn't. I haven't even been on board. I offered to help him unload, and he wouldn't let me, because he said he'd promised you.'

'I'm glad to hear it,' snapped Catherine.

'Well, I wasn't,' said Milo, suddenly deciding to speak out.

'*What?*'

'He needed help, Mum, — and I was ashamed not to be able to give it. He was humping all those baskets of crab and lobster on to the jetty, — and he's not getting any younger. He looks *tired*. I was . . . I'm a bit worried about him . . . '

'Well, he's only himself to blame.' Catherine's firm mouth was one bitter straight line. 'He could leave the sea, and stop trying to drag you into his way of life, too.'

Milo looked at his mother in despair. How could he get through that bitter anger? 'It's his living,' he said sadly, 'and you know it. He doesn't *know* any other way of life. How could he? He loves the sea.'

'More fool him.'

'That's as maybe. It's his choice.' Milo sounded suddenly adult and authoritative. He took a deep breath and dared to go on. 'And it was Dad's choice too, remember? He *chose* to work on the sea, — just as he chose to go after his mate when he went overboard. It was Dad's *own* choice — not Gramp's — and I — I'm proud of him for what he did!'

Catherine stared at her son in surprise. It was the first time he had ever dared to speak of Kitto's death in such terms. 'Well, I'm not!' she snarled. 'Wasting a good life for nothing.'

Milo laid a hand on his mother's stiff, unyielding arm. 'For *nothing*? He did save Bucco's life, remember?'

'I remember,' said Catherine, her voice like bitter ashes. 'I remember everything . . . ' Including the long, lonely years without him, she thought, and the struggle to bring up Milo alone . . . and the growing dread that Milo will be just like Kitto, and go off to sea and squander another young life . . . and I remember how Kitto's father — Gramp-the-Champ — *stayed on board and watched it happen.* 'including the fact that your grandfather — ' she began.

But Milo interrupted her then. 'He was the *skipper!*' he said fiercely. 'He was trying to manoeuvre the boat to pick them up or throw a life-raft . . . It was terrible weather, and he had a whole crew to get safely home . . . It wasn't his fault. Why can't you see that? It's the kind of accident that can happen anywhere at sea — a freak wave — someone not holding on to the lines — and Dad the only one near enough to see what happened.' He sighed, and rubbed a weary hand over his eyes, trying to hold his own sadness at bay. 'We've been into all this before,' he said. Over and over again, with Catherine, his obstinate mother, getting ever more ensnared by her own bitter anger.

He tried once more to reach her, his voice very young and gentle. 'It's all right, Mum. Dad did what he thought was right . . . what he had to do. Can't you let him rest in peace?'

Catherine did truly love her young son (perhaps too much, and too possessively) and something of his gentle, sad persistence seemed to reach her for a moment, and soften her angry mood. She reached out a hand to brush her fingers over his tousled hair. 'You're a good boy, Milo . . . I just . . . it's just that I don't want to lose you, too.'

'But you won't,' said Milo, smiling. 'I'm going to college, remember? Not the sea. That is, if I get the right grades . . . Don't worry about me!' He waited to see an answering smile on his mother's face, and then turned away. He had warded off yet another scene — and perhaps got a little sense into her head. It was all he could do for now. Then he thought of something else that might distract her. 'Do you remember Cressy? Cressy Latimer?'

Catherine stared. 'Yes — a nice young family. They took the Wrecker's Cottage several times, didn't they?' She looked at Milo in a puzzled way. 'What made you think of her?'

'I don't know,' said Milo. 'I found an old photo of her and the gang, that's all . . . Those were happy summers . . . '

'Yes, they were,' said Catherine, still in that softened tone. Perhaps now she'll remember some of the good times for a change, thought Milo. And the dancing shadow of little Cressy Latimer was still in his mind as he looked down at the beach. 'I must see to the bird,' he said, and went off down the rocks to look for some food for the famished Storm Petrel.

He found a few small crustaceans and took them back with him to the shed. The bird was still sitting there in the colander, but she looked a little more alert. 'Try some of this,' he said, and patiently tempted her with tiny morsels of fishy flesh . . . It wasn't very successful, and he decided to leave the bits for the bird to try on her own. But first he got out the liquid feed and managed to get her to swallow a little when he dribbled it drop by drop into her beak.

'That'll do for now,' he told her. 'I'll kill you with kindness if I'm not careful . . . You rest now, my dear, and get your strength back. You've a long way to go before you've done.'

The bird seemed to look at him out of her bright, beady eyes, and her head even turned to watch him as he moved away to leave her in peace 'I'll leave the door open,' he told her. 'No cages for you . . . The wild, free air is out there — and the sea's just beyond . . .' He gave the bird one last, valedictory smile, and crept softly away.

But when he went back the next morning to see how she was, the bird had gone.

★ ★ ★

There began then, for Cressy, a wearisome, grey time of tests and scans and more tests and more scans, and two ambulance rides across London to a famous eye hospital for consultations (and more tests) with their most experienced and well-known eye specialists.

The general opinion among the doctors and specialists seemed to be that the optic nerves of both eyes had been damaged by the blow on her head. They might well recover on their own in their own time — or they might not. Time was of the essence. Only time would tell. There was also the question of shock and grief resulting from the accident and her mother's death. What Cressy needed now, they said, was a long, quiet convalescence and as much rest and good fresh air as possible. Everything needed time to heal. Maybe, after a long rest, her eyes would recover by themselves, or maybe, later on, some kind of operation might be possible.

In the meantime, they told Stephen kindly, the best thing for Cressy would be a peaceful time at home with her father to look after her. And there were training sessions to arrange, too, where Cressy could be taught how to manage blindness and how to use a white stick to tap her way forward into independence . . . She was a clever and co-operative patient, they told Stephen. She would learn to adapt very quickly. Children were better at this than adults. But she would need her father's help a great deal at first.

It sounded like a pretty grim prospect to Cressie — for both herself and her father. But she tried gamely not to let her doubts show, and to accept everything the doctors said without too many anxious questions.

For a time, they left her to recover in the Children's Ward (though she was a bit old for it, and curiously adult in her acceptance of what was happening to her) and this at least gave Stephen a little respite. For Cressy realised all too clearly that having to care for her at home would put Stephen's job on the line. She hadn't dared to raise the subject yet — there seemed so much else to deal with, but she knew she must tackle her father about it soon.

Meanwhile the staff and the other young patients in the ward went out of their way to be extra kind to Cressy, and there were occasional cheerful distractions when she almost forgot her own problems. And one such moment was when she distinctly heard the sound of a chord — a rich, plangent, reverberating bass chord on the strings of a guitar.

'What's that? she asked, turning her head in its direction. 'It sounds like music.'

'It is music,' said a deep, cheerful voice close to her. 'Or it will be in a minute — when everyone's made up their mind what they want to sing.'

Cressy could not see the face in front of her, but she was learning fast how to get past this barrier.

'Describe yourself!' she commanded. 'I want to know who you are — and what you look like!'

The long young man in faded jeans laughed and took Cressy's hand in his. 'Feel me, then, and I'll give you a running commentary . . . One nose, fairly thin and straight. One mouth, smiling at the moment, in spite of talking too much! Two eyes, blue, ordinary brown eyebrows and ordinary brown hair. Anything else?'

'Two ears,' said Cressy, happily entering into the game, 'which, I presume are musically on the ball . . . and two hands that can play the guitar?'

'Spot on,' said the pleasant voice, laughing now. 'Oh, and one voice that can sing a bit. Important that, because it's my only excuse for being here.'

'But you haven't answered my question,' Cressy complained, laughing with him. '*Who are you*?'

'Name of Robin,' laughed the voice. 'Friend of the Children's Ward — for life.'

'Why?'

'Because they fixed me up good and

proper once when I had an argument with a tractor.'

'A *tractor*?' Cressy was very quick at reaching the point. 'How old were you then?'

'Too young. About your age — fifteen? ... Shouldn't have been driving it on the farm, really. Turned it over on top of me ... Smashed my leg. But they put me together again, good as new.' The voice seemed to grow suddenly warmer and deeper then as it added gently: 'They're good at that, you know, in here.'

'Yes, I know,' agreed Cressy, and felt somehow strangely comforted. This stranger beside her knew what she was going through — he had been through it all before. Not blindness, perhaps, but lameness ... and loss of independence? 'Can you walk *now*?' she asked, suddenly brave.

'Oh yes. With pins in. It'll always be stiff. Want to feel it?' He carefully guided her hand down the length of a denim-clad leg, past a knee than Cressy could tell would never bend freely again. 'It serves,' he said. 'Lucky to have it at all ... Now, what shall we sing today?'

Pandemonium broke out as everyone tried to put forward their own favourite pop song, until Robin quenched the arguments by starting up one of them on his own, and they were off. Soon the whole ward was singing, and Cressy gallantly joined in. She might not be able to see the fun, but she could at least hear it. And it occurred to her suddenly that maybe Robin had deliberately chosen to talk to her, and to demonstrate that music was still a world she could inhabit whether she could see or not.

'Cressy, isn't it?' Robin's voice said, close again. 'Do you play anything?'

'The flute,' said Cressy. 'Or — I did.'

'Flute,' said the voice, considering, and there was a sound of scrabbling in a bag among things that rattled and rang and chimed together. 'Here you are!' he said triumphantly. 'Only a penny whistle, but you'll be able to manage that. What shall it be?'

Cressy was inclined to try the old song 'Where have all the flowers gone?' which her mother, Sally, used to like, but she thought it would sound too sad and too obvious, so she launched into the Skye Boat Song which she thought everyone would know. Once again the whole ward joined in, and Robin's guitar wove a skilful accompaniment round the thin, clear sound of Cressy's penny whistle. Then she tried 'Over the hills and far away', remembering that the current TV hero

Sharpe had taken it for his theme tune, and most of the children knew it.

They tried several more after that, and then it was time for Ward Tea, and Robin had to go. But he stopped for a moment by Cressy and said softly: 'One road still open, Cressy. Don't forget!'

She lifted up her pale, fragile face then, and held out her hand, reaching out to touch his face again. 'Thanks,' she murmured. 'I won't forget.'

The young man in the shabby jeans, who was really very personable in spite of his limp, stooped suddenly and kissed the child-woman he had been at such pains to help. 'Well done!' he said, as if she had just won a great marathon or climbed a great mountain. Then he wandered off out of the ward with his guitar slung across his shoulder.

Cressy sat on in silence, amazed that life could suddenly feel so much better, — even with no eyes to see it.

* * *

The other strange thing that happened in the ward — or rather, outside it — was in the middle of the night when Cressy couldn't sleep. She lay listening to the night sounds of the ward — deep breathing, an occasional cough or a sign as someone turned over, a faint whimper of pain as someone moved incautiously under the sheets, and even someone softly crying somewhere . . . I'm not the only one in trouble here, she thought, and tried to identify what sound it was that had woken her.

There it was again — a faint tapping on the window beside her. She knew there was a window there, because one of the nurses had told her so, and had even paused to describe to her what could be seen from it, high up above the busy town below.

'What's the matter, Cressy? Can't you sleep?' asked the gentle night nurse, stopping on her rounds to soothe down any restless child who needed comforting.

'I can hear something,' said Cressy, tilting her head towards the sound. (Her hearing, she thought, had got much sharper since she couldn't see). 'Something tapping on the window.'

'Tapping? Oh, surely not. Up here? . . . ' She came across and stood beside Cressy's bed. 'Though we have sometimes had a pigeon or two,' she admitted doubtfully. 'Shall I look?'

'Please,' asked Cressy, in a strange,

insistent voice. 'It — I thought it sounded urgent.'

The nurse went over to the window and pulled back a bit of the curtain, and stood looking out. Below her, the town was still awake — street lights glowed in sultry chains and cars whizzed past in skeins of tangled light. The night sky shone with the reflections of a myriad homes and streets and floodlit buildings and sky-signs . . . No room, she thought sadly, for the stars in this crowded sky, — and since I work all night, I never have time for the stars, anyway.

'Nothing there,' she said, and then leaned forward to look intently at the thin ledge of stone outside the hospital window. 'No, wait, you're right. There is something there.'

Cressy, greatly daring, got herself out of bed, and felt her way across to stand beside the friendly nurse by the window. 'What is it?' she asked. It seemed suddenly enormously important for her to know.

'I think it's a bird,' said the nurse. 'Yes. A tiny bird. It looks all crumpled up and tired. But it's alive . . . Yes, it's moving its head, and you're right, it is trying to tap its beak against the glass.'

'Why?' wondered Cressy. 'Are there insects there or something?'

'Can't see any,' said the nurse, intrigued.

'What kind of bird?' Cressy asked. 'A sparrow?'

'No. It's black, with a white bit on its tail ... And it's beak is a funny shape, — kind of thick on top. I think it looks like some kind of sea-bird. But it's very small ... Yes, it must be a sea-bird, — it's got webbed feet.'

'I wonder where it's come from?' Cressy said, her voice sounding strange and distant.

'It's a long way from the sea,' admitted the nurse. 'Maybe I'm wrong. But there is the river nearby, and those gravel pit lakes always have a lot of birds on them ... Maybe it's come from there.'

'We can't do anything for it, can we, up here?' asked Cressy sadly.

'No,' said the nurse, also sounding sad. 'These high windows don't open. I'm afraid it will have to manage to fly away again on its own.'

'Poor thing,' said Cressy in a dream-laden voice, 'to be so far from home ... '

The kindly night nurse remembered her duty then and patted Cressy on the shoulder. 'I'll get you a cup of tea, shall I? Maybe it'll help you to sleep. I think you'd better get back to bed now ... At least your little bird is safe up here till morning.'

'Yes,' agreed Cressy docilely, allowing

41

herself to be led back to bed, and trying to appear as willing and obedient as a good patient should. 'Perhaps it will feel better when the sun is shining . . . '

But in the morning, the bird had gone.

★ ★ ★

It was soon after this that the doctors pronounced her ready to face going home and trying to get used to moving about on her own in the real world outside. It was a daunting task, and Cressy was a little afraid of it, but she did not say so. She only protested to her father about his own life being limited by his care of her.

'Are you sure you can cope with me?' she asked, trying in vain to sound brave and confident.

'Of course I can,' answered Stephen stoutly.

'But what about your job?' she asked, being now the only really practical one of the family.

'I can work at home,' explained Stephen. 'I've got my computer and my fax and my drawing-board. We'll manage. And I'd better teach you to use the computer, too, hadn't I? There are lots of useful gadgets we can get to help you to get around.' He looked at his young daughter's troubled face, and suddenly put his arm round her and hugged her close. 'It'll be good to be home again, won't it?'

'Yes,' agreed Cressy dutifully. 'It will.'

So they went home. But the trouble was that 'home' was full of Sally. Her house, still warm with her loving presence — her clothes in the wardrobe, her furniture, her flowers from the garden she loved put in a vase by Stephen for Cressy to smell . . . It all ought to have been a comfort to them, but somehow it hurt more than it healed. Gallantly, they both tried to make a life together, patching over the silences with bright conversation, and doing their best to laugh at Cressy's frequent tumbles and small collisions as she learnt to feel her way around. But it wasn't easy.

During this difficult time of re-adjustment, Cressy's world seemed to shrink and grow ever darker as her sight deteriorated. Sometimes there were fuzzy outlines of unknown objects, shifting shapes and shadows, glimpses of light and strange shafts of colour that quickly faded and became a grey, smoky fog. And sometimes there was nothing there at all, and Cressy put out her hands into darkness, groping for tangible outlines and solid shapes to hold on to . . . and sometimes, when there seemed to be no end to blank distance and empty space, she began to panic and called out in black terror for her father to come close, to give her back her sense of reality, and the comforting reassurance of human contact.

Stephen did not fail her. He was always there, always trying to anticipate her needs, her uncertain steps into the encroaching dark, and her painful progress towards sightless independence. When she was too rash and fell down again, he picked her up and dusted her off, and when she was too cautious and afraid of the next step, he coaxed her forward, building renewed confidence. Whatever would ease her way forward, he would try to give, however much it hurt him to see her so held back, so vulnerable in a heedless world.

It was not easy for either of them, and they tried with achingly careful consideration and kindness to help each other through the long, difficult days.

Cressy still went uncomplainingly from one hospital appointment to another, from one eye specialist to another, from one set of tests to another, and from one cautious and regretful consultant to another. No-one could say that they didn't try to find a cure, or at least some kind of treatment. But none of it did any good. The verdict was always the same. They said it all over again. Time was the essential factor. There was no certain outcome. They would just have to wait and see. (*See?* thought Cressy. *When?*) . . . And in the meantime, they said, as kindly as ever, and all over again, they would put Cressy in touch with all the people who could help her most.

She accepted everything they suggested without protest, relying on Stephen's gentle encouragement to see her through each interview, each new challenge and each new set of instructions, — listening to Stephen's voice with thankful acceptance, and trying to identify each new voice of each new friend or adviser as they became part of her strange new sightless world. She did not say to her father that none of these new voices or new experiences could dim the aching sense of loss that filled her days without Sally's loved and loving presence. Nor did she comment on the same sound of bewildered pain that she sometimes heard in her father's voice.

They both tried very hard to spare each other, and did their best to cover up the empty spaces of their lives. But it seemed to become increasingly difficult to bear the hidden griefs and tensions of their changed world. And when Stephen's mother decided to move in to help them, it got even harder.

Grace Latimer was a tall woman, and fair, like Stephen, but unlike her son she was bossy, managing and exceedingly sure of her own convictions. She had always ruled her little kingdom with brusque and unheeding competence, taking over her gentle husband's life to such an extent that he only finally escaped her rod of iron in an early death from heart failure. She had always been sure in her own mind that Stephen took after his father in being too gentle and self-effacing, and would have done much better in life if he had been a lot more forceful. She had been rather surprised when he had insisted on pursuing a career in commercial art (against her wishes), and even more surprised when he married Sally, — a young and radiant blonde with apparently nothing to recommend her except a pretty face and a happy smile.

But there had been a lot more to Sally than Grace ever discovered, — though she soon did discover that the smiling face contained an indomitable spirit, incurable optimism, and an ability to overcome all of life's little problems and perplexities without getting overpowered by them. She had somehow brought order and purpose

46

into Stephen's life, produced for him one beautiful daughter, and surrounded the two of them with the kind of warm and cheerful family atmosphere which made all their days seem to glow with happiness. But now she wasn't here, and it was different. And Grace Latimer decided that it was her job now to look after the pair of them and put their lives in order.

She was kindness itself to Cressy — helping with everything, from dressing her in all her best matching clothes, to cooking special meals for her, and taking her for brisk walks in the Park, (one arm held firmly in hers). She even persuaded some of Cressy's schoolfriends to come round to tea, and thoughtfully laid on extra cakes and doughnuts on their behalf. But it was no good. She could not dispel the bewildered sadness in Cressy's unseeing eyes, — or the equally sorrowful despair in her son Stephen's gaze as he watched Cressy trying to cope with her restricted life. They were polite to Grace, they did what they were told, but somehow, a lot of the time, they simply were not there.

'Cressy,' she said, pushing her neat hair behind her ears in a gesture of half-contained exasperation, 'is there anything particular you would like to do today? Shall we go to the Park again?'

'No, thank you,' said Cressy politely. 'I — I think I'll listen to the radio for a bit in my room ... ' and she fled from her grandmother's uncomprehending kindness. She could not say: 'Leave me alone. Let me work things out for myself! Let me learn to do things *on my own!*' Grace Latimer would not have understood. Stephen, Cressy's father, understood all too well. But he didn't like to hurt his mother's feelings either. So he said nothing. And Cressy said nothing. And Sally, dear Sally, who was really there all round them, could say nothing, and was being dusted and tidied away with every breath!

★ ★ ★

There were three people in Cressy's life just then who were in their several ways her life-lines. One was the young doctor who had first dealt with Cressy in the hospital — Euan Morris. His responsibility really ended when Cressy left the Intensive Care Unit, but he had somehow got attached to this brave, uncomplaining child, and had so far broken his own strict rules of non-involvement with his patients to come and see her several times in the Children's Ward during the painful waiting time while the eye specialists deliberated on her condition.

Euan was worried about this dangerous business of hope. It was always a doctor's worst dilemma — to send his patient home hoping for a miracle, or to quench that hope by allowing them to face the worst that might happen. Which was the best way? People needed hope, — of course they did. But sometimes it was worse to go on hoping day after day when nothing was happening at all . . . He felt, unhappily, that he ought to warn Cressy not to expect too much. And with that in mind, he arranged to see her at her final follow-up appointment after she had been trying to manage at home for a few weeks.

Cressy dutifully presented herself at the clinic appointment with Grannie Grace in tow, already on the warpath about her grand-daughter being harassed or bullied into any further useless treatment. It was clear to Euan Morris that he was going to have a difficult time, unless he could insist on seeing Cressy alone. Which, of course, he could.

'I think, Mrs. Latimer,' he said kindly, 'it would be better for Cressy to talk to me on her own. There may be . . . medical problems to discuss, or private worries.'

'Oh,' said Grace, looking none too pleased,

her straight no-nonsense mouth clamped rather too tight for comfort. 'Very well. But I don't want the child blinded with science . . . ' Then she realised what she had said, and actually blushed, not having had any intention of being so clumsy.

'It's all right,' said Euan, smiling at her confusion. 'Nothing you or I can say will frighten Cressy. She's much too brave . . . and I think we understand one another.' He leant forward and laid a light hand on Cressy's shoulder, knowing she could not see the wink he would have liked to share with her behind her grandmother's straight back.

Cressy laughed. She was not slow in the uptake at the best of times, and now, somehow, all her other faculties seemed to be working overtime. 'Go on, Grannie Grace,' she said, still laughing a little. 'I'll be all right with Doctor Euan. He's special!'

Grace looked from one to the other of them in surprise, and had to admit that there *was* something special about young Doctor Morris. A warmth and compassion she had failed to take account of, — and a decided glint of humour, too. Yes, he would do. So, having satisfied herself on that score, she had the sense to retreat, and allowed the nurse to usher her tactfully away.

'Now,' said Euan, settling Cressy in a chair

and putting his own chair beside her, instead of sitting behind his desk, 'we can really talk. Tell me how you've been?'

Cressy turned her head in his direction. Though she could not see him — even the vague fuzzy images of human bodies or the dark mass of solid objects had gone now — she still liked to establish some sort of contact with the disembodied voice in front of her. 'I'm all right,' she said slowly, trying to answer his question honestly. 'I mean, I'm learning to get about a bit on my own — if Grannie Grace will ever let me!'

Euan laughed. 'Yes, I can see that might be a problem.' He waited, and when she did not say any more, he prompted her gently. 'And what else is a problem?'

Cressy sighed. 'Oh . . . I suppose it's the *greyness*. I miss the colours . . . I mean, we walk in the Park, but the grass isn't green . . . the sky isn't blue.'

'You can remember it though, can't you?' Euan spoke with sudden urgency. 'You haven't *forgotten*?'

Cressy looked startled. 'No, of course not.'

'It's important, Cressy,' he insisted. 'You are at least one of the lucky ones *who have been sighted*. You *know* what the world looks like — so you can remember it, always. Just think how it must be for someone who has never seen a blue sky or a green field?'

Cressy was silent, taking it in, and instantly going beyond it. 'Are you saying,' she asked at last, 'I may have to depend on memory for ever?'

Euan's voice took on a warmer, more reassuring not. 'No. But I am saying that you must preserve what you've got *now*. And I think you ought to pursue all the ways of help that are open to you *as if* you might not get better. That way, you will learn a lot about how to be independent, and how to hold on to the thoughts and feelings and images of a sighted person, even if sight doesn't return. Do you understand?'

'Yes,' said Cressy after a pause. 'Yes, I think so.'

'You will realise, Cressy,' explained young Doctor Euan, in full earnest now, 'that we doctors and specialists don't know everything! We don't know nearly enough to say yes, you will get better, or no, you won't get better. We don't know the answer . . . We can only wait and hope, just as you can only wait and hope to see again.' He sighed and then unexpectedly took her hand in his to give what added support and contact he could as he went on. 'But hope, Cressy, can sometimes be more terrible to live with than not hoping.

I want you to try very hard to accept what has happened, and make the very best use of it you can, — so that if nothing good happens to your eyes, at least your life will be as full and rich and rewarding as it can be . . . You've got nothing to lose — and if things *do* go right in the end, you'll be no worse off. In fact you'll be better off, because you'll have developed other skills and other perceptions, — and you'll always look at blue sky and green grass in a different way. D'you follow me?'

'To the letter,' agreed Cressy, sounding curiously adult and calm. 'Do you think I should learn braille?'

'Not unless you want you. Today, with tapes and records and discs and all the computer paraphanalia available, life is much easier.' He gave her hand an encouraging pat. 'There are talking books, too, to listen to, if the actual use of braille text is too much to learn all at once. You are not so cut off from communication these days. Nothing like so much as someone profoundly deaf.'

'No,' agreed Cressy, working it out slowly. 'I'm very lucky, really.'

Young Doctor Euan felt a sudden rush of shaming tears behind his eyes. Here was this gallant, blinded child saying '*I am very lucky, really,*' and he could offer her no real hope of a miracle cure. 'That's my girl,' he said, allowing his young voice to sound unmistakably warm with approval. 'Now I *know* you'll be all right. But I should like you to come back to tell me how you're doing from time to time. Will you?'

'Yes, please!' smiled Cressy. 'You are my life-line, — keeping my world in focus.'

'That's it!' said Euan, getting to his feet after a last reassuring pat. 'Keeping the world in focus. It's still beautiful *inside*.'

And he went back to his duties, having done the very best he could to help Cressy come to terms with her new, grey world of shadows.

★ ★ ★

The second of Cressy's life-lines was her flute teacher, Emmy Dickson, (known to all as Dickie) who had made it her business to come and visit Cressy in hospital several times, and had since continued to call in at her home from time to time, and also to organise a few out-of-school visits from some of Cressy's friends. She was also an ally of Stephen's, — liking this quiet, sad man and his concern and care for his young daughter, and well understanding his problems with his bossy mother, Grace, who always tried

54

to do too much for everyone in her charge and never let them do things for themselves in their own time or in their own way.

Dickie was a talented musician herself, and a warm-hearted teacher who respected her young pupils' minds, and did her best to encourage them to think for themselves and play for themselves and their own satisfaction, not hers. And Cressy's problem troubled her.

She was a slim, fairly elegant forty-year-old, with well-cut hair with auburn lights in its thick brown bob, and clear hazel eyes that saw a lot more than they let on. She was fond of Cressy, who was a receptive student and who also had a serious sense of responsibility about the younger children in the school. Her reaction to that dreadful accident outside the school gates was typical of her quick thinking and generosity — just like her mother, Sally, whom Dickie had also known and liked. Now, she felt she must try to bring some practical offerings of help in the musical field for Cressy, while at the same time fending off Grace Latimer's insensitive dictums about 'not letting the child give up learning,' or 'keeping to school routine' or 'making some attempt to have an education' and so on.

Stephen, listening to all these arguments, had shrugged his shoulders at his mother's fierce demands, and said gently: 'Give her time, Mum. She's still in shock. There's plenty of time for education later, and anyway — ' with a sidelong glance at Dickie's intelligent and sympathetic gaze 'this is all — er — a kind of education in a way.'

'Yes,' agreed Dickie, readily accepting the challenge. 'Learning how to cope with blindness in everyday life is a whole new ball game.' Her eyes strayed to the window and the green garden outside, where she could see Cressy sitting on the old garden swing, swaying gently to and fro in the fitful sunshine. 'But at least playing the flute is familiar ground,' she murmured.

'Shall I call her in?' asked Grace, half-rising from her chair.

'No,' said Dickie. 'I'll go out to her.' She turned to smile at Stephen. 'I'll just leave these tapes with you, Stephen. You will know which she'll like best, — and she can put them on for herself when she likes.' She did not exactly glare at Grace, but her meaning was clear. Cressy must be allowed to do her own thing, make her own decisions, and — eventually — look after her own education, like all the rest of her new tasks that she must learn to cope with.

'Thanks,' said Stephen, with a glinting

smile. 'She'll have fun with these.'

Dickie stopped for a moment, and looked at Stephen hard. 'Yes,' she said. 'I hope she'll have a lot of fun, one way or another, before she's done.' And she went out to find Cressy in the garden. 'It's only me,' she said, sitting down in the nearest deck chair close to the swing.

'Oh, Dickie — hello! I didn't hear you come.'

'I crept in,' said Dickie, smiling. 'Hoping to avoid a lecture from your grandmother about Higher Education.'

'Did you succeed?'

'No. But I — er — managed to sidetrack a little.'

Cressy grinned. 'She means well,' she said tolerantly, in a voice that sounded far too old and wise for its years.

'I know,' agreed Dickie, who had more reason to sound wise and old. 'We all do, Cressy, that's the trouble.'

'Is it trouble?'

Dickie sighed, not misunderstanding her. 'I only meant — we try too hard.'

'Yes,' Cressy admitted. 'We all do. I try too hard as well, and — and somehow it only makes things worse.'

Dickie's glance was sympathetic. 'Is it so hard to relax and take things as they come?'

'It is when they expect you to be perfect!'

Dickie was shocked. 'No, Cressy! Surely not?'

'You'd be surprised,' said Cressy sadly. 'Dad expects me to be brave and resourceful, like my mother was. Grannie Grace expects me to be entirely docile and grateful for her attentions. The doctors expect me to go ahead with all sorts of training, and be eternally patient! And they're right, of course. And you are right — and Dad is right — and Grannie Grace is right, but — but, oh Dickie, I'm so *tired*!'

Dickie nodded her head to herself as if she had found out something important. 'I thought so,' she said softly. 'Of *course* you are. It's far too soon to worry about any plans for the future. I think you should take yourselves off for a holiday, you and Stephen, — *on your own*!'

'Do you?' Cressy thought about it. Would it be a good idea? 'I thought — doesn't Dad need to be here . . . where Mum was?'

'Do you?'

Cressy thought some more. 'N-no,' she said at last. 'She'll always be around, won't she, wherever we are? I needn't — we needn't hold her to this place, need we?'

'Of course you needn't,' agreed Dickie. 'I can't imagine your mother being held in *anywhere*, can you?'

Cressy didn't bother to reply to that. She understood Dickie's thoughts, and agreed with them. Maybe Stephen, her father, would think along those lines, too . . . If she dared to ask him, would he be hurt? Upset? Think Cressy had forgotten her mother already? Be angry? Outraged? Shocked? . . . No, surely not. Surely he would know how Cressy felt? How Sally herself would feel?

'I don't know . . . ' she said aloud. 'I could ask him?'

'Why not?' Dickie's voice held a smile in it that Cressy could hear quite clearly. 'He won't bite, will he?'

Cressy sighed. 'No. Sometimes I wish he would.'

'Bite whom? You? Or Grannie Grace?'

'*Anyone*,' Cressy said explosively. 'He's too quiet. Too patient, Dickie. Too good to me. But I just wish he'd . . . let go a bit, or even *hate* something or someone!' She paused, and then went on, deciding she could confide this to her attentive teacher. 'D'you know, when I asked what had happened to the boy who drove that car, Dad suddenly got so furious he could hardly speak!'

'What did he say?'

'He said the boy had walked off with hardly a scratch, — and he wanted to kill him! Or at least to make him come and look at what he'd done to me — and then make him go and see my mother in the mortuary . . . ' She sighed again and shook her head doubtfully. 'I don't know . . . it might've done the boy good, I suppose . . . And it might have made Dad feel a bit better . . . but I doubt it.'

'I doubt it, too,' agreed Dickie sadly.

'Anger doesn't really help, does it?' Cressy still sounded doubtful. 'And it made Dad sound quite different — all wrong, somehow, not a bit like him . . . But at least — at least he sounded *alive*.'

Dickie was silent for a moment. 'He's alive all right, Cressy. And hurting. Just like you. It just takes different ways . . . '

'I know,' said Cressy. 'Only I don't know how to help him.'

There was another pause. Then Dickie said gently: 'I think you are helping him — with every day that goes by — with every small victory you have over managing your life.'

'Even boiling a kettle?'

Dickie laughed, and Cressy laughed with her. 'Exactly,' Dickie agreed. And finding something to laugh at, she added to herself. But she did not say it.

Instead, she went off on another tack, — one she had been carefully preparing for. 'Or playing the flute?' she said, a clear challenge in her voice.

Cressy smiled, almost dreamily, as if remembering something good. 'It's funny you should say that . . . I actually tried a penny whistle in hospital.'

'Did you?' If Dickie was surprised she did not say so. 'Did it work?'

Cressy made a small, pouting face. 'More-or-less. But there aren't enough notes!' She laughed a little. 'Robin covered for me with his guitar.' A thought suddenly struck her. 'Do you know this Robin?'

Dickie hesitated. 'Yes . . . a bit. I know the good work he does visiting the Children's Ward.'

'Did you ask him to talk to me?' demanded Cressy suspiciously. (She was still a bit too proud and touchy.)

'No.' Dickie was quite short and definite. 'Robin does his own thing, with no prompting from me.'

'I'm glad,' said Cressy, feeling a little ashamed. 'He was lovely to me!'

'I'm not surprised,' said Dickie warmly, 'if you played for him.' She hesitated again and then added softly: 'Music needn't stop for you, Cressy. You know that, don't you? There's a lot you can do from memory — without needing braille notation or anything.' She paused and added thoughtfully, 'Memory is going to be very important to you, isn't it?'

'*Very,*' agreed Cressy.

'You'd be surprised what you can pick up from ear,' went on Dickie. 'Or improvising, like with Robin.'

Cressy nodded. 'I was amazed, really, at how easy it was!'

Dickie laughed. 'Good. So don't stop experimenting, will you? There will be new ways open to you, and always more to learn, one way and another . . . '

Cressy smiled in the direction of Dickie's kind, wise voice. 'I'll try,' she said humbly.

'You could take your flute with you on holiday,' Dickie added slyly. 'Think about it.'

'I will,' agreed Cressy. 'Between learning to boil kettles and pleasing Grannie Grace.'

'Quite a task,' admitted Dickie, and laid a gentle, consoling hand on Cressy's sun-gilded head. 'Don't fret, Cressy. You're doing fine!'

Cressy turned her face up to the sun (wherever it was) and smiled. But she made no answer, — and Dickie tiptoed away across the green grass that Cressy could not see and left her to her dreams.

$$\star \ \star \ \star$$

Cressy's third life-line was a little old lady called Florrie who lived in a caravan at the bottom of the hill below their house. She had been there a long time, alone in her mobile home, making a beautiful garden round her, and — as she told everyone frequently — minding her own business and offending no-one. She and her late husband, Frank, had bought the land long ago, intending to build their dream retirement bungalow on it, but they had never got round to it before Frank got too ill to do it anyway. So they had been content to stay on in the comfortable old caravan, given temporary planning permission for it by the local authority till such time as building should take place. After Frank died, the Council had once or twice tried to remove her, but in they end they had relented and renewed the temporary planning permission, which worked quite well, though — as Florrie pointed out — no-one knew quite what 'temporary' meant.

Florrie was a friendly soul. She always spoke to Cressy when she went by, and used to call out to Sally, too, if she was passing her door. She kept three old iron chairs, painted a shabby green, on the strip of grass near the caravan door, and if it was fine enough and warm enough, she invited anyone in who would come for a cup of tea and a chat.

Cressy had discovered that she could manage the walk from her home to Florrie's without any help from anyone, and she could negotiate the green chairs, too, and settle down for a cup of tea and a cheerful gossip without any supervision. It was bliss, she said aloud to Florrie, to do things on her own, and Florrie nodded her fluffy white head (which Cressy could not see) and said sagely: 'Independence is best, any road. No-one to blame but yourself!' She poured out a cup of tea and put it in front of Cressy. 'Sugar's beside you,' she added, nonchalantly, and carefully did not offer to put it in for her.

'Florrie,' said Cressy, successfully managing the sugar bowl and giving her cup a good stir, 'my flute teacher, Dickie, thinks Dad and I ought to go away for a bit of a holiday? What do you think?'

The old lady considered the matter, head on one side like an enquiring robin. 'Do you want to?'

Cressy hesitated. 'I don't know. I don't want to upset Dad. I don't want him to think — ' She paused again, not sure how to put it.

'That you've forgotten your mother already?'

Cressy looked in Florrie's direction. 'You're quick off the mark, aren't you?'

'Stands to reason,' said Florrie. 'Rush off to the sun somewhere, without a care in the world?' She peered with bright boot-button eyes at Cressy's expressive face and added in a curiously soft and gentle voice: 'But it isn't like that at all, is it?'

'No,' said Cressy. 'But somehow every moment in that house reminds us of — of how things were. I even — I keep on expecting her to come in the door . . . '

The old lady nodded again and patted Cressy's hand. 'Course you do. So does your Dad, I shouldn't wonder. I reckon a holiday would be good for both of you.' She took a long, rather noisy slurp of tea. 'Mind you,' she said artfully, 'you aren't trying to run away, are you?'

'Of course not!' Cressy sounded absurdly indignant.

'I mean,' said Florrie, giving her own tea a vigorous stir, 'you don't want to shut Sally out, do you?'

'Of course not!' said Cressy again, even more indignantly. 'It's not like that . . . I told Dickie that we — I mean, — she'll be with us, won't she? Wherever we go?'

'Well then, what are you worrying about?' asked Florrie, and got out the biscuit tin and held it in front of Cressy. 'Here, biscuit coming up.'

Cressy reached out a hand and found the tin. 'I don't know,' she said.

'Don't know what?' asked Florrie, smiling fondly (and invisibly) at Cressy's troubled face.

'What I'm worrying about!'

Florrie laughed. Then she put her mind to the matter in hand. 'Isn't there somewhere nice you used to go to — the three of you — where you were all extra happy?'

Cressy thought hard. 'Yes. The cottage in Cornwall. We loved the holidays there.'

'By the sea?'

'Yes. Just a small, sandy cove. Very quiet. Only two cottages and a couple of boats . . . Lovely.'

'The sea might be difficult?' wondered Florrie doubtfully.

Cressy was not perturbed. 'Oh, I don't think so. It's all small enough to find your way around, — and you can't fall into the sea unless you go over the rocks, and I wouldn't do that . . . And there was a family there — a boy who would probably still be around to help . . . ' Her voice was suddenly soft with memory. 'You know, Florrie,' she added dreamily, 'I've been thinking about that place, ever since the bird came . . . Did

I tell you about the bird?'

'No,' said Florrie. 'What bird?'

'It arrived outside the hospital window, in the night. High up. I heard it tapping on the glass with its beak . . . It might have been looking for insects, the nurse said . . . '

'What kind of bird?' asked Florrie, sounding curiously insistent.

'I don't know. I couldn't see it . . . But the nurse said it was small and crumpled-looking, and black with some white on it, — and a funny beak . . . A sea-bird, she thought.'

'The very same!' said Florrie triumphantly.

'What do you mean?'

'There's been one like that on my bird-table every day this week. Couldn't make out what it was. Not one I know, — and I know most of 'em . . . But I've got a bird book indoors. Frank was keen on birds.'

'*Is it still there?*' asked Cressy, also sounding strangely insistent.

'Wait a bit,' said Florrie. 'I'll get the book first. Then we can compare it.' She shuffled off in her old carpet slippers, and presently returned with Frank's bird book in her hand. She stopped beside Cressy's chair and took hold of her hand. 'Come on. We'll go and look. It's at the bottom of the garden . . . Mind the rough grass.'

They walked down the path together, Cressy tapping her way cautiously, Florrie waddling along at a comfortable pace beside her. 'There!' she said at last. 'Yes! There she is!'

'How d'you know it's a she?' asked Cressy.

Florrie seemed puzzled by the question. 'Dunno. She looks like a she.'

'Well, what *does* she look like?' Cressy's voice was almost sharp with urgency.

'She's — your nurse was right — she's crumpled-looking all right . . . and sort of blackish, not dead-black like a blackbird or a crow, and white on her tail feathers and a bit of white underneath when she moves . . . and yes, the beak is funny.' She paused to have a closer look. 'Don't want to go too near,' she muttered. 'Frighten her off . . . '

She was quietly leafing through Frank's book among the many different sea-birds. 'Not a gull,' she murmured. 'Much too small. A bit like a swallow — or a swift . . . Perhaps it's a tern?' She turned another page. 'No! There she is! Absolutely right. Even the funny beak. And small enough. She's a Petrel. A Storm Petrel.'

'All the way from Cornwall?' said Cressy, in a voice of wonder. 'Now I know I must go back there!'

'Mm,' said Florrie, considering the matter

seriously. 'Sounds as if you should.' She seemed to hesitate and then decide to speak of things that she had long kept hidden. 'When my old Frank died,' she said in a dreamy voice, 'I decided to stay on here, you see. He loved this place. We had a lot of happy times here. We bought the caravan as a holiday home first, when he was working in the factory. It was the best we could afford — and nearest to green fields, you see . . . He loved the country — always wanted to retire here and build our dream home on this site. But he just didn't make it . . . ' She sighed, and dunked another biscuit in her tea. 'But, you see, Cressy, he's here all right. And every flower I grow here, I reckon he sees it too, and enjoys its smell!' She leant forward and picked a small spring of honeysuckle that was growing out from the hedge close by the bird-table, and put it into Cressy's hand. 'Smell that! There's country for you!'

Cressy lifted up the sweet creamy flowers, and a waft of heady fragrance drifted round her head. 'Lovely!' she murmured.

' 'Tis so,' agreed Florrie. 'And I can see old Frank around the place whenever I shut my eyes, and whenever I smell that smell!' She leant forward again and took hold of Cressy's arm in a hard, firm grip. 'Listen to me, young Cressy. Can you remember what your mother looked like?'

'Of course I can!' said Cressy, outraged.

'Well, *picture* her. To me, I mean. The most vivid time — the one that sticks in your mind. Tell me how it was.'

Cressy hesitated, bewildered. 'The most vivid? . . . ' It was, of course, that brilliant moment before the crash. Her mother, Sally, smiling in the sun, and then —

'Go on,' said Florrie. 'Say it!'

'She was standing by the car,' said Cressy, 'in the sun. Her hair was all shiny, like a — like a halo, with the sunlight behind it . . . and she was smiling at me and waving . . . And then — '

'No!' commanded Florrie, gripping her arm even harder. 'Stop! Stop there! That's the most vivid. That's the best. Guard it, Cressy! Keep it bright, see? Polish it every day. Live with it in your head all the time. Every day. Whenever you want to! That way you'll never be blind at all!' She gave Cressy's arm a final shake and released it, saying nothing more.

Cressy, for the first time in many grey days, felt real tears prick behind her eyes. 'Oh Florrie!' she said. 'You clever old thing! What would I do without you?'

'Humph!' snorted Florrie. 'Tell that to the bird!' But when she looked across the garden again at the bird-table in the bright sunshine, the bird had gone.

★ ★ ★

After that, it somehow seemed right to suggest the idea of a holiday after all . . . Perhaps her father would understand and not be upset. Perhaps he would even like the idea. Anyway, she had to try.

They had just come in together from a careful little walk in the Park, — white stick tapping, Stephen's hand always close to her elbow in case she stumbled, and a couple of Cressy's kind-hearted schoolfriends doing their best to be cheerful companions without sounding too over-helpful.

'Dad,' said Cressy, laying her stick down against the sofa, and standing still in the middle of the familiar living-room, 'let's go away.'

'Away?' Stephen sounded totally uncomprehending. 'Away where?'

'*Anywhere*,' Cressy said, sounding unguardedly desperate.

Stephen looked at his daughter's face and saw the pain in it. 'Why, Cressy? I thought — familiar surroundings would be easiest for you.'

'In some ways they are,' she conceded,

still sounding driven and curiously uncertain. 'But — '

'But?' Stephen's voice was gentle.

'But — they're *too* familiar. I keep on expecting Mum to come in through the door . . . ' and for a small moment of shameful weakness she allowed her own voice to wobble.

Stephen laid a warm and reassuring arm round her taut shoulders. After all, he had the same problem — Sally's home, Sally's belongings, Sally's presence was all around them. It should have been comforting, but somehow it was not. It was a constant reminder, a constant anguish of loss. He knew how Cressy felt.

'Where would you like to go?' he asked, for it was suddenly clear to him that Cressy was right.

'I thought — could we go back to Cornwall? To Crocker's Cove? . . . We were all so happy there.'

Stephen stared at her in consternation. 'But — could you cope with the sea? I mean, the path down to the beach? And the rocks?' His anxious voice was full of doubt. 'And — could you bear *not* to see the sea?'

'Yes,' said Cressy firmly. 'I could hear it, couldn't I?' She could feel him still hesitating, and went on quickly: 'And the Trevelyans will still be there, won't they? Milo will be there. He can shepherd me around. He's good at that. He always was.' She sounded strangely eager and wistful, — like the child she had been four years ago when they had spent their last Cornish holiday in the Wrecker's Cottage at the head of the Cove.

'*Why*, Cressy?' he said again, not sure whether it would be a good idea for her, or only cause her more heartache and frustration.

'Because they won't pity me,' she said with flat calm. 'Down there, they are all much too busy living dangerously to waste time on being sorry for people. It would be such a rest!'

Then Stephen understood. After that, he could not refuse. So he re-arranged his life yet again, so that they could return to Cornwall, where Cressy could listen to the sea.

★ ★ ★

'It's a bit odd, you finding that photo of Cressy Latimer,' said Catherine Trevelyan to Milo, holding a letter in her hand, and looking at him rather hard. 'And remembering her so clearly, out of all the others.'

'Why?' asked Milo, busy with a bit of chicken wire and some staples for a new cage for one of his patients.

His mind went back to the little fair girl with the sea-green eyes who had so enchanted him during those long, care-free summer holidays . . . Of course there had been other visitors to the Wrecker's Cottage since then, but none had been quite so close a companion, so willing an ally in Milo's adventures, so devoted to him, or so cherished and protected by him in the gallant, careless company of his boyhood friends.

'It was a long time ago . . . ' said his mother sadly.

'Not too long to remember Cressy!' Milo answered, and sudden sparks of sunlight seemed to glow deep down in the deep blue eyes. 'She was my best mate in those days, — almost my first girlfriend, if I remember right!' He looked back at his mother, seeing something in her face that was not altogether happy. But then nothing about Catherine Trevelyan was altogether happy these days, as he well knew . . . And try as he might, he had not yet succeeded in lifting the cloud of dark anger and hidden grief from her.

Milo was a soft-hearted boy, — 'too soft!' his mother often told him, especially when he was worrying about one of his injured animals . . . And he could not tell his mother that to him she was yet another injured creature who needed care and attention — and love. Yes, love, — like his other wounded charges. But while they accepted his ministrations mostly without protest if not all that willingly, and even sometimes showed signs of becoming mysteriously attached to him, — his mother would accept nothing, fended off all attempts at approach, and would not give an inch in spite of all his efforts, and even snarled just like some of his other defenceless patients when they felt hurt and frightened.

That was it, of course, with his mother, and Milo recognised it. Catherine was deeply hurt by her husband, Kitto's death, — as were all of them, but with her the outrage of hurt took the form of flailing anger . . . and she was frightened of a future without her young husband, and possibly without her young son as well, if the sea took him away from her, like most of the young men of St. Quentin Harbour. And knowing all this, wise young Milo always spoke to her softly, always tried to turn away her anger, and always waited hopefully for the day when she would at last let go and turn to him for the comfort and care he was longing to give.

But this look of uncertain distress in her face seemed to Milo to be something different, and he questioned her then in an even gentler voice than usual. 'Mum? What is it? What about Cressy?'

'They want to come down,' she told him, speaking almost reluctantly, 'she and her father.'

Milo's sunburnt forehead creased in a small frown. 'Not her mother?'

Catherine shook her head. 'No. It's bad news, Milo. Tragic, really. There was an accident . . . ' She hesitated so long that Milo prompted her.

'And?'

'Sally Latimer was killed, and Cressy — I'm afraid Cressy is blind.'

'*Blind?*' He sounded shocked beyond belief.

'He says — Stephen Latimer says it may be only temporary, they don't know . . . She hit her head, you see.'

'*Blind!*' repeated Milo, seeing again in his mind's eye the little dancing figure of ten-year-old Cressy racing along the summer sands, climbing recklessly over the slippery rocks, plunging into the blue-green sea in a scatter of diamond-glinting spray, calling after the bigger boys, and most of all after Milo, '*Wait for me*! and laughing, always laughing in the sun. 'Oh God,' he said, low-voiced and shaken, 'how absolutely awful!'

'Yes,' agreed Catherin shortly. Then, being a practical woman, and not unkind in spite of her own suppressed problems, she went on to give Milo instructions that might help young Cressy, and would certainly give Milo a useful way to express his own distress. 'I was thinking, could you rig up a kind of rope guide-line along the path down to the beach? It isn't steep or dangerous, is it, as long as you keep away from the rocks, and if Cressy could keep to the sandy path and hold on to the rope, she would soon get used to managing on her own, wouldn't she?'

'I'm sure she would,' agreed Milo, instantly enthusiastic. 'She aways was wildly independent — and she'll probably remember it all anyway.'

'How will she know about the tide?' wondered Catherine, still crisp and practical.

'By getting her feet wet,' laughed Milo. But then he added more seriously: 'But I can extend the rope path down as far as high tide mark to where I beach the *Gannet*.'

Catherine nodded. 'That makes sense.' She paused, thinking. 'I'd better re-arrange the cottage a bit . . . She could have her bed downstairs — that crooked little stairway is pretty lethal at the best of times, anyway. What do you think?'

'Give her the front room — it opens on to the path,' he said. 'That way, she can feel independent . . . The back room is quite big enough for a living-room. I can move the furniture around and put the dining table in there . . . ' It was typical of Milo that he instantly thought of what Cressy would want most — her own private place and an independent way of escape. Most of his charges felt like that. He glanced up at Catherine's serious face. 'How long have we got?'

'The weekend. They want to come down on Monday.'

'We'd better get a move on then,' said Milo, and began to stride up the sandy path that led to the Wrecker's Cottage.

★ ★ ★

When they had done what they could with the cottage and the rope-walk, Milo decided to walk round to Port Quentin to see Gramp-the-Champ.

There were two ways over to the little fishing port round the headland. One was the steep way over the rocks that he had come hurrying down with the Storm Petrel in his hands, straight to the sanctuary of his workshop shed behind his mother's cottage. But there was another, slower way that wound up the little valley beside the trout stream and crossed the heathery flanks of the cliffs at a lower point in a cleft between the rocks. There had been an old slipway down to the beach once, but this was broken and pitted now, and had become merely a smoother bit of track than the rest. No boats came up higher than the sandy ridge above the tide-line in the cove these days. The small inshore fishing boats preferred a safer berth in the harbour of Port Quentin, round the point in the next little bay.

But a few landrovers and four-wheel drives belonging to the local farmers came down the track and parked near the old slipway from time to time, and Catherine kept an old jeep in a corner by the rocks as a backstop means of transport for serious shopping or visitors' luggage. The other approach to Crocker's Cove by the high cliff path from the other side was even more steep and dangerous than the Port Quentin side, and not many visitors ventured down it. They took the rough inland cart-track, like the farmers, and came down through gorse and heather and gouged-out rock to the fallen stones and darting lizards above the little stream.

Milo set off up that way, too, having in mind to call on a few of his special friends on the way. For there were other denizens of the cove, of course, living secret lives of their own up here in the wild country above the shore; but only someone patient and watchful, like Milo, really got to know them. Apart from the few tame gulls who hovered about waiting for Catherine's household scraps to be thrown their way, there were a couple of shy and secretive otters who lived further up the trout-stream where it widened into a brown, peaty rock pool. And across the clifftop down the other side towards Mermaid's Pool, there was a certain rock at the edge of the sea where the seals hauled out to sun themselves in fine weather . . . And there were a pair of barn owls who had managed to bring up a brood of downy chicks in the corner of a deserted cowshed further on up the inland track. Milo had designs on that cowshed. It would make a bigger and more private sanctuary for his animals, — especially the bigger ones like foxes or badger cubs or hares, who needed more space and larger cages. He was only waiting for the young owls to fly before he moved in and started knocking cages together.

Now he stopped to look up at the hole in the rotting beams of the cowshed roof, and called out softly: 'Are you there, Barney? Is all safe and well with you?' He could see the mother owl's head looking down at him over the rim of the beam, but all he could hear was a contented purring, and a few snores from the chicks. Father Barn Owl was probably out daylight hunting to feed those voracious youngsters.

Satisfied, Milo moved on, saluting a basking slow-worm on the way, and stopping to watch a lark rise suddenly out of the gorse and mount, singing, towards the sky. His clear, observant gaze followed it till it was only a speck in the sky, but he could still hear its joyous song. Contentedly, he walked on, at one with his world. Oh, plenty of friends Milo had, even without his cronies in the nearby town — the sons of his grandfather's crewmen who all lived by the sea, and loved and feared it and rejoiced in its many moods as Milo did.

Plenty of friends to keep him happy — even before Cressy came back into his life and changed his world for ever.

★ ★ ★

Gramp-the-Champ remembered Cressy, too. He was getting old enough now for the passing years to flow into one another as a continuous bright pattern of remembered days, — days of sunshine and shadow, of tranquil smiling seas, and towering storms that were mighty and magnificent, days of success and triumph when the trawl nets came up full, and the encroaching foreign marauders got driven away from the fishing grounds by Gramp-the-Champ and his little fleet of belligerent trawlers, and days when the catch was far too low and the pirate Spanish factory ships became too big and powerful to be intimidated . . . days of fearful gales and flat calms, days of mountainous seas that nearly forced his boat — his lovely *Crystal Rose* — to turn turtle and capsize, held upright, sometimes, simply by the trawl nets acting as makeshift stabilizers just under the surface on either side, and days when the sun shone on a flowing tide and the winds whistled him home . . .

He did not quite know why all these memories seemed to be so bright, and so full of successful endeavour, or at least triumph over adversity. Surely there must have been black days when nothing went right and danger came too near, and he hated his pitching boat and his grumbling crew, and the threatening, implacable sea . . . But he didn't remember them.

Except, of course, the one most awful day of all, when Kitto — his brave and loyal son, his future and his immortality — had leapt into the sea to save a friend and drowned in the attempt. But that was a sorrow that went so deep that it had no place in the placid stream of sunlit memories. It belonged in a place apart, dark and aching with the kind of impotent grief that nothing could assuage, — except that even at its deepest, there was something in that bitter loss which he recognised as acceptance, the patient, sorrowful acceptance of the final choice, the final hazard that every man of the sea must face for himself, and no-one, not even Gramp-the-Champ, could face it for him. This he knew and understood, deep down in his own dark pain, and never spoke of, but never forgot.

For the rest, the past had somehow grown gentle and golden, complete in itself, and he let it flow past him in a comfortable haze of brightness, leaving him free to concentrate on the fierce storms and sudden calms of today, and whatever present challenge came up . . . He was used to challenges and he liked them. It suited him to be stretched to the limit, to find that his life was a continuous war that was never won, but never entirely lost ... That was how he wanted it to be. He would never change it.

But Cressy — little dancing golden-haired Cressy — was part of that flowing tide of bright memory, and he answered his grandson Milo's question with an affectionate, reminiscent smile.

'Yes, I remember Cressy.' He observed Milo's troubled face with instant recognition. Those two understood each other very well, and he knew trouble when he saw it. 'Why? ... Is there something wrong?'

'Yes, I'm afraid there is,' said Milo, and promptly went on to tell his grandfather all that he knew so far, — about the accident, about Cressy's sudden blindness, about their proposed visit to Crocker's Cove.

' ... so I was wondering,' he said, sounding a little shy and doubtful, 'if you would let us borrow Bo'sun ... He's such a clever dog, and I'm sure he'll remember Cressy ... He could be a sort of minder. I know he's not trained as a guide dog, — and maybe Cressy will have to have a real, trained one of her own some day — but Bo'sun will know by instinct how to look after her if we tell him ... and I'm sure he'd bark if she was in any kind of danger, — wouldn't you, Bo'sun?' He bent down to stroke the head of Gramp's favourite companion (apart from Milo himself, of course) and the old dog thumped his wavy tail in response, and looked up at him out of liquid amber eyes. 'Wouldn't he, Gramp?' Milo persisted.

Gramp was smiling at Milo's eagerness. 'Yes, he probably would,'

Milo looked at his grandfather pleadingly. 'After all, you let him stay with us while you're away at sea, anyway, — since you won't let him on board *Crystal Rose* because it's too dangerous for dogs under your feet. So it would be almost the same, wouldn't it?'

'Yes,' agreed Gramp, nodding cheerfully, and trying to stem the flow of Milo's anxious pleading. 'Of course you can borrow Bo'sun. I'm always glad when I know he's safe and sound with you while I'm at sea.' He paused, wondering how to tell a young and vigorous boy on the threshold of manhood about the limitations and liabilities of old age . . . 'But, remember, Milo, he's not a young dog any more . . . He may not find it so easy to dash about with young people, or to take new orders, or to change his day-to-day routine. Dogs are creatures of habit . . . I'm sure he'll be happy to go anywhere with Cressy, — she won't be able to do anything too risky anyway — and I expect you'll be there yourself mostly to keep an eye on her, won't you?' There was a decided twinkle in his eyes now. Gramp didn't miss much.

Milo did not blush, but he grinned back at Gramp's innocent face. 'Yes, I shall,' he told him cheerfully. 'I've more-or-less finished with school, now that the A-levels are over. We're let off the hook for the last few days. So I'll have lots of time to take Cressy about.'

'That's good,' nodded Gramp. 'And as for old Bo'sun, all I'm saying is, don't ask too much of him. He needs a quiet life these days!'

It was on the tip of Milo's tongue to say: 'Like you?' But he did not say it. How could he? Gramp-the-Champ would never be happy to settle for a quiet life. The sea and all its hazards was in his blood. He would never be willing to admit it was time to stay ashore . . .

'No,' said Gramp, following his thoughts with perfect ease. 'A quiet life is not for me, Milo. Not yet!'

His grandson laughed. He was looking into Gramp's horizon-searching blue eyes and suddenly realised that the two of them were level in height now. Gramp was quite a tall man, as Cornishmen go, and his son Kitto had been much the same height, with the same distance-blue eyes and the same fairish hair that could glint in the sun. And now here was the third generation, already nearly a man and as tall as the others, — and ready and willing to join Gramp as one of his crew whenever the need arose . . . Milo's eyes were blue, like his father's, but his hair was like Catherine's, dark as a raven's wing, — and his mother had set her mind and heart implacably against the sea and the hazards of a trawlerman's life. It had taken Kitto, her young husband, and she wasn't going to let it take her son as well . . . The two factions warred within Milo with ceaseless pain. He loved his mother — he would like to do what she felt was right for him. But he loved his grandfather too, just as he had loved and admired his own father, and he loved the sea . . . It was bred in him just as surely even in this third generation, and it would never let him go, never give him any peace . . . And he had no idea how to please both sides, or how to fulfil his own dreams and plans without hurting either of them . . .

'Don't fret, lad,' said Gramp softly. 'Things will resolve themselves in due course . . . Give them time.'

Milo nodded, always comforted by Gramp's instant comprehension, but also almost thrown by that clear gaze that saw so much.

'Now then, 'Gramp went on briskly: 'Let's concentrate on how to help little Cressy.'

'She's not little any more, Gramp. I've been working it out . . . If I'm seventeen, nearly eighteen, she must be fifteen, nearly sixteen now!'

'Almost a young woman,' murmured Gramp, as if envisaging a different set of hazards ahead. 'Well, let's see . . . She can *hear* everything, so you'd better teach her to recognise the different bird calls. Plenty of those, at sea and inland . . . And then there's music . . . Didn't she play something?'

'Yes. The flute. But I don't know if she still does.'

'We'll find out. There's Ollie Winters, and Joe and Sue. She'd fit in well with them. They were part of the old gang, anyway, weren't they? . . . They could make up a kind of quartet.' He was thinking ahead.

'But she won't be able to read the music,' protested Milo. 'Even if there was braille music or something, she wouldn't know it — not yet, anyway.'

'No, but there's *memory*,' said Gramp. 'And improvising — spell-binding, free style. She'd like that.' He grinned. 'More of a challenge . . . If I remember Cressy aright, she was never one to refuse a challenge.'

'No,' agreed Milo sadly. Even when she was dared to jump into Mermaid's Pool and nearly drowned . . . And he wondered if that was still true, now that the challenges were so much more difficult and daunting.

'After all, the others don't read music much,' ruminated Gramp. 'They mostly play off the top of their heads!' He laughed a little at the thought. 'And then there's Hetty,' he went on, caught up in the planning now.

'Hetty?'

'The garden,' his grandfather explained. 'Scented . . . You know, she grows all that stuff for the shop and the pot-pourri market as well . . . Rose petals, lavender, herbs . . . At least Cressy could smell them . . . She might even like helping Hetty sometimes. We'll have to see.' He smiled back at Milo's doubtful face. 'Don't worry. We'll find plenty of things for her to do. And there's all your creatures. She'll love those, — especially if you let her hold them . . . The sense of touch will be very important to her now.' He gave Milo's arm an encouraging shake. 'You'll just have to learn to *talk*, Milo.'

'Talk?'

'Describe. Tell. If she can't see it, you must paint her a picture of it, so that she *can* see it. You always were a bit of a poet,

Milo, — lots of imagination, and lots of fine words, I remember! Well, — use 'em!'

'Yes, I see,' said Milo, aware suddenly that he was taking on a huge and frightening task.

'People her world . . . Fill it with everything she might miss without your words to clothe it. Understand?'

'Yes,' Milo said again, privately thinking that Gramp sounded like a bit of a poet himself. 'Yes, I'll try . . . ' But he turned his head and looked away at the sea beyond the little harbour of Port Quentin, and wondered how he could begin to describe the myriad colours of the ever-changing ocean, the huge, far skies, the flickering cat's-paws of chancy winds on the water, and the sun glinting like pieces of eight on every wave crest. 'But it won't be easy,' he murmured.

'Who said anything worth doing was ever easy?' countered Gramp, and winked at his grandson in case he sounded too solemn.

After a moment's doubt, Milo grinned, and winked back. And they went off, laughing, arm-in-arm, with Bo'sun following faithfully behind.

Part Two

Crocker's Cove

In the end, Stephen and Cressy came down by the steep cliff path, much to everyone's horror. Catherine had gone up in the old jeep to meet them at the top of the cliff where Stephen had parked his car, but Cressy had flatly refused to go down to Crocker's Cove tamely by the back way, in spite of everyone's arguments.

'I can't go down to my favourite Cove with my ears shut to the sea!' she explained. 'Dad will hang on to me. I shall be perfectly safe!'

Catherine was prepared to argue, but she caught a warning flash from Stephen's watchful blue eyes, and for once held back her spate of indignant words. Stephen, she thought, looked older and sadder, but just as pleasantly good-looking as ever, — but there was a certain authority and patient resolve about him now as he dealt with Cressy's latest reckless demand. She got the impression that he was doing a lot of this lately, — Cressy, she remembered, had always been a bit reckless, heedlessly running about the rocks after Milo and his friends with no concept of its dangers.

'All right,' said Stephen to Cressy, smiling. 'But you must let me hold on to one hand — *all the way down.*' He turned back to Catherine Trevelyan for a moment with careful courtesy. 'I'm sorry to change your plans. Will it be all right to leave the luggage with you, while we walk down slowly?'

'Of course,' agreed Catherine, charmed by his gentle, faintly old-fashioned courtesy. 'I'll meet you down there,' and she climbed back into the jeep and drove rattling away down the rocky track.

Cressy held her hand out blithely to Stephen, and clutched her white stick in the other. She had got her own way, but she was much too aware of her father's constant anxiety about her — and his equally constant care and kindness — to crow over him. 'I'm sorry, Dad,' she explained softly. 'It's important to me not to come back crawling!'

Stephen gave her hand a squeeze of understanding and encouragement. 'I know,' he said. 'Best foot forward, then. We'll go down with our heads high! . . . But not too high to find the way!'

Cressy laughed. And step by step, white stick tapping, she negotiated the steep rocky path, and step by step Stephen walked beside her, swinging her hand in his for reassurance, protecting her from any slip or fall or obstacle that might come her way. And presently they came to the top of the lower cliff edge where the first glimpse of Crocker's Cove and its white cottages and the open sea beyond came into view. Cressy remembered this place, her feet knew it at once, though she could not see it, and she paused, tugging at Stephen's hand to make him stop beside her.

'Listen,' she said. 'I can hear the sea . . . I think I can tell you if the tide is in or out . . . ' She stood still, her head tilted towards the distant shore-line below her and the encircling rocks at the foot of the steep cliff path. The roar of the surf was faint up here, but it was still clear and distinguishable. 'It's over the edge of Gull Rock,' she said, her voice suddenly certain. 'I can hear it in the blow-hole . . . Can you?'

Stephen listened, too, and found that he could hear the pounding surf against the rocks, but he could also hear the sudden hiss and slap of the tide as it poured into the blow-hole and blew out again in a cloud of spray. 'Yes,' he said, marvelling at Cressy's keen hearing, and her memory of the little Cove and its special wonders. 'Yes, I can!'

Cressy turned her head and smiled in her father's direction. 'You see? . . . I can remember everything about Crocker's Cove. I'm going to be all right here, Dad. Stop worrying.'

'I'm not worrying,' said Stephen, and suddenly found that it was true. There was something about Cressy's triumphant confidence, — and her instant, joyous recognition of the place she loved — that made him feel sure, at last, that this was right for her. Yes, it was the right thing to do!

'Come on, then,' Cressy said. 'We'll soon be down. I want to put my toes in the sea!'

And together they made their cautious way over the tawny rocks and tufts of heather, the clumps of thrift and sea-campion and golden samphire, the little tufted outcrops of devil's bit scabious and stone crop and sudden brilliant patches of mesembreanthemum clinging to the sheer walls of the rock. And, knowing Cressy's mind by now, each time they met a new flower, Stephen stopped and picked one for her, and described its shape and colour so that she could identify it. Just as well, he thought, smiling a little to himself, that I've got an artist's eye for colour and form, though I'm no botanist. At least I can make things reasonably vivid for her.

96

' . . . like wide-open daisies, hanging down from the rocks in a tangle of red, fleshy sort of stems, and very bright colours — all pinks and oranges and golds and bright crimson, with yellow middles . . . Dazzlingly vivid colours . . . '

'Mesembreanthemums!' said Cressy, and fingered the small daisy-like florets and found the yellow eye in the centre. 'Are there lots of them?'

'Curtains of colour — all down the rocks.'

'Just as they used to be!' nodded Cressy, and took another deep breath of satisfaction. 'Are the rocks still all those amazing colours, too?'

'Yes.' Stephen's eyes followed the slope of the cliff to where the richest outcrop of serpentine rock glowed in the sun. They were famous for their colours, these jewel-like rocks, especially when they were within reach of the sea-spray which sprang up over them and brought each jewelled vein into vibrant life. 'Reds and greens — and yellow, though that may be lichen — and silvery grey-blue, and a sort of tawny gold like a lion's skin . . . '

'Lion Rock is just down there,' said Cressy, pointing a finger towards the rocks she could not see. But her aim was perfectly accurate.

'Yes, you're right,' said Stephen, delighted.

'And it is as tawny as ever, too.'

'Sea-birds nesting on it?'

Stephen screwed up his eyes against the glare of the sun on the water. 'Yes. On the seaward side. Myriads of them . . . Rocks white with gulls' wings!'

'Good,' said Cressy, sounding absurdly pleased and happy. 'Come on, come on! . . . It's waiting for us!'

Smiling at her incandescent happiness, Stephen led her safely down from rock to rock.

★ ★ ★

The Cove was indeed waiting for them, and so was Milo. He had not tried to go up in the jeep with Catherine, making the excuse that there was not really room for four people and the luggage, — but in truth he was already half-convinced in his mind that Cressy would insist on coming down the cliff path just as she always had, and would refuse to let the mere fact of her blindness hold her back from what she wanted to do. He knew that it was dangerous, though — who better? He had climbed up and down those cliffs since he was a small boy (and in recent times, Cressy had climbed after him). But he understood why she would want to come

98

back to Crocker's Cove in her usual way, and not as a fumbling, nervous shadow of her former brave and reckless self.

He tried to say so to Catherine, who by this time had come back with the jeep and the luggage, and was saying in outraged concern: 'It's madness to let her climb down! I don't know what her father is thinking of!'

'He's thinking of Cressy!' said Milo, almost snapping, and when he saw no real comprehension in his mother's eyes, he turned away and went off by himself to wait for Cressy at the bottom of the cliff where the high-tide was just lapping the gold-flecked rocks. He did not try to climb up to meet them. He didn't want Cressy to feel too protected — too hemmed in with care. Let her at least feel a little freedom — a little of the wild, sweet winds and crashing waves and calling gulls that had been hers to play with long ago . . . So he waited patiently at the bottom, looking up to see them come as they rounded the last steep flank of the last tall golden rock.

'Milo's waiting for you,' said Stephen softly, knowing it would mean instant comfort to Cressy in her darkened world.

Her face lit up. 'Is he? . . . Oh, how lovely! Is he — is he very different?'

Stephen looked down. 'I don't think so . . . Taller, of course . . . He's nearly grown up now, Cressy, do you realise?'

'Yes,' she agreed readily. 'I've been thinking about it. I know he will be changed a bit . . . He's seventeen — nearly eighteen — now.' She turned her face towards Stephen for a moment, as if he had spoken his inward fears, and added gently: 'I — I won't expect too much!' But her smile was still lit up from within like a candle-flame, and in spite of her promise to Stephen, she almost danced towards the last few steps down to the sand.

'Be careful!' said Stephen, having willed himself not to say it more often than he could help.

But he needn't have worried. Milo had suddenly come forward, saying softly: 'Hello, Cressy, — it's me,' and Cressy stepped off the last rock straight into his arms.

★ ★ ★

Behind her façade of unbending coldness and pent-up anger, Catherine was really rather a shy person, and she was finding it hard now to welcome Stephen to the Wrecker's Cottage and to offer him the sympathy and support she would like to give him. She understood — all too well — the sudden emptiness of a life that had been full when a loved and loving companion had been there. And on top of that there was Cressy's blindness to deal with, and — she supposed — a totally new way of life to get used to. Even his working days must be changed and disrupted by his new responsibilities.

'We've altered things round a bit since you were here last,' she said awkwardly. 'We thought Cressy might be safer down here, and not have to climb up those steep stairs . . . Do you think she'll like this room? She can get out to the path without any steps, and Milo's put a rope-walk for her to guide her down to the beach.'

'It's ideal,' said Stephen warmly. 'She needs to feel as independent as possible now.'

Catherine nodded. 'That's what Milo thought . . . And the bathroom is downstairs, anyway — next to the kitchen . . . We've turned the back room into the living-room. It's easy to carry food in and out, and so on. Will it do?'

'Of course it'll do,' Stephen assured her, smiling. 'Don't sound so anxious.' He saw her stiff shoulders begin to relax a little at his words, and went on cheerfully: 'As a matter of fact, Catherine, we've actually escaped from too much cosseting and over-protection from my dear mother, who has been looking after us far too well . . . It'll be a relief for both of us to manage life more simply.'

Catherine almost let herself smile in relief. 'But what about your work, Stephen?' (Since he had used her Christian name, like in the old days, she supposed she could, too.)

'I've got it all laid on,' he told her. 'That is, if there is somewhere I can plug in my computer and my fax and so on . . . I can do nearly all my work at home, — and maybe once or twice go up to London on the train from Penzance, if you and Milo could keep an eye on Cressy for the day?'

'Of course we could!' At last he was asking her to do something practical, and she was absurdly pleased. 'And it looks as if Milo has taken charge already!'

They both looked out of the window at the smooth wet sands of the little cove where Milo and Cressy were walking together close to the small breaking waves of the incoming tide.

'He's always good when anything or anyone is injured,' she said softly. 'And he was always very fond of Cressy . . . '

'Yes,' agreed Stephen thankfully, 'I know.'

Catherine wondered then if it was the right

time to say anything to Stephen about all the recent tragedy, and decided, somewhat nervously, to try. 'Stephen — I haven't said anything — but I am so sorry, — and you know I'll do anything to help. We both will.'

'I know that, too,' said Stephen simply. 'That's another reason why we came back!'

They both laughed a little then, both shyly, and Catherine covered her sudden lapse into honest feeling by getting very busy and practical about explaining all the gadgets in the kitchen.

Stephen understood her, and went cheerfully along with her explanations. It was clear to him that he and Cressy would be left in peace here, but with a back-up of real and unassuming kindness to support them.

' . . . and I wondered whether you'd like me to provide one hot meal a day while you're here? Say in the evening? I've got to cook for Milo then anyway, and two more would be no trouble.'

Stephen sighed. 'You're making it too easy.'

'Am I?' She took him seriously. 'I should think you've got enough to contend with without having to cater and cook as well . . . This way, you'd only have breakfast and odd snacks to do — and Cressy could probably help with those . . . ' She hesitated, not wanting to sound too managing. (Not too like his mother!) 'I could easily bring the main meal over from our place, — or, if you think Cressy would like the company, you could come over to us.'

Stephen, with his eyes still on the two young people on the shore, said smiling: 'I think she'd like that.'

Catherine relaxed a little more. At least she hadn't offended him. She knew Stephen was a man who liked his privacy, — and Cressy was probably the same, and maybe extra touchy at present about being offered too much help . . . But at least Catherine could point out to her that this arrangement would be easier for Stephen, and really, Cressy herself ought not to tackle real cooking yet — it would be much too dangerous.

'That's settled then,' she said, and managed a wintry smile as she added with sudden renewed shyness: 'So I'll expect you both for supper about seven?'

Stephen looked at the tall, awkward woman with the closed, unhappy face, and wished he could think of a way to make her smile a bit more. It made her look much younger. 'We'll be there,' he said, smiling back out of tired, kind eyes. 'And Catherine — '

'Yes?'

'I'm so glad we came.'
'So am I,' she said.

★ ★ ★

'I want to go everywhere,' Cressy said, as she walked along the sands hand-in-hand with Milo. 'To all the special places!'

'Not all at once,' said Milo, laughing. 'They'll keep. We'll find them one by one . . . and take our time.' He glanced sideways at her mutinous face and added gently: 'Cressy, they won't go away . . . They've been here a couple of thousand years or more — '

Cressy began to laugh, too. 'I know — I know I sound impatient. But oh, Milo, I've missed them so!'

He swung her hand cheerfully in his. 'All the more reason to savour each one in turn! . . . I can see I shall have to give you a complete run-down of every place — in minute detail. Where would you like to start?'

Cressy paused, and then turned directly in his direction. She was remembering Robin in the hospital ward, and his kind, friendly voice saying 'Feel me then, and I'll give you a running commentary . . . '

'With you,' she said, — and then, more

shyly, 'Can I?' Milo did not misunderstand her. He stood still, and guided her two hands till they framed his face. 'Feel free!' he said, smiling.

She remembered how Milo's face had looked — he was a boy then, thirteen and freckly, brown from summer sun, but even then, the faint, stern lines of the man he was going to be had been there for her to see. She hadn't noticed them much then, but now, in recollection, she remembered them. His jawline was stronger now, and the planes of his cheekbones seemed firmer, the bones a little more prominent under his eyes. 'Are your eyes still blue?'

'Of course!' he laughed. 'I'm not a chameleon!'

'Aren't you?' Her voice was teasing. 'I seem to remember you could change your skin to suit every need then. Can't you still?'

Milo thought about it. 'Well, maybe I can . . . ' he conceded doubtfully, 'if it means putting some creature at ease . . . '

'Like me?' asked Cressy, and neatly caught the hand that came out in a playful cuff.

Milo allowed her to capture his hand and laughed again. 'For someone who is blind, you're very quick off the mark,' he said.

Cressy was pleased at that. 'I could feel

you coming!' she told him. 'But sometimes
. . . I think instinct takes over.'

'So it should,' approved Milo. 'It does with
wild creatures, you know. If they have an
injury, something else takes over and helps
them to manage.'

Cressy was still for a moment, acknowledging
and accepting strange comfort. She had
known Milo would not fail her. Then she
lightened her sudden stillness by saying
mischievously: 'Aren't I a wild creature?'

'Yes, you are!' Milo told her, laughing.
'Very.'

Cressy laughed, too, and pursued her
explorations. 'Is your hair still as dark as
ever?'

'Darker, I think — and it won't lie down.'

'I can feel that!' She pulled a curly tuft
in strong young fingers. 'But you've got so
tall! . . . I can hardly reach you.'

'I can always stoop,' said Milo, still
smiling.

'No, you can't, Milo. You *mustn't*.
Don't you understand? You mustn't make
concessions for me! I couldn't bear it.'

'All right,' he said gently. 'All right! Don't
pull my hair out! I'll be as tough and
unrelenting as you like — so long as you're
happy,' he added in a different voice.

She relented then. 'I am happy, Milo.

Very, at this moment . . . To find the Cove just the same — and you the same . . . ' She hesitated for a moment, and then decided to be serious. There was something she wanted to explain to Milo, if only she could find the words to do so, and it was important that she should say it now before Milo began to be too kind to her.

In truth, Cressy had done a lot of growing up in those dark days since the accident, and one thing she had discovered was the power of words. Since she couldn't see, she had to clothe the images and thoughts in her mind with words to make them come alive for her. It was a new way of expressing herself, and since she was already a bright and intelligent creature and had been brought up by both Stephen and Sally to look about her and appreciate all the beauty around her and all the curious and exciting things that she saw, words had become very important to her as a means of reaching out to the few real friends who came close to her dark world.

And Milo was one of them — perhaps the best and most important of them — for already she was aware that nothing much had changed between them over the years, and he knew and understood her better than most — better than anyone except, perhaps, her father . . . So she took a deep breath and asked her leading question.

'Milo, can you tell me why you stay here? Why you are perfectly content to be here?'

Milo turned to look at the pale, flower-face raised towards him and tried not to flinch at the flawless innocence of those sightless eyes. 'Why did *you* come back here?' he countered softly, not touching her, but knowing she felt his gaze upon her.

She smiled in the direction of that gentle voice, started to speak, and then paused, as if pursued by many conflicting thoughts. 'Because . . . because life is simple here. Not easy, I mean, but straightforward. There is the sea — there is danger — there is space and air and light, though I can't see it . . . ' Her voice took on a dreaming quality. 'But I can *feel* it all round me, somehow . . . And there is fierceness which I can hear when the surf pounds on the Manions on storm days, and — and gentleness when the slow tide laps the sleeping rocks . . . Everything the heart needs is here. But — ' and here she turned her face towards Milo again with sudden emphasis, 'but there is no time for frills and noises off and — and tightly-packed human beings screaming their heads off at nothing in smoky discos and pop concerts . . . all the things my town friends liked and I can't stand.' She sighed, and went on more slowly. 'I mean, you are all too busy working the sea and staying alive to waste time on trifles . . . And — and though you are kind and — ' she hesitated again, wanting to use the word 'compassionate' but afraid it would sound too highflown, 'and helpful to people in a practical way — especially you with your animals — you have no time to waste on pity. You would not so insult your friends.' She gave him a sudden, impish, sideways grin, and added unevenly, 'Sounds a bit solemn, but that's why I've come back.'

Milo was staring at her in spellbound silence. But at last he said what he knew she was waiting to hear. 'And that's why I stay.' It was a simple answer, but it was entirely true. He stooped down to the sand and picked up a golden-brown convoluted fan shell and laid it in her hand. 'Feel it,' he said. 'Perfectly formed, timeless and beautiful, — but hard as the rock it came from and the busy sea-creature who made it . . . and when the sea smashes it to pieces it turns into sand — just as golden and just as indestructible, but suffering a sea-change . . . The sea is always changing, Cressy, but always the same. We live by it, we love it and we fear it, but we could not live without it . . . And that's where the roots of my life began, and probably where they'll end.' There was a curious note of love in his voice, but almost a sense of warning, too. He didn't understand it quite himself, and he thought Cressy would not either. But he was wrong.

She held the shell still in her hand and turned from the sound of Milo's voice towards the deeper and more powerful sound of the sea against Mermaid Rock. More powerful, she thought, but not more potent. Milo is a poet. 'It's all right,' she said softly. 'If your roots are sure, mine will become so one day. And where could they be but here?'

Milo looked at her strangely, and took her hand in his. 'In that case,' he said, allowing the smile in his voice to become clear, 'we know where we stand! So we can stop trying to find words for miracles, and enjoy each one as it comes!'

And, laughing quietly together, in perfect accord, they walked on along the empty sands.

★ ★ ★

That evening, just after Catherine's well-cooked supper, Gramp-the-Champ arrived with Bo'sun. He stood outside the cottage, being very careful not to intrude on his daughter-in-law's privacy. He knew, all too well, what her reaction to his presence might be.

But Milo was quick to see him there, and he wasn't going to have any nonsense from his mother. Gramp-the-Champ was coming in to meet Cressy and her father again, — and so was Bo'sun.

'Gramp,' he said, coming out of the cottage door with a couple of quick strides, 'come on in and meet Cressy and her Dad again. You're just in time for a cup of tea.'

Gramp's shrewd gaze caught the determined gleam in his grandson's eye and he decided to go along with it. But before he could make any move, Cressy did it for him. She came out of the door unaided, white stick tapping the way forward, and walked steadily straight up to Milo and his grandfather, holding one hand in front of her to reach out and touch them as soon as they were within reach.

'Hello, Gramp,' she said, her clear young voice warm with welcome. 'Now the day is perfect! Crocker's Cove hasn't changed at all!'

But it had, of course — or the people in it had — and Gramp was almost as shaken by Cressy's fearless, sightless gaze as by his own loss, and Catherine's, and Milo's. The

112

absence of Kitto — young, vital Kitto, his son — from that little gathering left an ache on the air, — and so did Cressy's and Stephen's loss with Sally's bright presence gone, and Cressy herself in the dark.

This will never do, Gramp thought swiftly. Can't have us all moping in the shadows. Not what I came for at all. So he stooped and kissed Cressy's upturned face, — very gently and tenderly for an old, grizzled fisherman — and said: 'You look more beautiful than ever, young Cressy. I daresay the Cove is as glad to see you as I am!' Then he took her hand and guided it towards old Bo'sun's silken head. 'I want you to meet old Bo'sun here. He's coming to stay with you for a few days while I'm at sea. Milo and you can look after him for me, can't you?'

'Of course we can,' Cressy was delighted, and her hand lingered on the dog's wise old head. 'How old is he? Can you — could you describe him for me?'

Gramp laughed. 'Easily, — since I've known him nearly fourteen years! . . . Well, he's a golden retriever that somehow got a bit mixed up with a collie, I think . . . He's sort of golden-yellow, with a white bit on his chest that ought not to be there by rights, but we call it his cravat . . . He's long-haired, more-or-less, but going a bit scruffy at the edges, and there's a bit of real grey round his muzzle now.'

'What colour are his eyes?'

'Golden, — like his breed. Or topaz, you might say . . . And he's got one ear higher than the other.' Gramp was still smiling.

'But he can hear anything a mile off!' put in Milo, also smiling. 'And if anyone tried to hurt Gramp, I think he'd kill them!'

Cressy's hand was still caressing the listening head. 'Won't he mind being away from you?'

'He's used to it,' Gramp told her cheerfully. But he approved of Cressy's instant understanding of Bo'sun's needs. He also noted thankfully that Bo'sun's tail was wagging hopefully and he was looking up at Cressy with a curious air of recognition and acceptance. Did he really remember her? At any rate, it looked as if the new allegiance was already given — and maybe there would be no conflict of devotion for the poor old boy to come to terms with after all.

'How long will you be away this time?' asked Milo, (though it was not a question any practising fisherman would dream of asking these days.)

Gramp-the-Champ shrugged. 'As long as the fish keep coming. But with the quota and all that, we can only do about four days on and three days off!' He watched Cressy still stooping over the dog and whispering into his ear, and winked at Milo. All was well with their little plan, — it seemed to be working like a dream.

'You can show me where the crabs are in the rock pools, Bo'sun . . . Can you catch crabs? . . . And I can throw balls for you, but you'll have to bring them back, won't you? . . . And maybe Milo will take us up the trout-stream track into the heather country . . . Would you like that?'

Bo'sun's liquid gaze assured her that he would like anything she suggested, but in case she did not understand him, he gave one short, approving bark to make it clear, and lifted one paw (the white one) for her to shake.

Cressy could not see it, — but Milo, with instant unspoken tact, guided her hand towards the outstretched paw, and left the two of them to make that final contact together.

'That's it then, Bo'sun,' she said, shaking his paw up and down, and laughing. 'We're mates for ever now.'

'Your tea's getting cold,' called Catherine, none too graciously, and as they turned to go in, Stephen came to the door to meet Gramp, holding out his hand. He didn't understand

Catherine's sudden change of manner, but he had always liked Gramp-the-Champ, and he thought it was time someone made him welcome.

'It's good to see you again,' he said. 'And everyone is being so kind.' He glanced back at Catherine, still puzzled by her withdrawal into her old uptight stance of cold disapproval. 'Cressy and I feel at home already. We're going to be very happy here.'

'I hope so,' agreed Gramp in his deep sea-dark voice. 'The Cove can be a very soothing sort of place when it likes.' Then, looking back over his shoulder at Milo, he added slyly: 'Mind you, Milo's quite an expert, too.'

'Expert in what?' asked Cressy, immediately interested.

'Soothing things down,' said Gramp, with intent. But then enlarged on it kindly: 'With his patients — his injured creatures, I mean.' He and Milo exchanged a rather guilty look. They both knew they were treading on dangerous ground, — and Catherine was much too bright not to understand.

Catherine is an injured creature, too, thought Gramp sadly, just as much as young Cressy . . . So are all of us here, one way and another . . . But he did not say it. Instead, he made himself as charming and agreeable as he could, — and when Gramp chose he could be very good company — talking to Stephen about his work as a commercial artist and how he would manage to pursue his craft down here . . . And fascinating both Cressy and her father with descriptions of other coves, other shores and islands that he had seen and admired on his many different adventures with *Crystal Rose*. He did not talk much about the sea itself, — though he could have done, with passion and fierce devotion — but he knew that would upset Catherine. Instead, he focussed his attention on inshore recollections that might appeal to Stephen's artist's eye, — and light up Cressy's darkened world with clear bright pictures that her quick mind could easily imagine and absorb.

'You make them all sound so alluring, maybe I shall want to paint them for myself,' said Stephen, laughing, 'and forget about the commercial world for a bit.'

'Would you like to?' asked Gramp, smiling at Stephen's enthusiasm.

'Oh yes, I always want to do my own thing — who doesn't? But money counts too, you know . . . ' He paused, thinking that perhaps it might trouble Cressy if he sounded too driven by the necessity to earn a living. 'Though as a matter of fact, I do get book illustrations too from time to time, and

I like those . . . I've got one now, actually, and that means I can suit myself what I paint — up to a point . . . '

'What's it about?' asked Cressy, only too willing to get her father talking about his work. He spent so much time looking after her these days that she wondered how he got anything done at all.

'Oh . . . it's mostly countryside, and a river estuary — even a bit of seacoast, too . . . I thought we might look for it round here, as we wander about . . . What do you think?' He was at such pains to include Cressy in everything he did that it almost hurt somehow, and she was still always surprised and touched at his constant care for her.

'Sounds exciting,' she said. 'You can read me the story first, and then describe the sort of place you've found, — and I'll tell you if it sounds right or wrong!'

Stephen laughed, and turned back to Gramp, meeting his sympathetic and discerning eye with a reassuring glance of his own. 'You see — ? Cressy's got it all worked out already! We're going to be quite busy.'

Gramp nodded approval, and got quietly to his feet. 'Well, I'm going to be quite busy too in a little while, I'd better be getting back.' He smiled rather hopefully in

Catherine's direction. 'Thanks for the tea. I'll come back to see how Bo'sun is getting on in a few days.'

'Yes,' said Catherine, unrelenting. 'All right.'

But Milo wasn't going to let Gramp go without a single word of goodwill. He got up, too, rather swiftly, and said: 'Did you bring the van over?'

'No, I came over the hill.' (Over the hill? he thought. That's me, I suppose.)

'Then I'll come a bit of the way with you,' Milo said. 'I want to check on the animals anyway.'

'Can I come?' asked Cressy at once. She had felt the strange pressures too, and wanted to send dear Gramp off to his fishing without any shadows pursuing him.

'Why not?' agreed Milo, smiling. 'I can introduce you to the patients.' And Bo'sun, sensing the moment of departure, got lumberingly to his feet and followed them out of the door.

Behind them, Stephen watched Cressy safely out on to the path, and then turned back to Catherine, wondering how to lighten her mood. But now that Gramp had gone, she seemed to shrug off her stiff manner, and return to her friendlier self.

'Let's have another cup of tea,' she said,

and sat down beside Stephen at the table, reaching for the teapot with a brisk and competent hand.

Outside, the three of them stood still for a moment, savouring the summer evening. The sea lapped gently on the shore in a quiet, persistent wash of sound — the air smelled tangy and fresh with salt and seaweed, and the scent of the cliff flowers drifted down to them in waves of heady, sundrenched fragrance.

Cressy drew a long, happy breath of release and freedom. 'Lovely!' she murmured. She could not see the sea, but she could hear it, and she was content.

They walked slowly towards the cliff path and Gramp said suddenly: 'What happened to the bird?'

'Oh, it recovered. It was gone by morning.'

'What bird was that?' asked Cressy innocently.

'A vagrant — blown off course,' explained Gramp. 'Landed on my boat. They do sometimes.'

'What kind of bird?' persisted Cressy, a strange thought in her mind.

'A Storm Petrel,' said Milo. 'Very small. Very tired.'

Cressy was staring in his direction, seeing nothing, but expressing a curious shocked stillness in her pale face. She stopped walking, and asked in a shaken voice: 'How long ago was that?'

Gramp was surprised at the question, — but Milo had also stopped suddenly and was looking at Cressy intently, saying nothing at all.

'I don't know . . . How long ago, Milo? Ten days? A fortnight?'

'About that,' agreed Milo, still looking at Cressy.

'I suppose — ' she began tentatively, 'they are ocean birds, aren't they? I suppose they can fly a long way?'

'Hundreds of miles,' agreed Gramp. 'Thousands, possibly.' Then Cressy's odd stillness reached him. 'Why?'

'I — I know it can't be possible . . . ' she murmured, and turned her head in Milo's direction again, seeking reassurance.

But Milo said gently: 'Go on, Cressy . . . What isn't possible?'

She was holding Milo's hand already, more for guidance than for comfort, but now she clutched it more tightly, and said in a breathless voice to both of them: 'You — you won't laugh?'

Gramp by this time was aware that they were on the edge of something unusual and disturbing, — and that it was somehow important to Cressy, so he spoke for both of them. 'We're not laughing, Cressy.'

She took a deep breath then, and began: 'The first time was outside the hospital window . . . ' and then went on to tell them all the rest. She could feel from the listening silence that these two gentle people were far too well-acquainted with the strange happenings in their sea-girt world to be surprised at anything, or to be too sceptical to accept it, but even so, she heard her own voice stumbling into lame excuses.

'I suppose — I mean, there could be several different birds . . . ?' she began weakly. 'But — but Storm Petrels? In London? . . . From the Channel, or the Bay of Biscay? . . . ' Then she gave up trying to explain it, and fell back on dear old Florrie of the deplorable carpet slippers, and their last little conversation. 'So I think I said something like *All the way from Cornwall? Now I know I must go!*' . . . And Florrie said: '*Sounds as if you should!*' ' She paused, and when neither of them said anything, she added quite simply: 'So that's why I persuaded Dad to come — the real reason why I came!'

The silence was long and strange, but in the end it was Gramp-the-Champ who knew what to say. Milo did not even try. 'Well,' Gramp said quietly, his voice even deeper than usual, 'the sea's a strange place. There's no knowing what she'll send you next ... But this time, she's done us proud!'

★ ★ ★

Milo did not say very much when he took Cressy to see the animals in their little sanctuary behind the cottage. But Cressy accepted his silence, knowing somehow that he was not unhappy about the strange happenings with the bird, but had quietly admitted them into the pattern of his life, as he seemed to do with most things that occurred to him or around him.

So now, still without comment, he left Bo'sun sitting dejectedly outside the shed in case his gentle, bumbling old presence frightened the injured creatures inside, and took Cressy quietly into the half-dark shade of the little shed.

'This is Foxy,' he said, leading Cressy up to the small wire cage. 'He's got a damaged paw — caught in a trap or something ... I shall have to dress it for him in a moment. But first I'd better put his muzzle on — he's a wild thing, you see, and he hasn't learnt that you mustn't bite the hand that feeds you!'

Cressy laughed. 'Can I hold him for you?'

'Yes, when he's got his muzzle on. But you must be very firm and hold him tight. That way he feels safer, and won't wriggle.'

Cressy understood his warning. Milo never wasted words on unnecessary directions. So she waited patiently till the scrabbling sounds behind the wires of the cage had subsided, and Foxy had been captured and muzzled and made safe to handle.

'Here you are,' he said. 'Put your hands under mine, — that's it, round his front legs and his neck . . . Now, sit forward so that his back legs are in your lap and you can hold him steady . . . All right?'

'Yes,' said Cressy, breathless and delighted to have the furry little fox-cub in her grasp. He was warm under her hands and smelt slightly musky, but with an added whiff of heather and wild thyme which Milo had used for his bedding.

'Hold still now, Foxy,' said Milo in his softest, most cozening voice, 'while we fix you up . . . You'll soon be running free again after those rabbits on the hill.'

'What does he look like?' asked Cressy, speaking softly, too.

'Well, brownish and reddish on top — very fluffy and fuzzy, — but you can feel that, can't you? That's his baby fur, — and he's white underneath and on the top of his brush . . . He's got a black nose, and black tips to his ears which are very pointed and perky . . . Can you feel those? Very sharp! . . . And his teeth, when you can see them without the muzzle, are very white and pointed, and even sharper than his ears! He'd nip off the top of a finger as soon as look at you!'

Cressy giggled, unperturbed by the thought, and held on even tighter.

'Now then,' said Milo sternly to the little cub, 'this may hurt a bit . . . but the new dressing will feel better, and you're not to eat it!' And he eased off the old bandage and pad of lint with skilled and careful fingers.

'What do you put on it?' Cressy asked, always interested in acquiring new bits of knowledge.

'This is an antibiotic cream which the vet gave me . . . The leg was a bit infected when I found him . . . But it's healing nicely now . . . He'll be ready to go in another week.'

He finished re-dressing and bandaging the paw, and wound the whole thing fairly tightly with a neat plastic binding to keep the little cub from tearing off all his good work with its sharp, impatient teeth.

'There now,' he said to Foxy approvingly, 'it didn't really hurt a bit, did it? You go back now and have a snooze, and it'll feel much better in the morning.'

Gently, he took the tense little body out of Cressy's hands and lowered it back into its neat wire cage, — and once it was safely inside, he whisked off the muzzle and withdrew his own hand rather smartly, and shut the cage door.

'Isn't there a titbit we can give him?' asked Cressy. 'He's been very good.'

Milo laughed. 'You're even softer than I am! Here — push a bit of puppy food through the wire — but don't let your fingers get too far inside.'

'There you are, Foxy,' said Cressy. 'All over now . . . Freedom soon . . . ' and if there was a wistful note in her voice (Oh, how she would love to be able to run free on the hills like Foxy when the time came) she tried to hide it by saying quickly: 'Who's next?'

'The little hedgehogs — they only want feeding. You can hold one of those if you like, — but they're prickly!'

'What happened to them?'

'Nothing. They were orphaned. The mother was killed on the road, poor thing. A lot of them are. I found these two curled up in the ditch beside her. They were so cold and hungry — I couldn't leave them there.'

'What do you feed them on?' she asked, and gave a small crow of pleasure as Milo put one small, warm, spiky creature into her hands.

'Well, they're getting on now, so they can take a special kind of milk. The vet gave me some stuff called Esbilac — it's got vitamins and egg yolk in it. But at first when they were very cold and collapsed the vet gave them Aconite, and then when they revived a bit, he put them on to a kind of fluid replacement called Lectade ... But now they can suck milk from a syringe, and soon they'll be able to lap it from a saucer ... And then they'll begin on worms and grubs and things ... '

'You'll be busy foraging for them!'

'Oh, I don't mind,' laughed Milo. 'So long as they survive! The only thing is, I have to remember which animal needs what! ... And to get them on to foraging for themselves in the long run.'

He filled a syringe, and carefully handed it to Cressy, guiding her fingers round it, and then directing the open end into the baby hedgehog's mouth. It instantly began to suck hungrily, and Cressy could feel its small, ravenous mouth tugging at the syringe. It was a strange feeling to be on the end of such a strong, instinctive urge

127

for life. 'It feels very much alive now,' she said, entranced.

'Yes.' Milo was busy feeding the other baby. 'They're doing fine now. I think they'll survive. But they've got to learn to find their own food before they go out into the wide world.'

'Will you have to teach them?'

'No. They'll find out. I'll let them wander a bit further, and maybe put a few grubs and worms in their way . . . We'll see how they get on.'

He put the baby hedgehogs safely back in their cage among the heaps of straw and bracken and heather where they could curl up and go to sleep again in peace. Time enough to worry about their future food when they were a little older. For the moment, this would suffice.

Then there was the angry grey squirrel, chattering furiously at him from its cage, and frantically trying to gnaw its way out of every corner . . . Once again he had to find a tiny, restricting muzzle for those sharp teeth. 'A squirrel can bite you to the bone in a flash!' he cautioned. 'But I've got to put some more stuff on his tail. It was very infected when I caught him. I think he must have got it caught in a door, or even got half-run-over by a car. Anyway, I'm afraid he'll never have a very handsome brush again. But at least he's alive.'

Cressy, greatly daring now, held the struggling squirrel tight in her hands while Milo dealt with the injured tail. The squirrel chattered with rage all the time, — but afterwards took a hazel nut from Cressy through the bars of its cage, and carefully turned it round in its paws until it found the right place to crack it, and then sat there contentedly munching as if nothing untowards had happened.

All of this Milo cheerfully relayed to Cressy, so that she would be in the picture, along with a lively description of the bedraggled grey squirrel with its absurdly heavy bandaged tail. 'If animals can look really cross, this one can!' he told her, laughing. 'Even the tufts in its ears are twitching! And most of its back fur is standing on end like a wire brush! . . . But it's settling down now, with the nut to keep it happy . . . The worst is over.'

'Have you given him a name?' asked Cressy, smiling.

'Yes, I call him Wily Willy — he's much too clever at escaping . . . And the little hedgehogs are Spikey and Spiney . . . Not that they care!'

Cressy grinned. 'Is there anyone else?'

'Yes,' Milo sighed. 'There's Boxer, the hare . . . only he's not boxing, I'm afraid, he's been too sick.'

'What happened to him?'

'I don't know, — a snare, probably, — anyway, something lethal with wire in it. I found him lying in a heap up there near the trout stream. He could scarcely breathe, the wire was so tight round his neck, and it had cut into the skin quite badly . . . ' He was reaching inside for the soft brown limbs of the hare, and it made no effort to escape his imprisoning hands. Either it was too tired and sick to care, or it had already learnt to trust Milo's gentle fingers. He didn't know which, — but he hoped it was trust not fear that kept the wild creature so still.

'You'll have to be very gentle with this one,' he said softly. 'I'm truly not sure if he's frightened to death, or very trusting . . . Hares are intelligent creatures . . . Maybe he understands that we only want to help him . . . I don't know.'

'I'll be very careful,' said Cressy. (As if she hadn't been already, but still!)

With slow, gentle movements, Milo eased the long, slender body out of the cage and laid it down on the old orange-box crate that served as a table.

'Just put your hands softly on his arms and

legs to keep him still,' directed Milo, 'though I don't think he'll wriggle much . . . I need to get at his head and neck to clean the wound and re-dress it.'

Cressy's hands rested on the warm, soft fur of his coat, and the hare did not resist her. She could feel his heart beating away in his chest, but he made no move, even when Milo took off the old dressing and fixed on a new one. 'You're getting better, you know,' he told the hare, in his quiet, reassuring voice. 'Really, you are. You're not going to die . . . The fields will soon be all yours again, young Boxer . . . and there may even be a lovely lady-friend waiting for you out there . . . Be patient now, be still and rest . . . You'll soon be well.'

The hare seemed to be listening to him, — its large, dark eyes were open, and the black-tipped ears were pricked, as if Milo's voice was a sound he recognised and did not fear.

'Is he listening?' asked Cressy, very quick to feel the conflicting vibrations in the air.

'I think he is,' said Milo, smoothing the last fold of the neck-binding into place. 'Let's put him back now. He's still very tired, — and handling him is a bit of an ordeal for him, even though he's so good about it.'

'Will he live?' she asked, for she could hear the doubt in Milo's gentle voice.

'I don't know,' Milo said. 'He needs the fields and the open sky . . . Hares don't like being caged. I wish I could let him go.'

'Could we build him a larger cage?' she wondered. 'Is there anywhere with more room?'

Milo looked at her in amazement. Really, Cressy was almost psychic! 'Yes,' he said. 'I do know a place . . . in the old cowshed . . . I could give him more room, and at least a glimpse of the sky where the roof has fallen in! I don't think the barn owls would mind.'

'Barn owls?' Cressy was confused. 'Explain!' she commanded.

So Milo did, and added hopefully: 'I believe we could move him up there, if I got everything ready first. Will you help me?'

'Of course,' said Cressy. 'When do we start?'

'Tomorrow?'

'Is that soon enough?' asked Cressy. And Milo laughed.

So they left Boxer the hare to sleep off his ordeal. (However skilful Milo had been, it had still been an ordeal) and went out into the summer twilight and took the path to the Wrecker's Cottage, with Milo keeping a guiding hand on Cressy's arm, and Bo'sun loping happily behind.

Cressy could not see the pearly gloaming settling over the hills or the last pale gleams of sunset light on the sea, but she could breathe in the scents and spicy airs of the summer night, and hear the sleepy sea-birds crying their last goodnights across the water. And beyond all the myriad small sounds of the settling evening world, she could hear the endless, comforting, soothing voice of the sea.

They reached the Wrecker's cottage and the door to Cressy's own room which stood open to the soft night air. Stephen was waiting for her, but he did not come out to meet her. Let Milo have the last word on this first, magical day.

'Sleep sound,' said Milo softly. 'Bo'sun will take care of you. It will all still be there tomorrow, — and so shall I!'

'Wonderful!' breathed Cressy. 'Thank you, Milo.'

'What for?'

'For making my world come alive again!' she said. Then she turned round and went inside, feeling strangely at peace, to where her patient father was waiting.

Bo'sun, after one puzzled look after Milo, followed dutifully inside and took up guard duty on the threshold of Cressy's door.

Outside, the sea-birds ceased to cry, and dusk came down on the sleeping world. But all night long the ceaseless voice of the sea coloured Cressy's dreams.

★ ★ ★

When Cressy came out into the morning, there was someone hammering outside her door. The trouble was, Cressy had no means of telling the time these days. Night was the same as day to her — though sometimes in very bright sunlight she could feel or 'see' a faint lifting of the darkness into a paler grey glow. But mostly she had to rely on alarm clocks and radio time-pips to tell her where she was and what part of the day or night she was living in, — and it was all rather confusing.

But someone would not be hammering something outside her door in the middle of the night, so it must be daytime, and, anyway, she could hear the gulls squabbling over something down on the shore, and they would not be fighting over scraps in the night, — not unless there was a boat out there somewhere, discarding bits of its catch, and that seemed unlikely off the treacherous Manion Rocks beyond Crocker's

Cove . . . So it must be all right to call out to whoever it was, and ask for news. Besides, Bo'sun hadn't barked.

'Hallo?' she called. 'Who's there? . . . Is it morning yet?'

And Milo's warm, reassuring voice replied: 'Yes, it's morning — a fine day, a mist on the sea, and all's well.'

Cressy laughed and took a couple of steps forward, with her hand on the rope guide-line that Milo had set up for her. 'What are you doing?'

'Extending the rope walk for you, so that you can come across to our cottage easily, too.' He gave one final thump with his hammer, and added cheerfully: 'Come and try it.'

Cressy turned to change course, but she was bewildered by the different angle, and Milo reached out his own brown hand and put it over her searching one, and placed it securely on the second line of rope stretching inland, away from the beach, towards Catherine's cottage.

'If you're coming over to supper most nights, you'd better know the way!' he said, laughing, and walked with her along the new rope-path till she reached Catherine's door. 'Now turn round and walk back,' he said. 'Then I'll know you're safe to be let loose!'

135

Cressy obliged, smiling at his teasing voice. Bo'sun, obviously coming to the conclusion that his human masters and mistresses were completely mad, trotted obediently after them, first one way and then the other.

'Well done!' said Milo softly. 'Now, try the one down to the beach. I'll be right behind you.'

Patiently, Cressy did as she was told. She showed no sign of fear at the unfamiliar path and the rocky terrain on either side. She just kept one hand on the guiding rope, and tapped her way down with her white stick until she was standing on the soft sand of the little cove. 'Where am I now?'

'On the shore. Can you tell where the sea is?'

Cressy lifted her head and listened, sniffing at the tangy sea breeze Bo'sun sniffed at it, too. It smelled interesting. 'There,' she said, pointing accurately straight out to sea.

'Follow the rope down,' directed Milo. 'I've kept it going till you reach just above the tide-line. That's where I usually beach my own boat, *Gannet*. She's only a small dinghy with an outboard, but she's quite useful for small trips. I'll take you out in her later, if you like.'

'I thought we were going to build a new cage for the hare.'

'So we are,' laughed Milo. 'First. After I'm convinced you can find your way about by yourself.'

'Is that what all this is in aid of?'

'Of course.'

Cressy shook her head reprovingly at where she thought he might be, and gave a rueful grin. 'I can manage perfectly well.'

'Yes,' said Milo's voice, still half-laughing. 'Well, we'll see about that.'

Cressy did not answer this. She just went on walking down to where the rope guide-line came to an end. There, she turned unerringly to the left of the last wooden post-rail and felt with out outstretched hand for the rounded planking of Milo's boat. 'I've found her!' she cried, pleased with her success. 'Is this *The Gannet*?'

'It surely is,' Milo told her, smiling at her delight. 'And since you're so clever, tell me where her bows are pointing?'

Cressy's hand explored the little boat from stem to stern, though she knew the answer already. 'Towards the sea, of course.' (Where else would the boat be pointing if Milo had beached her ready for the next trip when the tide came up?)

'You'll do!' Milo was laughing again, but his voice was warm with approval. 'Even Bo'sun thinks so. He's lying down by the boat and going to sleep!'

Cressy laughed, too. 'So I'm safe to be let loose?'

'I think so,' agreed Milo, but he sounded perfectly serious now. 'If you don't take too many silly risks . . . ' There was a pause, and then he added — still seriously, 'I'm giving you your freedom, Cressy. Do you understand?'

'I understand perfectly,' she answered gravely, knowing it was important to reassure him. 'And thanks for taking the trouble.' She also paused for a moment, and then said, with a hint of mischief creeping back into her voice: 'I'll try to be circumspect!'

Then Milo burst out laughing again and took her hand in his. 'Come on. Let's run down to the sea, — and you can stop being so well-behaved. You sound like a chastened schoolgirl.'

'I am a chastened schoolgirl!' laughed Cressy, a shade ruefully, but her feet followed his without any fear as they ran together over the morning sands. 'What does the sea look like today?' she challenged, standing beside him at the water's edge, and gazing outwards with her sightless eyes. (At least she could hear the waves rushing gently to and fro against the shore.)

' 'The sea today is like broken bottles, — ' '
began Milo.

But Cressy interrupted him, laughing. 'I know my Dylan Thomas too, you know! . . . Tell me what it really looks like.'

Milo paused to think. 'Well, — far out, almost on the horizon, there's a drift of mist which is turning pink with the sunrise.'

'Is it *that* early?'

'Oh yes. Can't you feel it? Everything dewy and fresh and still cool to the touch . . . And the birds still very noisy and busy. They get sleepier and lazier as the sun comes up.'

'Go on,' said Cressy. 'We've only got to the pink mist so far.'

Milo grinned at her persistence, and then, remembering that she could not see his grin, he said amiably: 'All right . . . Next frame: middle distance. It's a calm sea today, indigo dark, with green edges to the waves.'

'Are they high?'

'Not very. An easy swell — no white caps. And then, getting nearer to the shore, the colours get lighter — still green and turquoise, and deep blue and pale blue — even purple near the rocks in the shadow of the cliffs . . . and when it gets really close in-shore, the waves get up a little and they are like chunks of blue-green glass . . . with

139

little frills of spray landing like melting lace on the sands . . . '

'Milo!' she said, astonished. 'I thought you were a poet, even yesterday!'

'I've been practising,' he admitted, half-smiling and half-shy. 'Gramp told me I'd got to be your eyes . . . So — so I'm learning . . . '

'You certainly are,' agreed Cressy, and gave his arm a little hug of approval. 'I can see it all.'

'That's all right, then,' Milo said, in an absurdly matter-of-fact voice. 'Anything else I can do to oblige?'

'Yes,' said Cressy. 'Stop being so nice to me — and let's get on with that cage for Boxer.'

Bo'sun, having followed them down to the sea and sat himself down happily on a patch of sun-warmed rock, found that his rest was shortlived, for his people were off again up the beach, — and as his orders were to look after Cressy, there was no help for it but to follow them. Good-naturedly, with a faint arthritic grunt, he lumbered to his feet again, and set off after them, — a golden, devoted shadow.

★ ★ ★

140

Boxer the hare was asleep when they looked in on him, and they decided to leave him in peace till the new cage was ready for him.

Milo collected various tools and some wood and chicken wire, and Cressy actually felt confident enough to carry a basket of bits and pieces in one hand, while tapping along with her white stick in the other. Bo'sun was given a wooden strut to carry, which he managed very well until he tried to go sideways through the old cowshed door.

The little owls were still in their eyrie up in the crook of the old roof-beam, and snoring happily in their sleep until one of the parents came back with something to eat. Milo described them to her, as far as he could see or guess at the state of their development, — speckled and fluffy, all eyes and beak, and their parents white-breasted, long of wing, sandy-and-gold mottled plumage above, and once again those enormous wide-open gold-rimmed eyes.

'Won't they mind us?'

'I don't think so,' Milo said. 'The chicks won't notice, and the parents are both out hunting. So long as we don't disturb the nest — it's high up out of reach anyway — I don't think they'll be bothered.'

Cressy was fascinated by the snoring noise,

and so was Bo'sun, but Milo soon got down to work on the cage, and all Cressy had to do was hold the wire taut, or steady a piece of wood while Milo sawed it or hammered it. All Bo'sun had to do was keep out of the way, and avoid bits of off-cuts falling on his head. There was plenty to do, but also time to talk.

'Milo, can I ask you something?'

'Surely.'

'What's all this between your mother and Gramp-the-Champ?'

Milo sighed, and finished hammering in the next staple before he answered. 'It's — difficult, Cressy . . . I don't know if I can explain it.'

'Try,' Cressy commanded. She thought it might be better for all of them if the problem was out in the open.

'Well, — ' he hesitated, and then went on talking while he was working, his fingers busy, his eyes on his work, not on Cressy, — though she could not see his embarrassment or his distress, 'you knew about my father being drowned?'

'Yes, I did hear . . . It was soon after we left here the last time, wasn't it?'

'Nearly four years ago,' said Milo, and Cressy did not miss the pain in his voice.

'I'm so sorry, Milo.'

'Yes, well, — ' he said helplessly, 'you know all about that, too — losing a parent.'

Cressy made no comment on that, but when he didn't go on, she prompted him gently. 'So?'

'So . . . it was an accident — like yours — only this time it was nobody's fault.' For a moment there was stark anger in Milo's voice, as if he was thinking of Cressy's accident and her mother's death, and that senseless boy driver who had caused it. 'You see,' he explained, 'one of the crew — a mate of my Dad's — got swept overboard, and Dad went in after him.'

'Did he — rescue him?'

'Oh yes — just. It was a terrible night. The seas were horrendous. Dad got him back to the rope they had thrown, and they hauled him up, but when they came back with the rope for Dad, he'd gone.'

Cressy was silent. Then at last she said, remembering Sally, her brave and loving mother, 'terrible . . . but at least he chose what to do.'

'Exactly,' said Milo, sounding fierce and strange all of a sudden. 'He *chose*, — and I'm proud of him for choosing. But Mum — my mother — sees it differently.'

'How?' asked Cressy, not sure if she understood.

'She blames Gramp for not being the one to jump in.'

'But — but he was the *skipper*, wasn't he?' Cressy knew enough about the sea and the trawlers to understand what this meant.

Milo looked across at her in silent approval. But she could not see his relief at her quick understanding, so he answered: 'Yes, he was. In charge of his own boat and his crew, and in charge of the whole trawler fleet, really. It was his job to get everyone home, — and in a storm like that, it was a hard enough job, believe me.'

'I do believe you,' said Cressy.

'And even if he had gone in after the other crewman, Gramp was too old to be much use in a sea like that . . . I don't think he even considered it. And I don't think my Dad stopped to consider *anything*. He just went — and took his chance.'

'But Catherine still blames Gramp?'

Milo sighed again, and hit a nail rather too hard. 'Dad — Kitto was her husband, after all. To her, I suppose, it was the end of the world . . . She would think Gramp would be much less of a loss!' His voice was suddenly hard and full of angry bitterness. How could you reason with a woman like his mother? She could only see one side of it — her loss of a beloved husband, and her young son's loss of a devoted father.

'But you can't think like that!' exclaimed Cressy.

'No,' said Milo sadly. '*I* can't. But she can.'

Cressy was silent again for a few moments. Then she said quietly: 'You know, my Dad got like that for a while. He was so angry — about Sally — about my mother — and about me. He seemed to go absolutely stiff with rage. I couldn't reach him. I couldn't *touch* him, he was unapproachable.'

'What happened to change him?'

'I cried,' said Cressy simply. 'It wasn't intentional. I didn't *plan* it or anything . . . But one day, I just couldn't take any more, — being unable to see what was happening to him, and feeling so sort of helpless, and then — you know, Milo, the dark sometimes gets to me and makes me panic . . . and I thought — here am I, blind as a bat, and I don't know what on earth is happening to my Dad, or to me either. What is to become of us? And I just — just fell apart and cried myself silly.'

'I'm not surprised,' said Milo, and there was a new warmth and understanding in his voice. 'And that did the trick, of course.'

'Why, of course?'

'Because *you* needed comforting,' he said.

'Your Dad would know, when he thought about it, that you and your future were what mattered now.

'Yes,' agreed Cressy heavily. 'And it's the same for you, I suppose, with Catherine, only she can't see it yet.'

'Perhaps I should cry,' Milo said drily.

'Can you?' Cressy asked, greatly daring.

'No,' said Milo, and laughed to cover what lay behind that painful admission

'It's a bit of a burden, isn't it?' said Cressy.

Surprisingly, Milo laughed again. 'Oh Cressy! Trust you to get to the point!'

'Well, isn't it?'

'Yes,' he admitted. 'It puts me in an impossible position, really. Mum hates the sea and everything to do with it (or so she says) and won't hear of me making a living by it. Gramp — though he never says so — would dearly love me to join him on *Crystal Rose* like my Dad did, only he does not like to upset my mother. Catherine says she hates Gramp for encouraging me, — and I spend all my time trying to keep the peace between them.'

'So what are you going to do?' asked Cressy, always the practical one looking for sensible answers to every problem.

Milo laughed again. 'Compromise. If I get

146

my A-level grades, that is.'

'How?'

'I'm going to Exeter to read Marine Biology. That way, I'll be at university but near enough to get home to see Mum. But when I'm qualified, obviously, my work will take me back to sea!'

'Clever!' applauded Cressy, smiling.

'Yes, but I mean it, Cress. It *is* what I want to do.'

'All those animals and sea creatures . . .' murmured Cressy. 'Are you sure it's only *marine* biology you want?'

'No, I'm not,' admitted Milo. 'But it'll be a start. Biology first — marine second? . . . I don't know . . . But at least I'll learn how to help *some* of them!'

Cressy heard the stress behind Milo's gentle voice, and laid her hand on his. 'You've been a bit torn in two by all this, haven't you? . . . That makes two of us trying to pick up the pieces . . . Shall we go and fetch Boxer? That's one piece we can pick up at least.'

Milo suddenly put an unguarded arm round her and hugged her very close. 'Thank God you came down when you did, Cress! For someone blind, you see very clearly! And by the way, bats aren't blind — they've developed a kind of built-in radar, and I think you're acquiring it, too!' Then he released her, his special accolade given, and pulled her to her feet. 'Yes, you're right. let's go and fetch Boxer. He's only asking for what we want, too — a bit of freedom and a bit of sky!'

★ ★ ★

Stephen was glad that Milo had so readily taken Cressy under his protective wing, and glad that the whole new set-up meant that she had a great deal more freedom than she had been able to get at home in the busy, uncaring suburbs. He was a naturally generous man, and his whole concern now was geared in his mind to Cressy's comfort — Cressy's progress towards reasonable independence — and Cressy's happiness, if such a thing could be achieved. But all the same, he found himself curiously lonely when she was not with him. He had got used to being her guide and mentor in those difficult first days, knowing she relied on his judgement, his confidence in her ability to cope with her blindness, and even his touch to reassure her when she occasionally lost heart . . . Am I getting too possessive? he wondered, as he sat at his computer and looked out of the Wrecker's window at the lovely little cove basking in the summer sun . . . Would Sally disapprove? . . . It's so difficult to know how much I ought to let her take her own risks . . . I wish I knew what was right . . .

And then he heard her step and her tapping stick on the narrow, twisting stairs of the ancient cottage. It was on the tip of his tongue to call out: 'Cressy, don't try to come up. I'll come down,' but he suddenly thought: No. If she wants to come up, I must let her. So he sat on at his desk, waiting for those steps to hesitate or fail, or stumble — and of course they did not.

She came into the room, one hand outstretched and probing, white stick in the other, and went unerringly across to his chair, laying her free hand across his shoulders. 'I thought you might be wondering where I was.'

He smiled, and leant his head back for a moment against her encircling arm. 'You're getting very clever at finding your way about.'

Cressy laughed. 'Milo says I'm developing a built-in radar, like a bat!'

'So you are,' agreed Stephen, still smiling, and though she could not see his face, she could hear the smile in his voice.

'It seems so much easier down here,' she said.

'Does it? Why?'

'I don't know . . . There's more space — and there are more pointers, somehow.'

'Such as?'

'Oh . . . sounds — the sea, and the shore-wind, and the sea-birds calling, and — and scents . . . Maybe I'm becoming more sensitive — but everything smells simply marvellous!'

Stephen laughed. 'After London, that's not surprising!'

'No, I know. But it's amazing how many different scents there are . . . ' She hesitated, as if she was trying to say something quite different, and didn't know how to put it. 'Everything feels more open, somehow,' she murmured. 'The barriers are down.'

'Are they?' Stephen wondered if that was true. He had not yet been able to talk to Cressy about dear Sally without difficulty, and he wondered painfully if it would ever get easier . . . And for a moment another fleeting vision came into his mind — a picture of Catherine's stiff, unyielding figure as she confronted good old Gramp-the-Champ with cold, unforgiving eyes . . . Plenty of barriers there.

'You know when we were deciding whether to come down here or not, — I said familiar surroundings were *too* familiar?'

'Yes,' agreed Stephen bleakly.

'Well, I wanted to tell you — somehow Mum feels much nearer to us *here* — I mean, she's here because she loved being here, not because it's her place or her duty. Do you know what I mean?'

'Yes,' said Stephen again, and swallowed hard.

'I think — ' said Cressy, at last daring to say what she had come to say, 'she'd want to see us enjoying ourselves, — don't you?'

Stephen nodded, forgetting that Cressy couldn't see his choked-up agreement. 'Yes,' he said at last. 'She would.'

'Well then,' Cressy challenged, summoning gaiety into her voice, 'would you like to come out with us? Milo wants to take us out in the *Gannet* to look at a bird colony on some rock.'

'I'd love to,' agreed Stephen, thankfully relinquishing his work, and getting to his feet. And he was almost ashamed at the extra small spurt of warmth that crept into the cold wilderness of his heart as he realised that his young daughter did want his company after all. 'Away with work!' he said. 'Where are you taking me?'

'Over the seas and far away,' said Cressy. 'Won't it be fun?'

★ ★ ★

They walked down to the little beach together, with Cressy holding on dutifully to the guiding rope, and found Milo holding the *Gannet* steady for them against the high tide which was already lifting the little boat with every encroaching wave.

'You'd better take your shoes and socks off, he said, smiling at Stephen. 'I can carry Cressy.'

'Oh no you can't!' Cressy laughed. 'I don't mind getting my feet wet . . . Just give me a hand, will you?'

She was familiar with little boats from the holiday jaunts in earlier years, and she was still very neat and nippy despite her blindness. In no time at all, it seemed, she was sitting in the boat, and Stephen was rather more laboriously clambering in after her. Milo stayed in the water just long enough to give *Gannet* a push into deeper water, and then leapt in after them. In a few moments the little outboard motor was purring and *Gannet* was skimming merrily through the gentle swell of the Cove.

'It'll get a little rougher out of the Cove,' he warned them. 'But nothing much. It's pretty calm today.'

Cressy was sitting quite still with the shore

152

wind on her face, and one hand over the side trailing in the water, determined to be in touch with the sea even if she could not see it. Stephen thought she looked absurdly happy, even though she could only feel the small waves lapping the hull of the boat, and could only guess at the sparkle of sunlight on the water by the warmth of the summer sun on her uplifted face.

'No broken bottles today?' she teased Milo, and he began to laugh.

'No. Yes. There are always a few . . . But it's very silky today.'

'Colours?'

'A lot of very deep blue further out, — more green and gold here, over the shallows . . . It'll probably be even deeper blue when we get to Bird Rock . . . The real ocean begins out there.'

For a while Milo did not speak again, for the noise of the little outboard motor made it difficult for the others to hear him, and he concentrated on getting his little craft as swiftly and calmly to its destination without risks or delays. There were hidden rocks at the edge of the Cove, beyond each long enclosing arm of rocky outcrop from the descending cliffs, — but Milo knew them all and steered a clear course through the translucent waters of the sandy bay to the deep sea blueness beyond.

When they came near to Bird Rock, the sound of all those strident voices calling to one another came across the water to them like a wave of chattering conversation. Milo cut the engine and took up the oars, allowing *Gannet* to drift nearer — but not too near — the steep sides of the rocky islet.

'They sound like a crowd of people having a party,' said Cressy.

Milo laughed. 'Don't they? . . . You know, Gramp told me I ought to teach you all the different bird cries . . . I'd have a job here.'

'How many kinds are there here?'

'I don't know exactly . . . but there's gannets and kittiwakes, and fulmers and guillemots, and skuas, — and the arctic terns are usually here by now . . . ' He paused, squinting up at the wheeling circles of wings — white and black and grey — that wove constantly changing skeins and patterns along the cliff edge and over the sea. 'And then there's the gulls, of course,' he added.

'How many kinds of gull?' Cressy was nothing if not persistent.

'Um — black-headed, herring gull, black back and lesser black back — and what they call the common gull — and I expect there's others, too.'

'Not puffins?'

'No. Too rocky. They like to nest in burrows — like shearwaters. They need a bit of turf and sandy soil on top of the cliff . . . This is too sheer for them . . . '
He turned his head towards Cressy, who was still gazing upward towards the cliffside, not trying to see but trying to hear the different voices of the squabbling birds.

'You can probably make out the kittiwakes,' he said. 'They seem to come through the others. It's like their name, you see, *kitt-ee-wayke* . . . '

Cressy was listening intently. 'Yes. I think I can hear them — among all the rest . . . Any more?'

'I've forgotten the cormorants and shags. They mostly nest on the rockiest ledges, looking straight out to sea . . . But we've got them round the Cove as well . . . They come closer in-shore nowadays, — even into the rivers.'

'No storm petrels?'

It was a loaded question, and Milo understood it. 'Not here. At nesting time they seek out some remote spot that has turf for burrows, like the puffins and shearwaters . . . They are too small to compete with the bigger bird colonies . . . But most of the time, they're away over the sea, — never coming in to land . . . '

Cressy gave a quick nod of consent, and stopped trying to distinguish all the deafening babble of the birds, and turned her head towards Milo again. 'Describe, please!'

Milo in turn looked at Stephen. He, after all, was the expert with the artist's eye.

'No,' said Stephen, waving one hand at Milo, while the other was already busy with sketchpad and pencil. 'I'm going to work! This is fascinating!'

'Is it a place that would fit into your book illustrations?'

'It might be . . . I'll tell you later.'

Cressy accepted that cheerfully. 'Well then, come on, Milo.'

So Milo drew a deep breath, remembering Gramp-the-Champ's gentle old voice saying: '*Paint her a picture . . . People her world . . .*'

'Well,' he began, 'it's very tall, — the rock, I mean, and very black and sheer at the bottom. It rises out of the sea all smooth and glistening, like a seal's flank, only huge . . . And up above, where the ledges begin, it is almost entirely white with birds — all nesting, or quarrelling about nest sites, or sitting on eggs . . . And above the sitters, and there are *hundreds* of those, — the air is white with wings, — wings of all kinds, diving and circling, and trying to settle on the rock, or rising up again to look for

156

somewhere else, or being pushed off by someone who got there first, or fighting off marauders.'

'Marauders?'

'The skuas. They dive-bomb the nests and eat the eggs, or even carry off the chicks . . . They're real pirates, the skuas . . . And some of the bigger gulls do it, too . . . ' He paused, looking out at the wheeling bird colonies, and then his eyes came down to the deep-sea inky darkness round the edge of the rocky islet. 'And below . . . ' he said, 'where the sea is inky dark close to the rock, the auks and little auks are zooming over the surface like speed boats, and diving deep and catching fish and flying off, and coming back for more . . . and the arctic terns are there, too, diving down from a great height, wings folded and beaks outstretched, like an army of black-and-white swordfish, cleaving straight through the water without even a splash! . . . They're beautiful in the water, and so are the auks, — all smooth and supple and graceful — and the terns are in the air, too, but the auks are rather dumpy, awkward birds on land . . . ' He was looking up again, and suddenly his voice changed to excitement, and he added eagerly, 'and up there — way up above all the other circling and diving birds — is an osprey — a fish-eagle . . . I'm sure it is! You don't often see one of those down here . . . They mostly live round the coasts of Scotland . . . But I'm sure that's what he is!'

'What does he look like?' Cressy's head was tilted upwards, but she was not trying to see the bird, only waiting for Milo's words to make it come alive for her.

'Very wide wing-span,' said Milo, 'with 'fingers' along the edges . . . and a sort of wedge-shaped whitish tail, and a pale head, I think, though he's too high up to see clearly — the rest of him is all brown and mottled, and he's hovering, riding the air, quite still . . . waiting to strike . . . '

'What is he after?'

'Fish, probably. Not eggs or babies — though he might take those, too, even young fledgelings, given the chance . . . '

Cressy sighed. 'It's rather a cruel world out there, isn't it?'

'Yes,' agreed Milo. 'I'm afraid nature's like that! It's all a bit of a war of survival.' Then, feeling Cressy's sudden sadness, he reached under the duckboard of his seat and brought out a small wicker cage, which he had kept hidden from sight until now. 'I've got something here, Cressy, that I want you to help me with, will you?'

Her head came round, and her smile was

eager. 'Of course. What is it?'

'It's a Sooty Tern,' said Milo. 'Just about ready to be released . . . I thought you might like to do it.'

'What happened to it?'

'Crashed into the trawl-rig in a gale, and broke its wing. Birds often do, blown on to the trawlers in rough weather . . . The crew wanted to wring its neck, but Gramp brought it back to me.'

'Like the Storm Petrel?'

'Yes,' agreed Milo. 'But she could fly on when she was rested. This one couldn't.'

'Did you set it's wing?'

'No,' said Milo. 'It's a delicate job, setting a wing . . . But I've got a friendly vet who does the skilled work . . . ' He had got the wicker cage on the seat beside him now, which was difficult as he was still keeping *Gannet* steady with the oars so that she didn't get too near the steep sides of Bird Rock. He would have to get Cressy to undo the fastening of the cage, if her fingers could find it.

'So where has it been? It wasn't in the shed with the others, was it?'

'No. Not for the last week or so . . . It's been learning to fly again in the little flying cage I built further up the hill . . . We often have injured birds, you know, and they all have to get their wings strong again before we let them go . . . They have so many hundreds of miles to go . . . when they do take off!'

Cressy saw the sense of that. 'And now he's ready?'

'I think so . . . And I thought — with the other terns here, he might be happier and find a group to join . . . and find his way home.'

'Where is home?' Cressy asked, thinking of the Storm Petrel whose only real home was the endless ocean swell and its long-rolling, ceaselessly moving waves.

Milo nodded, as if she had spoken. 'Yes, a bit like the petrels. Mostly over the sea, and from a long way off . . . They aren't called arctic terns for nothing, — they are only visitors, here . . . ' He shifted the cage a little, resting his elbow on the lid as he still manoeuvred his oar. 'He can hear the other birds,' he said. 'He's getting restless. Time to go.'

'What must I do?'

'Undo the catch first . . . Then lift the lid very cautiously and put your hands inside. Take hold of the bird in a firm grip round its wings. Can you do that?'

'I think so,' said Cressy, and felt for the catch of the cage. But then a thought struck her, and she said: 'Tell me what he looks like before I let him go.'

'Well, the young birds are all sooty black with white speckles, but this is an adult, and he's a lovely glossy black on top, very white breast and under his wings, and the contrast of black-and-white sort of very sharp — very spick and span — white above his beak, but not all the way up to his head, and white tips to his tail feathers . . . He's a neat-looking bird, very smart when he's well, and he flies rather like a swallow with a forked tail, only he's better at diving than a swallow!'

'Lovely!' said Cressy, trying to picture it in her mind. 'And he's well and smart now?'

'Very — and raring to go!'

'Well, I'm ready now,' Cressy said. 'Tell me what to do.'

'Get your hands on the edge of the opening,' he said, 'and then put them straight in.' He watched her two hands find the right place, and then said sharply: 'Now!'

Cressy's fingers found the bird and clasped themselves round it, feeling its warm flesh under the silken feathers and its tiny heart beating away in frantic excitement.

'Hold him firmly,' Milo said. 'He'll feel safer that way — and he'll be able to fly better if you launch him straight up into the air . . . He's a gliding bird, not used to land take-offs!'

Cressy held the bird tight, as she was told. 'Can I stand up?'

Milo hesitated, and then said: 'Yes, if Stephen holds you steady.'

Stephen smiled and put down his pencil. He had purposely kept out of the action and the conversation up till now, content to let Milo do the talking (which he was enormously good at!) and direct the proceedings as skilfully and calmly as he usually did. But now, clearly, another pair of hands was needed if Milo was to keep *Gannet* steady and Cressy was allowed to stand up in the boat (which wasn't usually allowed!) 'All right,' he said. 'Hold on, Cressy, I've got you.'

Cressy stood up, still holding the bird. 'Straight up into the sky?'

'No,' said Milo. 'Upwards and forwards. Stephen's got you. Lean outwards.'

Cressy leant outwards, her face towards the sea and the sky, not towards the rising walls of the rocky islet. 'Now?'

'Now!' said Milo. 'Lift him up — and let go!'

Cressy lifted her hands and threw the bird forwards and upwards, — skywards. 'Go!' she cried. 'Go safe and happy!'

She felt a shudder go through the pulsing, warm little body, and then it was gone.

'Bravo!' said Stephen.

'Well done!' said Milo. 'He's well and truly launched.'

'Will he be all right?'

'I hope so . . . At least he's got a good chance.'

'Goodbye bird,' said Cressy. 'I hope you make it!' And she sat down again in the boat, steered safely back by Stephen, and found herself feeling suddenly a little tired and sad.

Milo did not miss it. 'Home now,' he said gently. 'You've done your good deed for the day. Are you ready, Stephen?'

'Absolutely,' Stephen smiled. 'I've made some splendid sketches! . . . And I think it's about time for tea!'

Milo smiled from Stephen to his gallant young daughter. 'I'm sure it is,' he said, and turned little *Gannet* blithely for him.

★ ★ ★

When they got back the tide was well and truly on the way out, and there was a long expanse of wet gold sand to walk up to reach the rope walk and the path to the cottage. Milo had meant to beach the *Gannet* just above the receding water-line and walk up the sands to fetch his boat trolley, so that he could wheel the dinghy up the beach to its usual safe anchorage above the high-tide line.

But an anxious and disconsolate Bo'sun was waiting for them, right on the edge of the water, gazing out hopefully, and beginning to wag his plumy tail when he saw the little boat coming in to shore. It was clearly a puzzle to his doggie mind to know what was required of him and where his duty lay. Should he have stayed on shore and let Milo and Cressy and the big tall man go without him? Or should he have tried to swim after them and guard Cressy wherever they were going? How could he look after her if she went away from him in a boat out to sea? . . . He was allowed in Milo's boat sometimes, on short trips round the cove, — but this time he had been told sternly to stay behind. And he was a little hurt and bewildered by the rebuff. What had he done wrong?

But when he saw Cressy coming slowly towards him over the wet sand, he forgot his hurt and ran joyfully to meet her, barking a welcome, and Cressy stooped down unerringly, blindly certain of his welcoming closeness, and laid a hand on his golden head.

'We're back!' she told him, crooning to him softly. 'Were you waiting for us? What a faithful minder you are. And you see I'm quite safe, aren't I? And so is Milo and so is Dad . . . You've got nothing to worry about now . . . ' She gave the smooth, uplifted head another warm caress, and though she did not see the devotion in his amber eyes, she could feel it in every hair of his head, and added an extra hug for good measure. 'There!' she told him. 'Now you're in charge again. Everything is quite all right.'

But it wasn't, of course, when they got back to the rocky path to the cottage and were confronted by an angry, rather frightened Catherine.

'Where have you been?' she demanded. 'Milo, how dare you take such risks with Cressy!'

'There were no risks,' said Milo calmly. 'The sea was smooth as a millpond, — and no bad weather forecast.'

'It was a *lovely* trip,' put in Cressy, speaking up for Milo and herself and her father, all in one breath. 'Wasn't it, Dad?'

'Marvellous!' assented Stephen, with enthusiasm. 'All those birds — all those bird-voices clamouring for attention — all those wings!'

'And those divers!' Cressy added, 'zooming

down like dive bombers, cutting the water like swordfish!'

Catherine was looking at her in amazement. 'How do you know?'

'Milo told me,' said Cressy simply.

Catherine rounded on Milo then. 'So you can talk well enough when it's about boats and the sea! Why can't you get it into your head that the sea is dangerous.'

'I know that, Mother,' said Milo in a voice of ashes.

But here, surprisingly, Stephen intervened. It was time someone stood up to Catherine's prejudices which made her considerably blinder than his brave young daughter, — and high time the voice of reason had its say.

'Milo took a lot of trouble to arrange things safely.' Stephen's voice was mild still, but quite firm. 'We all had a very happy, peaceful trip — and some exciting new experiences, especially Cressy. Please don't spoil them.'

Catherine's mouth shut tight in astonishment.

'Now I'm going to put *my* kettle on,' Stephen continued smoothly, smiling a little at Catherine's expression. 'So why don't you all come to tea with me for a change?'

And, of course, Catherine could not refuse. Cressy could feel Milo's secret smile, though she could not see it, and she reached out, quite instinctively, and took hold of his hand and gave it a reassuring squeeze. Bo'sun, having been a bit alarmed by the warring voices, agreed with Cressy that things were all right now, and lay down at her feet.

And it was while Stephen was gracefully playing host and dispensing tea and biscuits all round, that a young voice at the door said: 'Is Milo there? I've got a message for him.'

'Yes,' said Milo, 'I'm here.'

'It's Joe and the Group,' said the voice. 'I don't suppose Cressy remembers us, but we were part of the gang, weren't we, long ago?'

'Yes,' agreed Milo, his voice suddenly warmer. 'You were. So?'

'Well, we're doing a bit of a concert tonight. Not a band gig, but a bit of all sorts — and people can bring anything they can play. Cressy used to play the flute a bit, didn't she?'

By this time, Cressy had come forward too, to stand beside Milo at the cottage door. The boy looking up at her took a swift breath of surprise. For the little fair girl who had chased round the rocks with him four years ago had turned into a kind of sleeping beauty — wide sea-green eyes that saw nothing but were nevertheless extremely beautiful, long corn-gold hair that framed a perfect heart-shaped face, and a mouth that looked sweet and vulnerable and ought to have been sad, but was now smiling quite happily at a face she could not see.

'Which of the gang were you?' she asked.

'I'm Benjamin,' said the voice, 'but they used to call me Beano.'

Cressy laughed, and held out her hand. 'Of course I remember you, Beano. You taught me how to catch crabs, and I think it was you who helped Milo pull me out of Mermaid's Pool.'

Beano was overwhelmed. His round, freckled face was one big smile. From that moment he was, like Bo'sun, and like Milo (though he would probably not admit it even to himself) Cressy's devoted slave.

'Will you come?' Beano asked, pale with hope. 'And Stephen — Mr. Latimer, too, of course. You used to play a bit, didn't you?'

'Guitar, a little,' said Stephen, suddenly shy before this cheerful boy. 'Never any good, though . . . '

'Did you bring it down?'

'Yes, but only to strum for Cressy.'

'Well, you can strum for us, too!' said Beano. The beaming smile extended further. 'What about you, Mrs. Trevelyan?'

'Oh. Oh no, I don't think so.' Catherine

168

retreated headlong into her forbidding manner. 'I don't play anything.'

'But you used to sing,' said Stephen, remembering bonfires on the sands, and young voices raised in happy abandon ... Even Catherine had been young and happy then. And now she was becoming old before her time, — locked in her own bitter grief and anger. 'Oh, come on, Catherine,' he urged, seeing her hesitate. 'It sounds like a wonderful party ... Let's all go.'

He got a fleeting impression, as he turned back to the young people on the doorstep, that a small, surreptitious glance of mutual understanding passed from Milo to Beano, — as if they had fulfilled a task successfully. Were they acting under orders? And if so, whose? There was only one man who could see that far ahead, and know that music could be Cressy's salvation, — and that was Gramp-the-Champ.

'All right then,' said Catherine bluntly. And then, trying belatedly to sound gracious: 'Thanks, Beano.'

'We'd love to come,' reinforced Stephen warmly. 'What time?' he called after the smiling Beano, who was just about to turn away and get his long legs climbing over the cliff to Port Quentin harbour.

'Any time after eight,' said Beano, over

his shoulder. 'Joe and the others can get there by the . . . Milo knows the way.' And he was gone over the hill, with Milo and Stephen smiling after him. Cressy was smiling, too, but almost in a nostalgic, far-too-adult way.

'What does he look like now?' she asked Milo.

'Just the same, only taller. All legs and elbows still.'

'Freckles?'

'More than ever!'

'And a superbly mischievous smile,' put in Stephen, not to be outdone.

'Perfect!' laughed Cressy. 'What does he play, Milo?'

'The trumpet,' Milo told her. 'Very loud and clear!'

They were all laughing now, — even Catherine.

'I can't wait,' said Cressy.

★ ★ ★

To Stephen's surprise, the 'concert' did not seem to be taking place in a house or a hall, but on the shore of Port Quentin harbour, just underneath the balcony of the 'Fisherman's Arms' which overlooked the Hard and the quay beyond.

At low tide there was a lot of space on the sands between the enclosing harbour walls, and cars were able to park among the smaller beached boats, the stacks of in-shore lobster-pots and drying nets and market buoys and all the miscellaneous clutter that lay about in a fishing port at low tide. Catherine, after her initial reluctance, had decided to be reasonably unbending and helpful, so she drove them all over the rough track back way to Port Quentin and parked the old jeep on the beach among the other cars. There would be another four or five hours, she calculated, before the incoming tide reached the harbour sands.

There was a scattering of interested onlookers on the beach, and leaning on the harbour walls, and a more decorous bunch of onlookers had gathered on the pub balcony, deciding that music and beer would go very well together.

Milo took Cressy by the hand and led her across to the little group of musicians getting themselves organised on the cleared space of the concrete Hard. Beano, one of the busy group setting up instruments and mikes, looked up and smiled. 'Cressy!' he called, his freckled face lighting up with welcome. 'Look, guys, here's Cressy! You remember Cressy, don't you?'

171

A chorus of welcoming noises emerged from various directions, confusing Cressy a little, but Milo took her carefully from one to the other, making sure she knew what was needful to know about each one.

'This is Ollie Winters — you probably remember him? Hair like white wheat sticking up like stubble, large feet, and very good at whelking . . . A good rock climber, too, except that his feet were always tripping him up.'

Cressy laughed, and took the outstretched hand. 'Do they still?'

'Yes,' admitted a warm, friendly voice. 'All the time!'

The laughter became general. 'Ollie is head of the Group,' explained Milo, 'in so far as it *has* a head, but it's mostly headless and sometimes legless!'

'Do you mind!' said Ollie, laughing even more. 'I'm supposed to prance about with a guitar and sing,' he volunteered cheerfully, 'if my feet don't get entangled in the mike cables!'

'And we have to back him,' added another voice, a girl's this time, 'which is sometimes difficult when he takes off without warning!' She also took Cressy's hand in a warm, firm grip of reassurance. 'I'm Sue,' she told her. 'I play violin, and my brother, Joe, plays keyboard, and even a real piano when he gets the chance!'

Sue was a pretty girl, tall and slim, with a dark, sleek cap of hair curving round a shapely head, and very white skin which gleamed in the frame of her short black tunic. Her brother was equally slim and dark, and somewhat more intense of eye, but equally smiling and friendly.

'Describe!' commanded Cressy to Milo, and he laughed.

'Twins, Cressy. Dark and dangerous. Elegant to look at, but beware! They can get quite wild when the music takes them!'

'I can usually stir them up with the drums!' said an extra voice, and Milo made another introduction.

'This is Mags Porter — generally known as Portly.'

'For obvious reasons!' put in Beano's cheeky voice, and there were sounds of a slight scuffle.

Cressy grinned and said: 'Well, you need to be expansive for drums!'

There was a general giggle, and Ollie's voice said cheerfully: 'Milo, she'll do! Welcome aboard, Cressy!'

For a moment Cressy was a bit alarmed. What had she let herself in for? She fingered her silver flute nervously and said: 'I don't know if I — '

'Oh, don't worry,' said Ollie, swiftly aware, 'we're not into serious rehearsal stuff. We like to do our own thing, just as it comes . . . Just let go, and play what you feel like. You'll be surprised how well things fit together once we get going . . . '

Cressy thought desperately: Yes. I *will* be surprised! But she knew she had to try. It was a challenge Milo had set her — and she hated to disappoint him. She drew a deep breath. 'O.K.,' she said. 'I'll try . . . ' and prayed for inspiration and fingers that could feel the notes without her eyes to guide them.

Beano began things with a long and spirited trumpet solo, accompanied by Joe on the keyboard when he could catch up with Beano's erratic beat. Beano was actually very good, Cressy realised, but inclined to gallop into wildly brilliant passages of finger-work which occasionally produced a glaring blast on a gloriously wrong note, but mostly didn't — and nobody seemed to mind, anyway. There was even a burst of applause from the pub balcony, and a voice from above said: 'Go it, Beano!'

Then Sue began weaving a curious Celtic-sounding air on her violin, sad and strange and haunting, and Joe made a miasma of soft chords on his keyboard to frame it, and presently, to Cressy's surprise, she heard Stephen's guitar joining the quiet chords with his own gentle thrumming. Ollie did not use his own electric guitar this time, but occasionally broke into a sotto voce gentle humming, as if it was really a song but somehow too sad to sing aloud . . .

'*Now*, Cressy,' murmured Milo. 'Don't follow them — lead them . . . This is a sea song . . . '

A sea song? thought Cressy, and suddenly the violin's caressing voice seemed to be speaking to her of misty islands and distant seas, and ancient voyages in coracles and long-ships, and deep, dark forests that came down to unknown shores, and sea-birds crying overhead, and a white stag that ran on the shore, tossing his silver antlers in bright moonlight, and a traveller who had come on a long, long journey and who sang a lonely song . . . and her fingers found the song that he sang, and poured its sadness and loneliness out into the listening air.

There was an extraordinary silence when the song ended and the rest of the Group drew to a close. Then another burst of applause came from above, and Ollie said, close to Cressy's ear: 'Wow! Cressy. Talk about spellbinding!'

'You wove it for me,' she said, turning a dazed face in his direction 'What happened?'

'I don't know,' Ollie said. 'Sue started it!'

'And then we kinda gelled,' said Joe, sounding a little awestruck.

'Where did you go to?' asked Sue's voice, also a little shaken.

'I don't know . . . ' Cressy admitted, still sounding a little dazed. 'Back in time, I think . . . Didn't I?

'Don't ask me!' said Sue, smiling now, and making it very clear to Cressy that she approved. 'You were the leader — I just followed!'

'That's a mug's game,' said Cressy. 'It gets you nowhere!'

'Oh no,' said Sue, 'it got us somewhere all right!' And there was a small chorus of agreement from the others, which Cressy thankfully interpreted as a general vote of confidence.

After that it was easy. Somehow the small group of young musicians had reached a point of understanding and close co-operation that none of them had expected. (Except for Milo, who had remembered Gramp's prophetic voice saying: '*Spellbinding, free style . . . Cressy'd like that . . .* ' and who now knew he need do nothing more for

176

Cressy tonight except to murmur a quiet word of praise.) 'Well done,' he said softly. 'Go on exploring . . . It's full of magic out there . . . '

And Cressy smiled in his direction, and lifted the silver flute to her lips again, as Sue began another far-away voyage.

Stephen, standing back a little from the group, with Catherine, silent and astonished, beside him, knew he would never forget this moment, — or its equally magic setting. The summer twilight had dwindled almost to silver dusk, and the lights of all the little houses climbing up the slopes round the harbour were glowing like fireflies and casting golden reflections in the water under the dark cliffs beyond the harbour wall. The tide was turning now, and a sheen of pale water was creeping over the sands, — and more gleams and sparks of reflected light seemed to spring up and shine as the slow tide came.

The young musicians were all improvising as they went along — they did not need any light, but there was a small glowing street lamp just behind them, under the pub balcony, and this cast a gentle nimbus of diffused light round them so that they seemed like strange, mystical beings enclosed in a bubble of radiance. It only needed their music to make one bystander murmur: 'Out of this world!'

But there were merry moments, too. It wasn't all Celtic twilight. Beano and Portly got together and made an extraordinary amount of rhythmic noise with trumpet and drums, — Ollie sang a couple of current pop songs (with backing) in his light, easy tenor, happily pouring out the usual heart-rending phrases of unrequited (or requited) love . . . 'Now that you've gone . . . ' or 'Where do we go from here . . . ?' or 'What's it all for? . . . ' and so on.

Then Sue and Joe began an Irish jig and Cressy found her fingers flying to keep up and weave frilly embellishments round the tune, and Portly found a small light tabor-drum to tap with its own small insistent beat to keep the feet dancing, and Ollie and Stephen both strummed away on their guitars, and from there Sue suddenly turned the Irish tune into a very free version of the Helston Flora dance, and even Beano could join in then with his agile, perky trumpet, and it got so wild and exciting that all the listeners round the Hard and on the quay began to dance too, and the onlookers on the balcony clapped the beat, and one or two of the trawlers getting ready for the night's fishing let out a couple of cheerful blasts on their hooters to join in. Finally, when Sue's and Cressy's fingers were almost worn out. Beano let out one final, enormous, high trumpet blare, and the players collapsed in happy laughter.

The tide was coming in faster now, and people began to move their cars, and the pub landlord sent down a large tray of drinks 'on the house' for his free entertainment. It was almost time to go, but Ollie had one more surprise up his sleeve . . . A few of his friends strolled up casually and joined him near the mike, all of them members of their local chapel choir and used to singing together . . . And the rest of the Group got ready to play their last song.

Softly and very gently the young men's voices began on the famous old tune 'All through the night . . . ' The violin and the flute took up the melody and wove patterns round it, Joe's keyboard and Stephen's guitar made pulsing hushed chords round it, Portly's drum became nothing but a gentle whisper, and even Beano put a mute on his trumpet and made it sing soft and small. The voices, in close harmony now, sang true and sweet and quiet, fading at last to a gentle, dwindling hum on the final, loving chord, the flute lifted to one last pure silver note, and the whole group ended together in a dreaming, vanishing whisper of dying sound.

The silence came back then, and this time there was no applause, and Stephen was not the only one who had a lump in his throat. But then the voices from the balcony called out 'Goodnight!' and other voices all round the harbour joined in from every side, friend greeting friend and calling across the water. 'Goodnight! . . . Goodnight!'

'Time to go,' murmured Milo, and took Cressy's hand again, for he knew she would find it hard to come back from the place of enchantment to which the music had led her.

'Time to go,' echoed the Group, smiling and content now that their spell had been woven and made good.

'Cressy, we love you. Come again!' said Ollie, — and 'Come again!' the others repeated as they packed away their gear and went off into the night.

Catherine, still curiously quiet and shaken, went off after them to fetch the jeep. Stephen turned to help Cressy, but saw that he need not. She had fast hold of Milo's hand and was standing quite still with her head tilted towards the sky.

'Are there stars?' she said.

'A few faint ones — growing brighter every minute,' answered Milo, 'and gold reflections in the sea . . . a night for magic.'

'I know,' said Cressy. 'I can feel it all round me . . . ' She did not need her eyes to tell her that the night was enchanted. She had reached a new stage in heightened awareness without the help of sight, and somehow it was very comforting, and curiously exciting. 'It was the music that did it . . . ' she murmured.

'Not only,' Milo told her, his voice warm with praise. 'It was you.'

Part Three

Glimpses of Blue

The next day, Gramp-the-Champ came back with the trawler fleet, and as soon as he had got his catch weighed and boxed and sent off to the Newlyn fish market, he strolled over the hill to see how Bo'sun was getting on with Cressy. He didn't have any doubts about it really. Bo'sun was an obedient and affectionate dog, and he had clearly taken to Cressy when they first met. But all the same, Bo'sun was Gramp's dog, and it was natural for its owner to be a little anxious about him.

He needn't have worried. The three of them — Cressy, Milo and Bo'sun — were on the beach together, and Cressy was walking along at the water's edge quite fearlessly, without her white stick, but with her hand just resting on Bo'sun's silky head. The old dog was keeping pace with her, in perfect accord, and Milo, on the other side of Cressy, was guarding her steps against hidden rocks and boulders or sudden sunken pools in the smooth surface of the sand.

They looked so happy walking there that Gramp almost decided to turn round and leave them in peace, but Bo'sun heard his step and turned his head to look, his plumy tail wagging a joyous welcome.

'What is it, Bo'sun?' asked Cressy, feeling the sudden movement of his head. 'Is someone there?'

'It's Gramp,' said Milo, his voice as full of welcome as Bo'sun's tail. 'And Bo'sun doesn't know who to go to now. Shall we let him go?'

'Yes, of course we must. He's Gramp's dog. He'll be dying to say hallo to him.'

'Not dying, I hope,' said Gramp's deep voice close beside them.

'Go on, Bo'sun, go on!' Cressy said, not sure quite how near Gramp was, or whether the old dog knew what to do next. And Milo, smiling over Bo'sun's head at Gramp, stood still to watch what Bo'sun would do.

For a moment the old dog did nothing except look from Cressy to Gramp and back again, still not sure where his duty lay. But then he seemed to sense that Cressy really meant him to go, and he ran, barking joyfully, right up to Gramp's outstretched hand, and then back to Cressy, and then back to Gramp again, delirious with excitement and relief. Gramp, his god, was back in his life. He would do his duty, of course, and look after Cressy whom he loved, too, — but Gramp was the one, and Gramp had first call on his affections and his loyalty. Never was a dog so happy or so confused, or so filled with delight as he ran to and fro between them.

'I think we'd better all sit down together,' said Gramp, laughing, 'or Bo'sun will split in two!'

So they found a warm, protected spot out of the sea-wind, with their backs against the sun-warmed rock, and allowed Bo'sun to climb happily all over them and lick their faces and thump them with his tail in an ecstasy of devotion.

'What a welcome!' said Gramp, pleased and touched by the old dog's display of affection, — and he laid a soothing hand on the golden head. 'Calm down now, Bo'sun. We're all here together — no need to feel pulled in two!'

And Cressy, reaching out, put her arms round the dog and said: 'You've got us all where you want us, Bo'sun. Make the most of it!'

Milo, meanwhile, had proceeded in his usual quietly miraculous fashion to collect some driftwood and start a fire. Cressy wouldn't be able to see it, he knew, but she could hear the hiss and crackle of the burning wood, and feel the warmth of the flames on her face. Also, he had a few other things up his sleeve (or in his rucksack) and planned on providing a small feast for his friends.

'That feels lovely,' said Cressy, stretching her hands out to the fire. 'What are you going to do with it?'

'Cook on it,' said Milo, smiling. (Cressy could always 'hear' him smiling these days. It somehow got into his voice and was unmistakable). 'Just wait a minute while I fetch the last ingredients, and I'll give you a running commentary.' His footsteps receded as he went down the beach to the water-line.

Gramp took the opportunity to do a little morale-boosting of his own. 'I hear you've been distinguishing yourself with Ollie's Group,' he said, and his deep voice, like Milo's, also had a smile in it somewhere.

'Where did you hear that? You've only been back five minutes!'

'Oh, word travels fast round the port,' said Gramp carelessly. 'As a matter of fact, Cressy, you are something of a nine-day wonder at present. Everyone is talking about you.'

Cressy sighed. 'It's not so hard to play the flute by ear and not sight.'

'No,' conceded Gramp. 'But you did more

than that, by all accounts.'

'It was Sue who started it,' Cressy said, determined to give credit where it was due. 'I just . . . followed on.'

'I think you went a long way beyond that,' Gramp said, his rich, gruff voice sounding resonant with approval. 'And I'm so glad you could . . . It means you can adventure almost anywhere now — do you realise that?'

'Yes,' admitted Cressy slowly. 'I do now . . . I didn't at the time, though. I just got carried off on some magic carpet or something!'

Gramp laughed. 'Well, keep jumping on to it whenever you get the chance! Music makes your horizons limitless, you know — especially if you can create it yourself!'

'I know,' murmured Cressy. She reached out and took Gramp's hand for a moment. (She was getting quite uncanny about finding where people were), 'And I have a strong suspicion that you engineered the whole thing! . . . And if you did, Gramp-the-Champ, thanks for a new freedom! You really are champion!'

They were both laughing when Milo returned and dropped a live starfish into Cressy's hand. She gave a small, cheerful scream, and then her fingers felt it all round for identification. She could feel its suckers under the five arms as they sought for purchase on something solider than Cressy's soft hand.

'Are you going to cook it?' she asked, still laughing.

'No!' He joined in the laughter. 'I'll put it back presently . . . I just thought you'd like to hold a bit of sea-world in your hand, like the old days.'

'So I do,' she told him, smiling. 'But what are you going to cook, then?'

Milo crouched down by the fire, and as he unloaded his pack and spread out its contents, he told Cressy what he was doing. 'I have here a billycan for boiling water, — and a frying pan with a handle that can turn up and not get burnt.'

'So?' said Cressy, intrigued.

'And I have here a can of fresh water from the trout stream, and better still, three small trout that I caught earlier this morning. They are wrapped in rock samphire at the moment, and a bit of fennel — both of which I found growing on our cliffs.'

'Mm,' said Cressy, relishing the thought of fresh brown trout. 'Lovely!'

'And here,' went on Milo, 'I have some fresh mussels from the rocks, and a few cockles and a few shrimps. We can put them in the boiling water, they won't take long.'

'Sounds amazing.' Cressy said, laughing again.

'And here,' added Milo, with a final flourish, 'is some of Mum's fresh bread, baked this morning, which I stole off the kitchen table, — and a pinch of salt, a bit of butter, two tea-bags and a wedge of cheese.'

'Well, we won't starve,' said Gramp, chuckling happily.

'You can talk!' retorted Milo. 'Here you are, just back from three night's fishing, — and I bet you haven't stopped to get yourself a good meal before coming over to see Bo'sun.'

'No, I haven't,' admitted Gramp, unabashed. 'And it wasn't only Bo'sun I came over to see!'

Milo grinned at him, and went on getting the food ready, — and Gramp leaned forward to put a bit more wood on the fire.

'For greens,' said Milo, stirring something in his pan, 'we can have sea-cabbage, or sea-beet, or rocket. Plenty to eat round here!'

It became a most marvellous driftwood barbecue meal, and when it was over and they were all licking their fingers, Gramp unexpectedly produced a couple of oranges from one of his capacious pockets. 'We always keep some on board,' he explained to

Cressy. 'We're not exactly at sea long enough to get scurvy — but we do get parched with the salt!'

'Perfect,' said Cressy, as Milo peeled one and put some of the segments in her hand. 'What a super feast! Milo, you're a wizard with the cookpot.' In fact, she thought, Milo is a bit of a wizard altogether, one way and another, and so is his grandfather.

'Can you hear the sandpipers calling?' asked Milo. 'The tide's out, and they're feeding on the sands.'

Cressy listened, and sure enough she could hear the shrill piping voices of the little birds calling 'psee-psee-pee' across the wet, shining sands of the cove.

'They're very tame,' said Milo. 'Sometimes they come inland up the trout-stream, and you can almost touch them.'

Cressy would have liked to touch them, and she was thinking back to the feel of Milo's Sooty Tern in her hands, and the extraordinary shudder of power that seemed to go through his tiny body as she let him go and launched him into the wind.

'I wonder where your Sooty Tern has got to,' she murmured.

'Far out to sea with his friends, I hope,' smiled Milo.

'Like the Storm Petrel . . . ' Cressy added

dreamily. Really, all that food and the warm fire and the summer sun were making her absurdly sleepy.

'Whereabouts were you aiming for today?' asked Gramp, also sounding idle and sleepy.

'Nowhere much,' Milo said. 'I wanted to take Cressy up the stream to the otter pool. There's one there that needs a paw looked at — but I need another pair of hands to cage him. They're a bit obstreperous for Cressy to handle!'

'I'm sure I could manage him!' protested Cressy, outraged.

Milo laughed. 'You'd be surprised how they can wriggle, — and bite if they feel cornered . . . But they're usually friendly enough, if you leave them in peace!'

'I could lend a hand,' offered Gramp, right on cue.

Milo smiled with relief. 'Would you.'

'I thought you'd never ask!'

So they packed up Milo's rucksack, and scattered the fire, and made their way slowly up the beach towards the tumbling troutstream in the narrow valley between the rocky cliffs. Bo'sun trotted happily beside Cressy, allowing her to hold his collar or touch his head for reassurance, but he was glad to notice that his beloved Gramp was close beside him, too.

On the way, they stopped at Milo's workshop behind the cottage to pick up a biggish metal cage that could house the injured otter. 'We may have to take him in to my friend the vet,' explained Milo, 'so he'll need a stout cage in the jeep.'

He also paused to have a look at his other patients, and painstakingly gave Cressy a summary of their progress, so that she could picture them and not feel left out. 'Foxy's paw is nearly mended . . . He'll be ready to go in a day or two. He's looking more perky, too. His ears are more pricked. The little hedgehogs are getting stronger. They can eat worms and things now, so they'll soon be able to forage for themselves.'

'What will you do with them?'

'Let them go near a garden. The sea isn't the right place for them, — not enough green foliage and not enough grubs . . . But we'll find the right place for them soon, and they'll do fine.'

He moved on to another cage and laughed. 'As for Wily Willy here, I wonder he hasn't burst with apoplexy, he's still so cross. But I think he's almost ready to go . . . Once he's got the bandage off his tail, he'll be off up the nearest tree like a streak of lightning!'

Cressy said slowly and without any hint

of sadness in her voice: 'So it'll be Freedom Week soon.'

'It will,' agreed Milo, and took her hand for a moment in his. 'As for you, freedom began for you on the Hard last night, — I heard it!'

Cressy did not answer, but she gave his hand a squeeze of acknowledgement. Only, not even to Milo could she talk of the awful longing that came over her sometimes to be able to see again — to run again, heedlessly, wherever she wanted to — to be dependent on no-one — to be free to go anywhere in the whole wide world *by herself*! . . .

'Come on,' said Gramp, 'if we're going to get this creature into Port Quentin, we'd better shove off!'

He always knows when to distract me, thought Cressy, — kind, observant Gramp-the-Champ. And Milo takes after him! How lucky I am to know them!

So they went on up the path, carrying the cage, and this time they only stopped for a moment to look in on Boxer's new run with the sky above it. 'Another one who can go soon,' murmured Milo. 'Let's not disturb him. He's still scared of us humans, and I don't blame him!'

Above his head, the little barn owls were still snoring, and there was no sign of the parents. 'They must be hunting by daylight,' said Milo. 'Those youngsters are too hungry, these days . . . '

'When will they fly?'

'Not for a while yet. Poor parents! Another few weeks of hard slog for them.' He ducked his head out of the old cowshed door, and left Boxer and the little owls in peace. 'Nearly there now,' he said.

★ ★ ★

The otters' pool was a natural formation of the rock sloping down to a deep cleft lined by clean, water-scoured boulders. The stream tumbled headlong into it in a bright cascade of falling water, and settled and spread into a dark, still peat-pond with ferns and screening heathers and furzes leaning over it. Isolated and undisturbed, it was an ideal hiding-place for a family of otters, and they had learned not to fear Milo, who often visited them but never interfered with their games and frolics in the water. They had got quite tame, — as otters often do, being naturally friendly, social creatures — and they had often come over to have a look at him, and even accepted a small fish from his hand when it was offered.

This time, though, Milo thought grimly,

I shall have to betray their trust in me by capturing one of them, and I'm afraid they may never forgive me . . . But I can't leave that paw to fester and go gangrenous . . . He might die.

Before they settled down to wait for the otters to emerge, Gramp took Bo'sun a little way aside, upwind of the otters' holt, and told him sternly to stay there, out of sight and out of scent from the wary creatures. Bo'sun looked a bit hurt, but an order was an order, and he never disobeyed Gramp when he spoke in that stern voice, so he lay down where he was told and put his head on his paws, the picture of patient obedience. Satisfied, Gramp gave him a small, comforting pat of approval, and went back to join the others. He would be needed later on.

'Sit beside me,' Milo whispered to Cressy, 'and I'll tell you when they come out.'

They sat together in silence, while the little waterfall poured noisily over the rocks, burbling and splashing into the deep, peat-dark pool below. Above their heads, a lark suddenly rose from the heather, and flew, singing, into the sky, the bright, ecstatic trilling of its song rising higher and higher into the clear blue distance.

'Can you hear it?' whispered Milo.

'Vaughan Williams,' answered Cressy obscurely. ' 'Lark Ascending.' '

Milo laughed softly. 'There speaks the musician!' He went on, still speaking very softly. 'And there's a grey wagtail hopping and dipping on the stones by the pool, — so pretty and flirty . . . Ah! Here they come . . . ' His voice changed a little, but he was careful not to raise it. 'Mum and Dad and two young ones . . . The male is a bit darker than his mate, but they are all a lovely rich brown on top and paler underneath, greyish fur with some long guard hairs in it on their flanks, — and long, shiny, sinewy bodies, lovely and graceful in the water, a long, tapering tail, and clever front paws and strong webbed feet . . . Beautiful creatures, Cressy, — and so few of them left nowadays . . . '

'Which is the injured one?'

'The male — one webbed foot seems horribly crooked, and there's an open wound on it. I think it must be treated or the infection will spread, and he might die.'

'How will you catch him?'

'I don't know . . . I've got a long net, and Gramp has another one to throw over it . . . but I hate to cause him more fright and distress by being too violent . . . 'He paused, his voice trailing uncertainly. 'We'll have to play it by ear . . . ' he muttered at last, but he sounded none too sure about it.

They sat quietly together, waiting to see whether the otter family would accept their presence, or go scampering off again into hiding. After a time, Milo said softly into Cressy's ear: 'They're playing now — in and out of the water, over the rocks, under the waterfall, and diving deep in the pool . . . It's hide and seek . . . they don't seem to mind us at all . . . Can you hear the splashes?' He sounded relieved and pleased — but the anxiety was still there, and Cressy could feel it, too. Would it be possible to catch the male otter without scaring him to death? And what would the others do?

But then a strange thing happened, which even Milo with all his understanding of animals could not explain. The injured male otter came limping out of the water and stood up on his hind legs, looked across at Milo with his intelligent head cocked on one side as if assessing the situation, and then dropped to all fours and came loping towards him.

Amazed, Milo was at a loss, but just had time to whisper to Cressy: 'He's coming towards us . . . keep very still!' before Gramp took swift and decisive action. Moving behind the lissom body, making no sound, he simply dropped his net over the otter's back so that it covered him completely in its entangling folds. But even then the otter surprised them. He simply dropped to the ground and sat still, making no attempt to struggle, but looking up at Milo with the same, intelligent, demanding gaze.

'I do believe he's *asking* me for help,' said Milo, overcome with astonishment. 'Cressy, you can help, too. He's crouching quite still under the net. Could you stand on the edge of it and keep it taut while I get the cage into place?'

'Yes,' said Cressy. 'Just show me where.'

Gramp, meanwhile, had also straddled his side of the net under firm feet and was holding the rest of it in an equally firm pair of hands. 'He's quite calm,' he said. 'We can manage it without fuss, I think . . . He'll be all right.'

Milo fetched the cage, and together he and Gramp eased it under the net and pulled back its metal door. 'Be easy, now,' he said softly to the otter, 'I can see you know I'm only here to help . . . Let us do what we can for you . . . How can you look after your family with a bad foot? . . . It must make fishing and diving very difficult . . . We'll get you right, my friend, and bring you home again to your wife and babies . . . That's it . . . gently now, gently . . . easy does it . . . ' He went on talking softly, and the otter stayed still, with its head turned to the comforting sound of Milo's voice, and made no attempt to struggle . . . and before very long, Gramp and Milo had coaxed him into the cage, and he was safe and ready to be transported to the vet for treatment.

'He'll do now,' said Gramp, sounding as pleased and relieved as Milo. 'Let's get him away quietly.'

Cressy had not spoken throughout this difficult manoeuvre, content to listen to Milo's voice coaxing the otter into the cage with the minimum of stress. Now she said quietly: 'Is he all right?'

'Yes,' Milo told her happily. 'Not a bit afraid . . . I can't understand it . . . He's a lot cleverer than you'd think.'

'What are the others doing?' she asked.

'The kittens are still playing . . . Mum is sitting bolt upright on a rock under the waterfall, watching us . . . But she doesn't seem distressed either . . . ' His voice was still full of wonder.

Cressy thought: Milo is absurdly humble about his extraordinary gift with animals . . . He really doesn't know how good he is with them . . . But I shan't tell him so!

'I'll bring him back,' said Milo to the

mother otter, and turned to help Gramp with the cage. 'I'll go and bring the jeep up,' he said. 'We can all go in together . . . '

'And I'll let Bo'sun off the hook,' agreed Gramp. Then he too spoke to the other otters in his deep, soft voice. 'All will be well, my dears. He won't be long away . . . We'll bring him back to you good as new . . . '

Across the water, the mother stood up on her hind legs to look across at her strange friends. Then she called the kittens to her in a clear, peremptory squeak, and the whole family — minus their father — disappeared into the undergrowth behind the pond. Nothing was left except the sound of the falling water, and the grey wagtail still bobbing and dipping at the edge of the rocks.

'Come now,' said Gramp-the-Champ to Cressy, and took her hand in his, guiding her back to the path. Then, gently, he repeated his words to the otters, 'All will be well, my dear, — you'll see.'

And though he might still have been reassuring Cressy about the injured otter, he might be talking about something quite different.

★ ★ ★

Stephen had found working from home a great deal easier and more successful than he had dared to hope. This was partly due to the relaxed atmosphere of the little cove and the uninterrupted views from the Wrecker's window, which somehow seemed to release his artist's eye and imagination from the many shackles of urban life, — but more to the relief and freedom from anxiety that Cressy's stoical acceptance of her blindness and her happy relationship with Milo had brought to her father's troubled mind.

Cressy amazed him, really. She seemed so serene and so undismayed by the restrictions that her sightless existence put on her, — and Stephen knew that a lot of her increasing confidence and independence was due to Milo's compassionate and skilful handling. That, and the bluff but equally thoughtful contributions of old Gramp-the-Champ, who did a lot of quiet planning behind their backs, and usually had a comforting word of wisdom to say when the need arose.

Cressy did not complain, and did not argue about her condition. She accepted the doctors' verdict, and seemed content to wait. But he knew she missed her mother — dear, loving Sally — very much deep down, as he did, and once or twice she had woken screaming in the night from a nightmare re-living of that awful, fatal moment of the crash. And there had been one or two other occasions when he had tiptoed in to see her and found her awake and weeping in the dark.

Stephen was a naturally affectionate and devoted father, and he gave Cressy all the special care and kindness he could offer — which was a lot. But he knew that there were things he could not mend in his young daughter's life, losses he could not replace, just as there were in his own, and all he could do for both of them was make their lives as full and happy as possible, work hard enough to give them enough to live on, and never fail to hug Cressy close and hard when she needed comfort.

But he was constantly surprised at her resiliance and her discovery of new skills and new ways to enjoy life. The little concert on the Hard had been an astonishing experience for Stephen, and he looked at his daughter now with new eyes. She was developing a strange, visionary quality without her sight which she had never displayed before . . . And each time she came back to him glowing with excitement about some new experience, some new happening in Milo's company, and some new awareness becoming clear to her, he found himself rejoicing at her unexpected discoveries, and secretly admiring her for her persistence in trying to meet every challenge and learn to do new things, — and her absurd and touching courage when facing some new risk or some setback to her determined independence.

Yes, he thought, I am proud of my young daughter. I wish to God I could put things right for her — and maybe they will go right some day soon — but meantime, she is making a wonderfully brave attempt to enjoy each moment of this new life of hers, and I must make sure I support her in every way I can . . . And God bless Milo and Gramp for easing the way!

This time, he had watched them walking on the beach with Bo'sun, and seen them set off later up the narrow path to the tumbling trout stream, but he had not tried to join them. They looked happy enough, and he had his work to finish . . . He was about to return to his computer, when he heard raised voices outside Catherine's cottage, — Milo and his mother arguing about something, and sounding quite heated about it. *Milo sounding heated?* It seemed most unlikely. He was always so gentle and reasonable in his dealings with Cressy, and with his grandfather, Gramp-the-Champ. But with Catherine there always seemed to be a bit of hidden tension, and there was this curious unexplained coolness between her and Gramp ... Maybe he had better go across and see what the trouble was. He didn't want Cressy upset about anything.

He came across the path to the cottage in time to hear Milo say — as reasonably as ever — 'but it's only a few yards, Mum, and then Gramp can take over.'

'Gramp!' snorted Catherine. 'Encouraging you again. I won't have it!'

'Mum, he's not encouraging me. He's helping me take an injured otter to the vet. What's wrong with that?'

'And afterwards?' Her voice was shrill. 'Once he's got you over to Port Quentin, I suppose he'll be persuading you to go off on *Kittiwake* or *Crystal Rose*!'

Milo sighed. 'Don't be silly, Mum. I've got Cressy with me. He'll bring us straight back here. In any case, he's just in from a three-day fishing stint on *Crystal Rose*. All he wants now is a good night's sleep at home. He's tired.'

'Well, he's only himself to blame!' Catherine's voice was as acid as ever.

Stephen could not bear it. 'Can I be any help?' he asked sunnily. 'What is the problem?'

She turned to him crossly. 'The problem

is Milo. He wants to borrow the jeep, and I don't like him driving it alone on a provisional license.'

'It's only a couple of hundred yards up a cart-track,' said Milo, sounding distinctly exasperated. 'I can hardly crash the jeep in that space!'

'I could go with Milo,' volunteered Stephen, still maintaining his sunny untroubled expression. 'He's allowed to drive with someone beside him, isn't he?'

'Well, yes — ' Catherine admitted grudgingly, 'but — '

'That's all right then,' Stephen said, giving her no time to raise any more objections, 'Come on, Milo. Cressy will be waiting.'

'The keys, Mum?' prompted Milo, holding out his hand. And, to Catherine's own astonishment, she handed them over without another word.

'Phew!' said Milo, when they were bumping up the track to the otters' pool. 'Mum can be difficult at times!'

'Can't we all?' laughed Stephen. Then he added kindly: 'She's only anxious about you, really.'

'I know,' said Milo sadly. 'That's the trouble. She's *too* anxious!'

Stephen made no comment on this, though he would very much like to know what made

Catherine so bitter and so over-protective. But by this time Milo had arrived at the point nearest to the otters' pool, and there were Gramp and Cressy, with Bo'sun beside them, and a caged otter waiting safely under a furse bush out of the hot sun.

'Let's get him boarded,' said Milo, jumping out. 'The sooner he's in the vet's hands the better ... Are you coming with us, Stephen?'

Stephen wasn't quite sure how to answer this, but Gramp answered cheerfully for him. 'Good idea. Then you can all go home together, and leave me to get some rest!'

'That'll be the day!' grinned Milo, and Cressy laughed.

Carefully and quietly, they loaded the injured otter into the back of the jeep, and packed themselves in somehow as well.

'You can carry on, Milo,' said Gramp, as if he knew his grandson had been in trouble with Catherine. 'There are two of us here to make you legal.' There was a hint of faint mischief in his voice.

But, surprisingly, Milo said: 'No. I'll ride in the back and keep an eye on the otter. He may be scared of the jeep.'

'Can I come too?' asked Cressy humbly. (Shades of earlier days and earlier escapades requiring the same question and hopefully the same answer, many times over!) 'Or will I scare him as well?'

'Of course you can, — and of course you won't scare him,' Milo said, and immediately hoisted her up into the back of the jeep and leapt in after her. 'Otters really quite like company,' he told her. 'They can get quite tame, you know, and even make good family pets, provided they have a pool to swim in . . . ' He could feel Cressy's doubt and humility, and it touched him. 'You can talk to him,' he said, smiling. 'He'll like that . . . Your voice is softer than mine.'

Stephen looked across at Gramp and smiled. Both men thought how kind and tactful Milo was, — and what other seventeen-year-old, smarting with injured pride about his driving skills being questioned, would think first of the otter's comfort, and then Cressy's, — and last of all, his own vindication.

'Quite a lad, your Milo,' murmured Stephen.

'Yes,' agreed Gramp, letting in the gears as gently as possible. 'Quite a lad!'

★ ★ ★

When they came back, having left the injured otter safely with Milo's friend the vet, who promised to treat the damaged paw and let Milo know when it was safe to return him to the pool, Stephen made up his mind to have a quiet word with Catherine. Milo and Cressy had gone off to feed the baby hedgehogs, so he thought it might be a good moment.

He found Catherine in a flurry of furious baking and cooking for the evening meal. She knew she had been a bit unreasonable with Milo, and her instinct whenever she had been a bit too harsh with anyone, was to make it up to them by cooking a simply splendid meal.

'Am I interrupting?' asked Stephen pleasantly.

Catherine gave him a wild look and pushed her hair back with a flour-streaked hand. 'Not if you let me carry on.'

'Feel free,' laughed Stephen. 'Especially as we are going to benefit from all this activity tonight!'

'I hope so,' said Catherine dourly.

'I only called in to report us safely back,' he said, still smiling a little at her harassed face. 'And I don't think you need worry about Milo's driving. He's really very competent, Catherine, — and very safe. He'll easily pass his test — and I gather that comes up quite soon.'

Catherine put down her spoon and sighed,

once more pushing her dark wisps of hair out of her eyes in a fretful gesture. 'I know,' she admitted. She looked up at Stephen in sudden, frank appeal. 'I know perfectly well he can cope. In fact, Milo can cope with most things . . . I know I always worry too much, — and I know I'm over-protective . . . But, you see, Stephen, he's all I've got now.'

Stephen nodded calmly. 'Yes, of course. As a matter of fact, Catherine, we are in the same boat, you and I.' His voice was gentle, and so clearly full of understanding that Catherine was instantly disarmed, — so much so that she was in danger of dissolving into tears.

'I'm sorry, Stephen,' she said helplessly. 'I am such a fool! It is much harder for you. It must be almost impossible for you *not* to be too protective over Cressy.'

'Yes,' Stephen admitted. 'I do find it difficult. But Cressy is so determined to be independent, — and I have to let her try.'

Catherine sat down suddenly on the nearest stool, and looked up into his face again. 'You are saying I ought to let Milo have his head?'

Stephen nodded again. 'He's seventeen, Catherine. Almost a man. Older than Cressy — and a lot wiser. He'll be all right. He's a real credit to you already, — you know that.'

'Yes,' she agreed, on the edge of tears. 'I know that.'

'If you try to hold him back too much,' Stephen said, 'he'll only pull harder to get away . . . just like his own animals he is so clever with.'

Catherine gave a watery smile. 'You're absolutely right.'

'Children have to grow up,' said Stephen sadly, and hoped he did not sound too sententious. 'The best we can do for them is make them feel secure in our love and support before they take off!'

Catherine shook the tears out of her eyes, and reached out a shaky hand to Stephen. 'For goodness sake, sit down and have a cup of tea with me, before I disgrace myself altogether!'

Stephen laughed and sat down beside her. 'That's better! Now you sound almost human!'

She had the grace to laugh back then. 'Do I — do I really sound so inhuman?'

'Sometimes.' Stephen's voice was teasing now. 'Formidable, at least!'

She got up to fill the teapot from the kettle on the Aga, and made a protesting face at him. 'You make me sound like an old dragon.'

'A *young* dragon,' corrected Stephen, smiling. 'Breathing fire from time to time . . . But I dare say tea will quench it.'

She began to giggle helplessly, and set the teapot down in front of him with a small, rebellious flourish. 'All right, I'll be mild as milk in future.'

'Oh don't be that!' exclaimed Stephen. 'I wouldn't know you!' He accepted a mug of tea, and waved it at her in a teasing toast. 'Keep the home fires burning — in moderation!'

'In moderation,' she echoed, wryly smiling.

They sat together silently for a few moments, while thoughts of various unexpected kinds assailed them and then went by unspoken. Stephen reflected that he had given his gentle warning about Milo, but had done nothing yet to tackle her about her extraordinary antagonism to that good, kind man, Gramp-the-Champ . . . Well, that would have to come later. Better not go too far today. *'Anger never solves anything,'* he said suddenly, speaking out of his own knowledge, his own pain.

Catherine looked at him in silence, alert understanding clear in her dark, intelligent gaze. 'No,' she said at last, in a sad, reflective tone. 'But then I am not so forgiving as you.'

Gramp had issued an invitation to Milo and Cressy before he left them in Port Quentin, and this bright morning, Milo decided to take him at his word.

'Shall we go and visit Hetty Longhurst's garden?' he suggested to Cressy. 'Gramp says she's expecting us.'

Cressy was always game for any new adventure, — especially if Milo was in charge. She trusted him completely. 'Lovely. How shall we get there?'

'I thought we might take the *Gannet* round to Port Quentin — especially as Mum makes such a fuss about the jeep, even on an off-road cart-track!'

Cressy laughed. 'I think you'll find Dad has put that right for you.'

Milo looked at her incredulously, forgetting that she could not see his face. Then he amended it swiftly: 'You amaze me. How?'

'I don't know. He went and had a word with her before supper . . . Didn't you notice that she was in a rather sunny mood?'

'Yes, as a matter of fact I did,' admitted Milo. 'What happened?'

'A bit of a thaw set in, I think.' Cressy was still smiling. 'Dad can be very charming when he tries!'

Milo was impressed. 'Well, I wish he'd try a bit more often!'

'He probably will,' Cressy told him, with a roguish look in her expressive face.

Milo wondered about that. Could Stephen, with his kind, gentle understanding, really reach Catherine in her lonely, bitter pride, and persuade her to accept what had happened? It would take a lot of persuasion, — a lot of patience, he thought. But then Stephen was patient, — and very persistent in a quiet sort of way. He was wonderful with Cressy, always a support, even pushing her on a little if she seemed reluctant to try something new. He gave her a lot of freedom, and a lot of help . . . Milo sighed. 'Well, good luck to him,' he said. 'If he can persuade Mum to relax a bit, it'll be a godsend, — especially over Gramp. It bothers me a lot, this stupid feud of hers.'

'She'll come round,' said Cressy confidently. 'No-one could stand out against Gramp for long.'

'You'd be surprised,' muttered Milo. But he did not pursue it. Why darken Cressy's day any further with thoughts of family feuds? The sun was shining, the sea was calm, *Gannet* was rocking at her moorings. It was time for a new adventure to keep Cressy happy. 'Come on,' he said, taking her hand. 'Let's go. The tide won't wait!' And since the sea was smooth and glassy. and there was very little wind, he allowed the hopeful Bo'sun to scramble into the *Gannet* after them, and sit in blissful content beside them.

They puttered peacefully round to Port Quentin, and tied up close to the other small boats along the quay. Milo saw that both Gramp's boats were in, — he must have decided (at last) to have a real rest. But as they began to walk along the Hard, with Bo'sun carefully pacing beside Cressy so that she could touch his head for reassurance if she needed to, Gramp himself emerged from the depths of *Crystal Rose* where he had been busy fixing something, and fell in beside them.

'If you are bound for Hetty's, I'll come with you,' he said in his deep, warm voice. 'She's a very special sort of person, Hetty,' he explained to Cressy, 'and I don't see enough of her!'

'You intrigue me,' smiled Cressy. 'What's so special about her?'

Gramp paused to consider. 'I'm not sure, exactly,' he said. 'I think it's her tranquillity . . . She looks as frail and vague as a will-o-the-wisp, but she's as strong as a horse underneath. She manages that big garden and the teashop and the pot-pourri trade singlehanded . . . She never seems to get fazed by anything, or tired or cross with overwork . . . She's always smiling and full of welcome when you go to see her, — and she gives you a wonderful tea!'

Cressy laughed. 'She sounds almost too good to be true!'

Gramp took her seriously. 'She is, in a way . . . She's still very pretty, you know. She must be well into her sixties now, but she looks much younger, and she drifts about that garden, apparently doing nothing but admire the flowers, — but there's hardly a weed in sight!'

'She must have *some* faults!' Cressy was still intrigued.

'Oh yes,' agreed Gramp readily. 'She trusts everyone too much, and sometimes they rip her off, — and her house is wonderfully untidy, but she doesn't care!'

'Did she ever marry?'

'She did, indeed. Willie was a good mate of mine. And Hetty and my missus were always in each other's houses . . . ' He sighed a little. 'Hetty was very good to me when Jenna died.'

'Well, you were very good to her when Willie died,' retorted Milo, smiling affectionately at his grandfather.

'Yes, well, that's the way it goes in a small community,' said Gramp, his voice sounding a little sad and full of old memories. 'We help each other out when it's needed . . . '

Milo could have said: 'You do a lot more than that!' He knew the extent of Gramp's help to many of his friends and neighbours, — especially to the fishermen's wives, many of whom had lost their men at sea, or in some accident or other connected with the fishing business. And Hetty, Milo knew, had badly needed financial help when Willie Longhurst died . . . It had been Gramp's money that had helped to set up Hetty's garden and teashop and the pot-pourri business, — all of which was now a thriving business with all its initial debts paid off . . . But he said nothing more. It would only embarrass Gramp to be known as the good samaritan he really was . . . Better let it alone, he thought.

'Can we call it tea-time in the morning?' he asked hopefully.

Gramp laughed. 'No. But you can call it lunch-time. Don't worry — she'll come up trumps. She always does!'

They strolled on happily, with Cressy's white stick gently tapping, and Bo'sun padding faithfully beside her, until they came to a pair of tall, wrought-iron gates.

218

'Here we are,' said Gramp, and Cressy heard the click of the catch in his hand.

'They're beautiful gates,' said Milo, putting Cressy in the picture. 'They were made specially for Hetty by our village blacksmith, — well, he's more a wrought-iron man these days . . . They've got most of Hetty's flowers all winding round them — roses, honeysuckle, sweet peas, lavender, — all the ones that smell best and that she uses for her pot-pourri mixtures . . . and in the middle of each gate there's a sort of urn with petals spilling out of it, representing the scent of the flowers and the kind of essences and things Hetty distils from them . . . There's even a hint of smoke rising up, like incense!'

'Lovely!' said Cressy, and let her hand stray across the iron-work of the gates, tracing the curves and flower heads and entwining stems with sensitive fingers.

'They're not as delicate as the real thing,' said a soft voice from inside the gates, 'but he got all the shapes right.'

'You must be Hetty,' said Cressy, moving towards the gentle voice. 'Gramp has been telling me all about you.'

'He's been telling me all about you, too!' retorted Hetty, and took Cressy's seeking hand in hers. 'But he didn't tell me how pretty you are! Such lovely-coloured hair, — like primroses in spring . . . and those eyes, even if they can't see at the moment, they are still Port Quentin eyes — sea-green-and-blue, like the bay!' She drew Cressy inside the gates on to the garden path. 'Come in, my dears, all of you. The garden is waiting for you.' She kept hold of Cressy's hand for a moment and led her across the path to a chair set with a group of others under an apple tree. 'Sit there a moment and breathe. This is my most scented corner. Everything seems to come together here! And while you're sorting it out, I'll go and fetch us all a long, cool drink.'

'I'll come and carry things,' said Gramp with alacrity, and Cressy heard the two sets of footsteps diminish along the brick path.

'What is she really like?' she asked Milo, who was always her eyes these days.

'Like Gramp said, — still very pretty — though not so pretty as you,' he volunteered, in a moment of unexpected appreciation.

'Go on!' said Cressy, and left him to take it either way.

Milo laughed. 'Well, then — seriously. She's got silver-grey hair, sort of soft and shimmery, floating about round her shoulders — a pale face, rather dreamy, and big golden-brown eyes, very wide open, as if they could see visions, or at least all kinds of things we can't see at all . . . '

'Perhaps they can!' murmured Cressy. 'Flower visions.'

'I wouldn't be surprised,' agreed Milo. 'She has a kind of not-here look, — wispy and a bit vague, and she sort of floats along — not quite like an ordinary mortal.'

Cressy smiled. 'You describe her beautifully. I can almost see her.'

'She's wearing a sort of blue thing,' said Milo. 'Loose and flowing . . . like a smock, or a shift? . . . It's got pockets in it, crammed with bits and pieces, string and labels, and secateurs and things . . . '

'*Blue*?' said Cressy in a strange voice. 'Yes, I thought it was . . . '

Milo stared at her, instantly alert. '*Cressy*? What are you saying?'

She shook her head at him slowly. 'It's too soon, Milo. Too soon to say . . . But — but the doctors told me something — I mean, they talked to me a lot about colours . . . and how the optic nerves work, and how the injured eye loses the colours one by one — each on a different wavelength . . . They said red goes first, — and it did for me . . . then yellow, and last of all, blue . . . And when — I mean, *if* they come back, blue will come first.'

'Is that true?'

'They said so . . . ' She paused doubtfully. 'But I don't know if it really works like that . . . How can I tell? . . . I only know they said 'Watch out for blue,' and . . . ' Once again she hesitated.

'And — ?' he pressed her, because it seemed to him that something amazing and unexpected was happening to Cressy.

'I just thought — for a moment I thought I caught a glimpse of something blue . . . '

'*Cressy!*'

'No, wait, Milo. It was only a flick, — or a — a lightening of the dark for a second . . . It's gone again now — and I'm not sure if I imagined it or not . . . And anyway, we mustn't hope too much . . . It may very well be a — a sort of one-off blip, or a — a hallucination? It may never come again . . . But I'll keep on 'looking for blue' as they said . . . It *might* come back again, — or it might not.'

She reached out for Milo's hand and gripped it tight for a moment. 'Don't say anything — not yet. I don't want to build up anyone's hopes — especially Dad's . . . We'll just keep on looking — I mean, *trying to look* . . . At least the sea is blue, and it's all round us!'

Milo was silent, almost too moved to speak at all. Was Cressy's sight really coming back? Or was it just one freak moment? Or her imagination? He dared not guess at it any further . . . Better, as Cressy said, just to wait, and keep on 'looking for blue.'

But Cressy's quick ear had caught the sound of the others coming back. 'The scents!' she said swiftly. 'Tell me where the flowers are! She'll expect me to know!'

Milo drew his mind back from the miraculous possibilities and dreams-come-true of Cressy's startling revelation, to concentrate on the present. 'Lavender close by your feet on the path,' he began. 'Roses — several kinds — the old-fashioned shrubby ones. They smell best, very sweet and heady . . . You can't miss those . . . And sweet peas in clumps trained up a trellis . . . and something that looks like wild heliotrope, which grows in the hollows behind the cliffs . . . Maybe it's the garden variety . . . And sweet williams, — I know those . . . and those green and white tobacco plants — they are very strong-scented.'

'That'll do,' said Cressy, smiling into his face with those sea-green eyes that could not see even blue when it was in front of her, except in odd, chance snatches . . . 'You make my world come alive, Milo. It's enough for now!' She gave his hand one more grateful squeeze, and then sat back, head tilted, trying to identify the scents of the flowers he had described.

'Home-made lemonade for us,' said Hetty, 'and Gramp's got a home-made cider, so he'd better be careful! Well, Cressy, how does the garden smell?'

'Divine,' said Cressy, and dutifully (and truthfully) listed the scents she could identify. 'But Milo helped me,' she added honestly. 'And there's a funny lemony one somewhere near that I don't know . . . '

'Lemon verbena,' said Hetty. 'Here. Have a leaf and rub it in your fingers. It makes a lovely tea, as well . . . '

Cressy duly rubbed and sniffed and it was certainly a crisp, tangy, aromatic scent, — somehow extra green and fresh in the fragrant summer air. 'Hetty, when we go round the garden, will you give me a sort of running commentary?'

'Gladly,' laughed Hetty. 'I love showing it off!'

Gently, step by step, she led Cressy round her garden, stopping to smell a particular rose, and to guide Cressy's fingers round its velvet petals and its yellow pollen-dusted stamens in the middle. 'This one is deep crimson, Cressy, with pale yellow stamens in the middle, and its scent is so rich it's almost like musk . . . It was called the 'Old Velvet Rose' but its real name is Tuscany Superb . . . And here is a tall white lily . . . very heady scent, all right out of doors, but too strong indoors . . . And round this arch above your head is summer jasmine, — I expect you can smell that — and with it is an old-fashioned rambler rose called Seven Sisters because it has all sorts of colours ranging from cerise-purple to a sort of faded lilac and even nearly white . . . And a lovely scent . . . and over here is another rose called Fritz Nobis that has a scent like cloves . . . Can you smell that?'

'Yes . . . ' murmured Cressy, entranced by all the richness of scents around her.

Hetty stopped there for a moment, as if hesitating about where to go next, and perhaps assessing Cressy's endurance. She didn't want to overtax the gallant child who was trying so hard to take everything in. 'Let's sit down over here,' she said, 'and you can listen to the water . . . I have quite a lot of water in the garden, — all from a real stream that comes down from the hills above us, and I've managed to divert it into several different channels and several little waterfalls . . . This one has a fountain, too, in the middle of a small pond, — a stone dolphin with his mouth wide open to let the water flow down.'

'A bottle-nosed dolphin,' put in Milo helpfully, 'with a lovely pointed, beaky nose!'

Cressy sat back, listening to the soothing sound of falling water. It was peaceful here in the sun, with Milo and Gramp beside her, and old Bo'sun nudging her and laying his golden head on her knee . . . No pressures, no tensions, no dreams or hopes . . . just peace under a quiet sky . . . Only it wasn't entirely quiet, because presently a linnet began to sing from the tip of a branch above Cressy's head.

'I could almost fall asleep here,' she murmured.

'Well, you can if you like,' said Hetty, smiling at Cressy's pale gold head leaning back against the garden chair.

'No!' said Cressy, instantly waking up. 'There's too much to see — I mean smell! I don't want to miss a thing!'

So they wandered on, with Hetty describing yet more wonders, until they came to the herb garden in yet another sheltered corner of the sunny garden. 'If you sit down on this bank,' said Hetty, guiding Cressy on to a gently-sloping green mound, 'you'll have the scent of thyme all round you . . . It's a herb bench, you see, like the monks used to have in their herbariums. They were allowed to sit on these for a rest when they were gardening, — but not to sit down on a real wooden bench till the day's work was done!'

'Clever!' said Cressy, laughing, and let the sun-warmed scent of the thyme drift over her in langourous waves of perfumed air.

'At your feet, marjoram and sage,' said Hetty's soft voice, 'and apple-mint and summer savoury and fennel . . . If you stood down and brush your fingers over the leaves, they'll all speak to you!'

Cressy did so, in a strange dream-world peopled by velvet-petalled flowers and green, aromatic leaves which truly did seem to be talking to her in a clamour of different cajoling voices . . . 'I think I'm drunk!' she said at last, — and everyone laughed.

'In that case,' said Hetty, 'it's time for lunch. Gramp, will you give me a hand?'

'Delighted!' said Gramp, with alacrity, and got up from his chair.

'Milo, bring Cressy up to the table on the terrace,' said Hetty. 'We won't be long. It's all laid on. Gramp brought me a crab last night, and I've got my own salad . . . ' Her voice drifted off as she and Gramp disappeared up the sunlit path.

Cressy and Milo did not move for a few moments. They just sat there in the sun, savouring every scent, listening to the constant faint melody of falling water, and the sudden ecstatic trills and frills of the green linnet in the cherry tree.

'So much . . . ' murmured Cressy, in a dream-laden voice. 'I'd no idea there was so much! . . . Milo, I've been asleep half my life!'

Milo laughed at her softly. 'Well, you're truly awake now,' he said. 'And you can never go back!'

Cressy sighed, more in content than sadness. 'I never knew . . . ' she said in a voice of wonder.

'Never knew what?'

'I could be so happy!'

Milo did not answer. He was not sure if he could. And presently, without saying any more, Cressy took his hand again, and let him lead her back to the sunny terrace, and Hetty's garden table, now laden with food.

★ ★ ★

Over a delectable crab salad, and fresh strawberries from the garden with some of Hetty's own clotted cream, the conversation drifted vaguely and peacefully between flowers and Gramp's fishing trip, and Milo's otter patient, until Hetty said suddenly: 'Cressy,

I've got a favour to ask you. But I want you to know beforehand that you can say no if you like, and I won't be offended!'

'Sounds ominous!' said Cressy, laughing. 'What is it?'

'Well, every year I open the garden to visitors in the summer. We give the proceeds to a local charity for the families of fishermen. And I give teas up here on the terrace — just a few tables — I don't attract huge crowds, I'm glad to say!'

'Nor does anyone in Port Quentin, thank God!' added Gramp, smiling.

'So?' asked Cressy, wondering if she was going to be asked to serve teas, or make cakes or something (none of which seemed very likely or practicable).

'So . . . Hetty's voice was tentative now. 'I wondered if you would come and play your flute — with Sue and Joe, if you liked the idea. They would like it, I've asked them . . . Not the whole group, — a bit too noisy for my garden — but the three of you . . . winding the sort of spells you wove the other night . . . ?'

'Were you there?' asked Cressy, surprised.

'Oh yes.' Hetty's voice was suddenly warm with approval. 'I was there!'

'It sounds like a lovely idea,' said Gramp, his deep voice also full of warmth.

'But — the garden is magic enough as it is,' said Cressy, not sure if she could ever match again that strange moment of illumination in the twilight of little Port Quentin harbour.

'There can never be too much magic,' said Hetty softly. 'Can there, Milo?'

'No . . . ' agreed Milo slowly. 'But — ' he glanced at Cressy's doubtful face, 'it won't come to order, you know.'

'I know,' Hetty replied, as tranquilly as ever. 'I'm not asking that, Milo . . . I would just like Cressy to play . . . and dream her way through whatever comes . . . Sue and Joe are the same . . . They say they can only go the way the wind blows . . . '

'And the wind bloweth where it listeth,' murmured Cressy. 'Doesn't it, Gramp?'

And Gramp, the old, experienced sailor, who had known every mood of the sea, and every wind that blew, said softly: 'Yes. But if you go with it, who knows what realms you may reach!'

It was a curious conversation for a guileless sunny afternoon in a scented garden, but no-one seemed to think it all that strange. There was a gentle, considering silence, and then Cressy said quietly: 'Yes. All right. But don't expect too much!'

'I shall expect you to be happy when you're

playing, — that's all,' said Hetty, and patted Cressy's hand. 'What else is music for?'

And the linnet let out a little burst of song in instant confirmation.

★ ★ ★

Late that evening, when Cressy and Stephen were alone in the Wrecker's Cottage, Stephen said, rather awkwardly: 'Cress, I think I ought to go up to London on the Penzance train tomorrow.'

'Well, why not?' Cressy answered, hearing the anxiety in her father's voice. 'What bothers you about it?'

'You, of course,' he said. 'I don't like leaving you alone here.'

'But I'm not alone,' she said cheerfully. 'There's Milo, and Bo'sun, — and Catherine to keep an eye on me . . . And she's a lot less fierce since you had a go at her!'

Stephen laughed. 'I didn't 'have a go' exactly!'

'Well, whatever it was, it worked. She's softened up quite a lot. It makes life much easier for Milo.'

'Mm,' Stephen was thinking sadly: But not for Gramp-the-Champ. And then found himself saying it aloud.

'No,' agreed Cressy, sounding equally

troubled by the thought. 'It bothers Milo a lot.'

Stephen looked at Cressy's face and wondered how much she knew, and how much he dared ask. But she did not seem withdrawn into some dark secret or other. Her face was still open and concerned, — but not burdened with the need to keep another's confidence. 'Do you know what the trouble is?' he asked. 'Between Catherine and Gramp, I mean?'

'I only know what Milo has told me,' she admitted. 'And I'm not sure even he knows all of it . . . But it's about his father, Kitto, being drowned. Catherine blames Gramp for his death.'

'But he wasn't responsible, was he?'

'No. Kitto jumped overboard to save a mate of his. It was his own decision. Only, Catherine can't see that.'

'I see,' said Stephen slowly. And indeed he did. Just so had his lovely Sally leapt in front of a crashing car to save Cressy . . . and just so had he spent a long time and a lot of fruitless anger over blaming the driver, the perpetrator of the accident, who was indeed to blame, though it had been Sally's own choice — her own decision.

'Catherine thinks Gramp should have been

the one to take the risk.' Cressy's voice was a little bleak, now.

'But he was the skipper!'

'Exactly. He had to get the rest of the crew home safely — and the whole Port Quentin fishing fleet depended on him. He was their leader . . . ' She sighed. 'And anyway, Milo says Gramp was already too old to be strong enough a swimmer in that sea . . . And Kitto *chose*.'

'Just like Sally,' murmured Stephen, aloud. He had been at such pains to explain this to Cressy, — to make that brave, reckless decision into something honourable and heroic . . . And Cressy had said stonily: '*I don't want her life*.'

'Milo understands,' Cressy said quietly. 'He said he was *proud* of Kitto. I mean, he misses him badly, I think, but he doesn't grudge him his choice.' She turned towards her father then, and reached for his hand. 'And yes, I *do* feel the same way about Mum now. I understand what you were trying to make me see.'

See? thought Stephen, swallowing down quick tears, — whether of sorrow or relief he did not know . . . Dear God, how wise and grown-up my young daughter has become!

'Catherine is just angry,' Cressy said. 'Like you were at first, — remember?'

'I do, indeed,' he admitted, — and heard his own voice saying, half to Catherine and half to himself: '*Anger never solves anything* . . . I suppose it's just a way of expressing hurt,' he said slowly. 'You think blaming someone else will help. But it doesn't. It only makes the world seem blacker than ever.'

'Yes,' agreed Cressy, (and she should know, after all, what blackness meant.) 'And it seems very black to Catherine . . . Milo's very patient, and so is Gramp. But I wish she'd get over it, or forgive Gramp or something . . . It makes all their lives so painful and so fraught.'

Stephen sighed. 'It takes time,' he said. 'These things take time.'

'Yes, I know,' Cressy said, almost impatiently. 'But I keep on thinking Gramp hasn't got all that much time left. She mustn't leave it too late.'

Stephen glanced at her oddly. There was something a little strange and prophetic about her voice. But he decided not to pursue it then. There was something else he had to ask Cressy, and that was much more difficult. 'I was wondering, — do you want to come to London with me? Ought you to go and see those doctors again? They said they would always be willing to see you.'

'No,' said Cressy, sounding quite definite

and firm. 'Not yet. I've got nothing to tell them — there's no real change ... Better wait till — if — there really is anything to report.' She paused, and then added: 'Besides, I'm happy here, Dad. You know that ... I don't want to go anywhere else — not now.' (She wondered, fleetingly, if she ought to have told her father about that ephemeral glimpse of blue she had thought she saw in Hetty's garden ... but decided against it all over again, for fear that it was just a false alarm and would only disappoint Stephen. No, she couldn't say anything yet. It might never happen again ...) 'It's better for me to stay quietly here,' she told him gently.

'All right,' Stephen said, smiling at her determined face. 'If you're happy here, that's good enough for me. But you will have to see the specialist some time.'

Some time, never? thought Cressy. But she only said mildly: 'I will — when it's necessary.'

Stephen squeezed her hand. 'Good girl ... We'll leave it at that, — if you're sure you'll be all right while I'm gone?'

'I'll be fine,' she said. 'Stop worrying.'

'I'll only be gone for the day — just long enough to hand some work in and collect a whole lot more!'

'Dad, you can take longer if you want.'

'No, I *don't* want,' said Stephen. 'I want to come home. I'm happy here, too — like you.'

'Well, that's good news, at least!' said Cressy, laughing.

And Stephen, unashamedly wet-eyed, put his arms round her and hugged her. 'I am so proud of you, Cressy!' he said. 'So proud and glad!'

★ ★ ★

Cressy got up in time to help with the breakfast and wave her father off. She was getting quite good at small domestic chores. She could manage the toaster, and fill the electric kettle, though Stephen would not let her pour boiling water into the teapot. She could find the cornflakes, and take the milk out of the fridge, along with the butter, and locate the marmalade jar on the shelf. She couldn't yet manage to boil an egg (though she had plans about electric timers that pinged), but Stephen never wanted much breakfast anyway, and he told her cheerfully that he could get something on the train if he got hungry. It was somehow important to Cressy, now that Sally, her mother was no longer there, to be able to provide a bit of home comfort for her father, and to fill in that awful empty space that her mother had left, as far as she possibly could.

Stephen knew this, and he was always appreciative, always ready to praise every small triumph over intransigent material objects.

'Are you walking up the cliff path?' she asked, putting a last piece of toast on his plate with unerring fingers.

'No, Catherine is taking the jeep up. She says she's got some shopping to do in the village store.' Stephen had kept his car in the small car park at the top of the cliff, since the narrow, rocky cart-track round the back of the cove was too rough and bumpy for his car to negotiate. It was an easy run to Penzance, however, and he would be in plenty of time for the London train. 'The only thing is,' he said worriedly, 'you'll be alone for a bit, till Catherine gets back — or Milo comes over.'

'No, she won't,' said a cheerful voice at the door. 'Milo *has* come over,' and he was standing outside in the sunny morning, and Bo'sun had lumbered to his feet from his vigil by Cressy's door, and was wagging a joyful welcome.

'So that's all right, then,' said Cressy, smiling in her father's direction. 'Go on then, — no more excuses!'

'Mum's starting the jeep,' said Milo helpfully.

'Anyone would think you were trying to get rid of me!' grumbled Stephen, but he was smiling, too.

'Perhaps we are,' said Cressy darkly. 'A dastardly plot. We'll tell you all about it when you get back.' She leant forward and found her father's cheek and kissed him happily, and then came forward to stand beside Milo on the step. She couldn't exactly watch Stephen go, but she could wave a hand after his retreating footsteps, and look as confident and serene as even an anxious father could wish for. The two of them waited till they heard the jeep start up and go bumping away up the inland track, and then Milo said: 'So now they've gone, — and it's Freedom Day for us.'

'Freedom Day?'

'For the animals,' explained Milo hastily, in case it sounded too obvious a relief. 'Well, some of them, at least . . . Shall we begin with Boxer, the hare?'

'Yes, please!' Cressy sounded absurdly enthusiastic about it. 'He was the unhappiest of them all, being shut in the dark.' She hadn't intended any back-handed reference to her own plight, — though being shut in the dark was something she understood all too well. But Milo gave her hand an extra squeeze of encouragement, and said gently: 'Come on. You can let him go all by yourself . . . There's something special about being a *giver* of freedom!'

'Yes,' agreed Cressy, smiling. 'I know. I'm very privileged!'

They found Boxer the hare sitting very still and quiet in his grassy cage, his head tilted a little upwards and sideways, and his long, black-tipped ears pricked forward in urgent, acute listening.

'He's ready to go,' murmured Milo. 'All tense and strung-up, taking in the new scents of the day . . . But I must just make sure that wound in his neck has healed.' He reached inside the wire netting, and laid gentle hands round the long, silky body. 'His coat feels better,' he said. 'Less bristly and staring . . . I believe he's healed.' Then he directed Cressy, as once before, to hold the hare close and still in her arms while Milo took off the dressing and looked at the old neck-wound. 'Yes,' he confirmed happily. 'Healed and clean as a whistle . . . Boxer, my friend, you are free to go.'

So far, the hare had remained still under their hands just as before, but now — as if a breath of true wild air had reached him — he stirred a little in Cressy's arms, and the powerful back legs gave a small, involuntary kick.

'What must I do?' asked Cressy. 'Can we let him go right here? . . . Or should we take him further up the valley?'

'No,' said Milo. 'He's used to this sort of furze-and-heather cliff-edge country. He'll find his way . . . Can you stand up, still holding him, and come out of the door? I'll guide you.'

Cressy managed it, and the hare stirred again in her arms, and she could feel his body tensing with the longing for freedom that came with every new breath of fresh, scented cliff-top air.

'Now you're outside,' said Milo. 'Just kneel down. Don't let him go in mid-air, he might break a leg . . . Kneel down . . . that's right . . . and let him feel the ground under his feet . . . and then — just let go.'

Cressy did as she was told. She felt the warm, furry body of the hare straighten as his feet touched the ground. A shudder of excitement — of disbelief? — seemed to go through him. Were they really going to let him go? Was freedom so near?

'Now, Boxer,' said Milo softly. 'The world is all yours . . . Go free!'

'Go free!' echoed Cressy, and opened her

arms and let go. For a moment Boxer the hare sat still on the soft summer grass — still not quite believing his luck — and then a new wave of scented air washed over him, the beautiful ears twitched forward to pick up every inviting signal they could reach, and then settled back ready for instant flight, the strong back legs gave one, convulsive, mighty kick, and he was away.

'God speed, Boxer!' said Cressy, her face turned towards the wild, open spaces of the hidden valley, though she could not see them. 'Has he gone?'

'Yes,' Milo told her. 'Like a brown streak of summer lightning . . . Ears back, feet bounding, long and flat and swift . . . Straight as an arrow up the valley and into the heather . . . '

'*Over the hills and far away,*' said Cressy, and kept her voice light and teasing to hide the longing inside her.

'Now we'd better go and consider the others,' said Milo, knowing Cressy's hidden feelings, and instantly finding something else for her to do.

'Will they be ready, too?'

'Not sure till I look,' admitted Milo. 'Let's find out.'

'What about the baby barn owls?' asked Cressy, as they left the old cowshed and

Boxer's empty cage behind them.

'They're doing fine,' reported Milo. 'They look bigger and stronger.'

'And they're snoring louder than ever!'

He laughed. 'A good sign. It means they are well-fed and content . . . and I don't think we've disturbed the parents much. They still keep up their daylight hunting and fly in and out, — I've watched them.'

'Good,' said Cressy. 'So long as we haven't upset them.'

'Not a bit of it,' Milo said sturdily. 'And the youngsters will be flying soon and foraging for themselves . . . Then they'll all snore together in the daytime, and have their hunting parties at night.'

'Will you still keep an eye on them?'

'Oh yes,' he said. 'From time to time . . . Barn owls are getting scarce now, — they're precious! And rearing three young ones is quite a feat.' He gave Cressy's arm a comforting pat. 'You funny girl! You're quite concerned about them, aren't you? . . . I won't let anything happen to them.'

'I know you won't,' said Cressy, with supreme confidence, and she had a sudden picture in her mind of Milo standing outside the old cowshed door in the moonlight, watching the silvery ghosts of the barn owls glide by to their midnight feasts . . . It didn't matter that she had never seen the old cowshed in reality, or the barn owls, or even Milo himself since he was a thirteen-year-old boy, four long years ago, — the image in her mind was quite clear and quite beautiful . . . moonlight-silver and black shadow, with his known and remembered profile etched vividly against the shimmering night sky . . .

'Come on,' said Milo, unaware that he was posed in statuesque fashion in a bright moonlit idyll in Cressy's head, 'Let's get down to the others and see who else we can set free!'

They found Foxy sitting disconsolately in his cage, with his little black nose pressed to the wire, and Wily Willy still rushing round in circles and scolding furiously as soon as he saw them coming.

'I've got to get that bandage off his tail,' laughed Milo. 'He'll feel better-tempered then!'

'Can I hold him for you?'

'Yes, when I've got this little muzzle-thing tied on. He's in a decidedly biting mood!' Milo got the angry little squirrel safely subdued, and allowed Cressy to hold him again, as tightly and securely as she could. 'Don't give him a chance to wriggle,' he warned. 'Even when I've got the bandage off, he'll have to go back into his cage until we can take him further inland to let him go. He needs some trees and a garden or two . . . '

'Right,' said Cressy, and held on tight.

Wily Willy could not chatter with rage, but a kind of strangled grumbling emerged from behind the little leather muzzle. And if Cressy could have seen the rage in his malevolent black eyes, she would have been somewhat shaken. But she could not see it, so she held on quite steadily and confidently while Milo unwound the dressings and inspected the injured tail.

'Yes, it's healed,' he said. 'No more infection there . . . It'll never be a handsome tail again, — more like a bottle-brush with some of its tufts missing! But it'll serve. It will still act as a balance when he whisks up and down trees!' He put a last smear of penicillin cream on the bald patch, and said cheerfully: 'There you are then, Willy, — good as new! And don't be such an ungrateful brat! I've done my best for you!'

The squirrel grumbled even more behind his leather straps, and Cressy laughed.

'I'll put him back for now,' said Milo, carefully taking the cross little animal back from Cressy's tense fingers. 'We'll take him up the hill presently.'

'What about Foxy?'

'He'll be all right. I can see his paw from here. I'll just give him a final checkover, if you can hold him for me again . . . Then we can let him go.'

'Here? Just like that?'

'Well, maybe a little higher up the valley. But he's like Boxer, — he's used to this kind of terrain . . . He'll find his way back to where he wants to be.'

'But he's so little!'

'Not too little to know where to go, — or to smell it!' He took Foxy out of his cage, and once again showed Cressy how to hold him. And once again she felt the strong, furry body warm in her arms while Milo examined the injured paw. 'Yes,' he said, 'definitely freedom time in here . . . Let's put him back, and get them both on their way.'

'Who'll be left?' wondered Cressy.

'Only the little hedgehogs. But they don't mind. They rather like being made a fuss of. We can take our time with them.'

Cressy sighed. 'I'm glad . . . Don't you sometimes feel — pushed by their need to escape?'

'Yes, I do,' admitted Milo. 'But that's part of the job, isn't it? . . . You have to balance what they really need with what they think they need! After all, they're better off healed and well again. If they ran about injured and untreated, they would soon die.'

Cressy understood that, of course, but she also understood that Milo was often in quite a dilemma about his sick, wild patients, — and probably suffered more doubts on their behalf than he let on.

'It must be hard for you sometimes,' she said.

Milo laughed. 'You can say that again! . . . But now we've got two of them well enough to go. We can rejoice today!'

So they took the two cages between them, Milo with Foxy and Cressy with Wily Willy, and set off again, Cressy's stick tapping ahead of her from one hand, and Bo'sun keeping a respectable distance behind. He could smell Fox, and he didn't like squirrels, but if Milo chose to transport them somewhere, then it must be all right, and Cressy seemed to be all right, too, walking alone . . . All he had to do was follow.

They reached the twisting path at the head of the little valley beyond the otters' pool, and here Milo stopped. 'This will do for Foxy,' he said. 'Plenty of cover, — and rabbit tracks across the slopes. He'll manage very well from here.'

'What shall we do?' Cressy asked.

'Just open his cage. He'll go soon enough,' Knowing she would like to be the one to let him go, Milo guided her hand to the catch of the wire cage. 'Just lift it up . . . and stand clear! He'll probably go off like a bomb.'

Cressy stooped to the catch, lifted it clear, and obediently stood back. The little fox-cub snuffed the air, the pointed nose came questing to the open door . . .

'He's testing the air,' reported Milo. 'Not quite sure . . . Is it safe? . . . Yes, it is. He's put one paw outside — the good one. Now the other, — and — whoosh! . . . Did you hear him go by?'

'I *felt* him go by!' laughed Cressy.

'Just as I said!' Milo was laughing, too. 'Like a streaky red-brown bomb!'

'Can you still see him?'

'Yes, — just. But he's away up the hill already, among the gorse bushes . . . Now he's gone . . . Nothing left but a waving branch or two . . . and the crickets singing . . . '

'Good luck, Foxy!' said Cressy, and turned to Milo anxiously. 'Will he find enough to eat?'

'Oh yes, — now he will. He's quite a big boy now, and all the old hunting instincts will come out.'

'What will he find?'

'Mice — and voles — a baby rabbit now and then . . . Grubs and worms, — and sometimes bits of tourist sandwich!'

Cressy laughed. 'Oh well, — it sounds as if he'll do.'

'Of course he will,' Milo teased. 'You're like a mother hen with her chicks! . . . Let's get Wily Willy out of the way. He'll start eating the cage if we don't get a move on!'

They walked on, still higher up the valley, until they came to a small grove of stunted oak trees, their backs bent by the sea-winds, but their sturdy arms a perfect refuge for an adventurous squirrel.

'Here!' said Milo. 'Oak trees, Cressy, — a whole grove of them . . . They're smaller than the inland trees down here, but they'll do . . . Last year's acorns in the grass. Willy will have a feast.'

Cressy had set the cage down on the grass, and stood looking uncertainly in Milo's direction, waiting for orders.

'Bo'sun, sit still!' commanded Milo, knowing how the old dog disliked squirrels. But he needn't have spoken. Bo'sun knew his place. Had he tried to chase Foxy when he went? Or Boxer the hare, either? Of course not. He knew he must not. Why did Milo need to tell him? It was understood. No-one, not even a dog, would dare to chase one of Milo's animals. He knew that perfectly well. Gloomily, he sat on his tail and sulked.

'I'll open the cage this time,' said Milo.

'I'm a bit afraid of his teeth. He really is so cross!'

'Rather you than me!' agreed Cressy, laughing, — and waited to hear the click of the catch on the wire cage. The squirrel's angry chattering mounted and its furious paws rattled the bars of its prison.

'There you are, you ungrateful little beast! The door is open — the world's your oyster, and I suppose you'll be off without a word of thanks! . . . Don't mind me!' But his voice was gentle and full of warmth and affection even as he spoke, and Cressy smiled at his absurd attempt to sound stern. 'Off you go!' said Milo, and Cressy didn't even feel the wind of his passing as Wily Willy shot out of his cage and whisked up the nearest stunted oak into its comforting canopy of new green leaves.

'Gone?' asked Cressy.

'Like a shot!' laughed Milo. 'Listen! He's sitting on a branch up there, and *still* scolding!'

And Cressy could hear the angry chattering above her head, but she thought it sounded rather half-hearted now, as if Willy was only doing it for form's sake, as a final protest, — and really he was very cheerful indeed!

'All done,' said Milo. 'And I've walked you off your feet. Sit down here, under the trees, and I'll brew up some tea.'

'Out here?'

'Why not out here? I always carry my survival pack! . . . Never know when I'm going to get stranded, trying to rescue some creature or other . . . And there's a stream close by . . . Rest a while and dream, while I make a fire.'

'Honestly, Milo,' said Cressy, lying flat on the cool summer grass, 'is there anything you can't do?'

Milo didn't answer — but that was because he was already across the clearing, foraging under the oak trees for dead wood and twigs to start a fire. He could have said: Yes. I can't live in a city. I couldn't work indoors all day in an office. I couldn't give up my animals. And I couldn't ever live too far from the sea . . . But he wouldn't have needed to say it anyway. Cressy knew it already.

He came back with an armload of kindling, and found that Cressy had fallen fast asleep in the long sweet grass, and lay spread out in peaceful oblivion, with her face turned up to the filtered sunlight glancing through the leaves of the small oak trees. She looked very young and very vulnerable, fair hair spilling over the grassblades in milky primrose radiance, eyelashes making gold crescents below the sleeping lids that covered those sightless eyes, and her mouth soft and dreaming in her pale, still face.

Milo stood looking down at her, transfixed by her unconscious beauty, — and even more moved by her perilous fragility, and her simple trust in him. I love this child, he thought suddenly. This girl with the dreaming mouth and the sea-green eyes that cannot see the sea ... I have always loved her, I think, since she was a little thing, all flying hair and long legs, running over the sands and climbing the rocks and getting under my feet! ... and I shall always love her — whether she is blind or can see, wherever she goes, whatever she does — whether she needs me or not, remembers me or forgets me. I shall always love her till the day I die ... And I would give my own two eyes to make hers see again, if I could! ... And if I can't, — I'll make her darkness as light as ever I can while I have the chance ... so help me, God!

He did not say it aloud, of course ... Probably he would never say it aloud. But it didn't matter. It had been said in his mind. It was all settled — all complete, a vow to keep for his whole life, and he would never change. But now it was time to come down from the heights and be practical, to light a fire, and make Cressy's day as happy and full of comfort and new adventure as he could . . . Had he made her walk too far, he wondered? Tried her too hard? She was so determined to keep up, to be independent and self-reliant . . . (She always had been, even without blindness to contend with) . . . and he had felt he ought to let her do whatever she could, — not hold her back. But what if he was asking too much of her? She would never tell him, — never admit it.

'Stop worrying,' said Cressy's voice close beside him. 'I'm fine, thank you . . . Relaxed and sleepy, and rather hungry. Where's the food?'

Milo looked at her in amazement. She was still lying comfortably on the grass, but with one arm propping her up so that her head was turned in his direction. He knew she could not see his face, but her own expression seemed totally aware of both him and his thoughts. 'How d'you know I'm worrying?' he asked, half-laughing.

'Bad vibes in the air,' said Cressy. 'Zigzags on the sunlight . . . Bats can see them, you tell me. Well, so can I!'

Milo relaxed a little. She hadn't gone

that deep into his thoughts — not yet! But Cressy's uncanny sensitivity was becoming a little unnerving.

'I was only wondering whether I'd made you walk too far?'

'Of course you haven't!' she told him stoutly. 'I love walking, — especially with you when I feel safe to stride out a bit . . . I don't get enough exercise, really. It's one of the problems I have to work out somehow.'

'Yes, but — '

'No,' she said, cutting him off firmly. 'The trouble is, you see, I don't sleep a lot in the night. I can't really tell the difference between night and day, — and my built-in clock doesn't tell me it's time to sleep . . . So I lie awake, or listen to the radio . . . and then in the morning, when the alarm goes off, I'm tired.'

Milo sighed. 'Isn't there . . . any difference in the light? Or the dark?'

She hesitated. 'Yes. Sometimes. In bright sunlight, there's definitely a lightening of the dark . . . But I suppose it's not enough to trigger the waking or sleeping syndrome!' She had heard him sigh and was quick to reassure him. 'But it doesn't matter, does it? At least I'm listening to a lot of music! I'll probably be more use to Sue and Joe because

I'm getting so well educated — musically speaking!'

Milo laughed. 'If it makes you take off like you did the other evening, it's probably worth it!'

'That's what I hoped,' said Cressy demurely. 'And I've had a lovely sleep now, — and I feel wonderful. All right?'

'All right,' agreed Milo, smiling. 'You're a splendid liar. And the tea's nearly ready.'

For, in spite of his arresting thoughts and the sudden revelation of his own private feelings about Cressy, his hands had been busy, — the fire was lit and burning merrily, the billycan of water was simmering, and there were various things on sticks balanced over the fire, and packages laid out neatly on the grass.

'What have we got today?' Cressy asked, moving nearer to Milo's voice, and to certain delectable smells coming from the fire.

'Baked potatoes in the embers, sort of kebabs on sticks, with prawns and mushrooms and bacon . . . Toasted cheese and celery sticks, and sardines, and plums . . . '

'Another feast!' cried Cressy, laughing. She took one of the kebab sticks from Milo's fingers and held it out to the fire as he directed. 'This is the life for me!' she said.

'And me!' agreed Milo. And somehow their words seemed to echo and spread out in the still air, like ripples in a pond after the stone has fallen . . .

★ ★ ★

Stephen came back in time for supper with Catherine and Milo, and seemed in a cheerful mood, especially when he found that Cressy and Milo had spent a happy day releasing various of their captives, and rounded it off with what sounded like a rattling good barbecue under the oak trees at the head of the valley. He was interested in all the details and listened to Milo's account of how each freed animal went off on his own back into his wild free world. And he was clearly relieved and pleased to find that Cressy had been content and well looked after while he was away. But he did not say very much about his trip to London until he and Cressy were alone again in the Wrecker's Cottage. And even then it was Cressy who opened the subject.

'Dad,' she said, carefully balancing the late-night cup of tea he had just given her, 'do you miss London — and all your friends at the Studio?'

'No.' Stephen sounded quite definite,

255

though his voice had a smile in it to counteract Cressy's anxious tone. 'Not in the least, — rather to my surprise.'

'Why not?' Cressy persisted.

'Oh, I don't know . . . They all seem so — sort of obsessed with trivia, somehow. Their lives all seem to be governed by *things* — cars, and houses, and holidays, and all the paraphernalia of high living . . . D'you know what I mean?'

'Yes, of course I do. I felt the same with my friends from school. They did their best, but the things they were interested in seemed so — so pointless.'

'What things?' It was Stephen's turn to be persistent.

'Oh, — boys — discos — clothes — make-up — parties . . . all the things I couldn't share in, and couldn't care less about!'

'You don't miss them either?'

'No,' she said. 'Like you, I seem to have gone *past* them somehow. Down here, I mean, seems much more like real life — and much richer.'

Stephen sighed. 'I can't tell you how glad I am to hear you say that! I was a bit afraid — '

'That I'd want to go back to *that* — and being a teenage floosie!'

Stephen laughed. 'Oh, hardly that! But you

might have missed . . . extra company?'

'I have all the company I need,' she said, smiling, and thinking of Milo and his constant care and kindness, and his quick mind and how it seemed to flow with hers . . . 'And people down here do seem to be much more concerned with real happenings, — and big questions.'

'Such as?'

'Oh, life — and death . . . and making a living out of the fishing trade, and surviving on small incomes, and helping each other out in emergencies, like Gramp-the-Champ and Hetty . . . And — and finding something to sing about, or playing the trumpet! . . . And healing sick creatures and releasing them back to the wild . . . Isn't all that more real and comforting, somehow, than all that . . . trivia, you called it?'

'Yes,' Stephen said, sighing again, 'of course it is.' He was silent for a few moments, and then arrived at the subject he had been almost afraid to mention. 'I spoke to your eye specialist on the phone. He asked me to report back.'

'What did he say?'

'Much the same as before. Wait and be patient. Allow your eyes — or the optic nerves — to heal in their own time . . . and try to be as well and active and happy as you can in the meantime.'

'I am doing all that.'

'I know,' he agreed, his voice warm with approval. 'And he said one curious thing which I didn't quite understand.'

'Yes?'

'Tell her to keep looking for blue.'

Cressy did not ask what he meant. Instead, she nodded her head a little, and said rather guiltily: 'I ought to have told you . . . I did get one small flash . . . ' And she went on to explain to her father what the specialist had told her about the colours going one by one, and returning one by one when the healing process was complete.

Stephen knew about colours — he understood about their different wavelengths and the fragile mechanism of the eyes' lenses that made them come alive. 'And — you really *saw* something blue?'

'Yes — just a glimpse . . . But it was gone in a flash. It was so quick — so soon gone — I couldn't really tell if I saw it or not . . . I might've imagined it . . . That's why I didn't tell you.'

Stephen said slowly: 'You'd better tell me if it happens again, though, hadn't you? I think your friend the eye specialist would want to know.'

'Yes,' Cressy agreed, still sounding a little

penitent. 'I'm sorry, Dad. I just didn't want to raise your hopes — or mine. It might not happen again . . . or it might . . . and I was afraid to make too much of it. Do you understand?'

'Of course I do.' Stephen put an arm round her shoulders and drew her close. 'Don't sound so guilty. I can see why you kept it to yourself. But next time — if there is a next time — don't shut me out!'

'Dad!' Cressy was horrified. 'I didn't mean — '

'No, I know you didn't. I only meant, next time don't be so considerate!'

Cressy laughed. 'What an instruction to a rebellious teenager!' But she still felt a little guilty — because she *had* told Milo . . . Only, these days, Milo seemed to be so much part of her own thoughts that she could scarcely tell where one began and one ended . . .

Stephen had another question on his mind, but once again he did not quite know how to broach it. For it was a loaded question that assumed the worst . . . and maybe he'd better leave it a bit longer.

'I listen to the radio a lot,' said Cressy, as if he had asked his loaded question.

Stephen looked at her in amazement. 'I didn't speak!'

'You didn't have to,' she said, smiling. 'I know your mind, and I usually know what's worrying you!'

'That's a bit frightening, Cress!' He was smiling, too, relieved that she was making it so easy for him. 'But, yes, your future education does worry me a bit. It's such a — such a loaded question!'

Cressy laughed. 'Well, I don't feel over-loaded at the moment! I'm learning a lot about music ... and I listen to the schools programmes sometimes, and the Open University ... and I've got all those tapes the school sent me. My brain hasn't been idle ... And — like we were saying — what I am learning down here, with Milo and Gramp and everyone, is more valuable than all the rest put together.'

Stephen nodded silently, and then remembered to speak his thoughts aloud. 'That makes very good sense to me.'

'Good,' said Cressy. 'So maybe we can go on as we are for a while — and see what happens? ... Time enough to make serious plans when the summer is over?' *When the summer is over*, she thought. What then? Milo will go away to university ... Gramp-the-Champ will get too old to go out with the fishing fleet ... Everything will change — and I won't be able to bear it, *especially without Milo.*

But she did not say it. How could she? How could she tell her father how much Milo had come to mean to her? She scarcely even knew herself . . . except that he was now part of the fibres of her being . . . (Keeping things to myself again! she thought guiltily) and firmly changed the subject. 'What about your work, Dad? Was it all right?'

'Yes,' he told her cheerfully. 'All present and correct, — and I came home with a load of commissions and orders, and one more book illustration job.'

'That's good, isn't it?' She sounded genuinely pleased.

'Very. From the bread-and-butter point of view.'

'And the artistic point of view?' she asked shrewdly.

Stephen laughed. 'Oh well, — this is *commercial* art we're talking about. But the book illustration work is more fun!'

Cressy laughed, too, and then said solemnly: 'I wouldn't want you to — er — Bastardise your Art for my sake!'

Stephen took hold of a strand of her hair and tugged it. 'As if I would! . . . How dare you!'

She giggled helplessly. 'Oh, I know you're good at it. I've seen your work, remember?

It's just that . . . I also know you have to compromise sometimes when you don't want to!'

Stephen sighed, acknowledging her understanding of his constant dilemma. 'That's life, Cressy. A series of compromises.'

'I know,' his wise young daughter told him. 'But isn't it sad?'

But Stephen wasn't going to let her be sad. 'Not really,' he said. 'It's a challenge, — like everything else. How to get round things and do the best you can with them in the circumstances . . . And the best example I can give you at the moment is someone called Cressida Latimer.'

'Dad?' she exclaimed, surprised.

But he only hugged her and added gently: 'Enough moralising! Time for bed . . . And no doubt Milo will be waiting for you tomorrow!'

'Yes,' she agreed happily. 'Aren't I lucky?'

★ ★ ★

It was late in the night when she heard the crying. Or she thought she did. Was it crying? Or just the figment of her dreams? She sometimes woke and found herself crying — weeping helplessly for her mother, Sally, and the awful moment of no return from that fatal crash . . . But this time it was not her own grief that was loud in the night, — it was someone else's . . . She listened again . . . Yes, it *was* crying. Something or someone was crying out there on the beach, or on the rocks . . . It was a thin, pitiful sound, desperate and lonely . . . It sounded just like a baby crying.

Cressy lay listening to it for a little while, and then she simply could not bear it any longer. She got up, found her jeans and sweater on the chair by her bed, and reached a sure hand down to the floor for her sandals. Ought she to go out alone in the middle of the night? But what difference would it make? She was always alone in the dark — always cautious, always feeling her way with the aid of a white stick and a patient dog . . . It didn't matter if it was day or night . . . She was just as safe — or unsafe — by moonlight as by sunlight . . . And the thing out there was still crying in the night . . . She had to go and find it, — and see if she could help.

When she got to her door, Bo'sun got up from his sentry duty on the threshold, and looked at her enquiringly. She could not see his puzzled face, but she knew he was there, and put out a reassuring hand. 'It's all right, Bo'sun,' she said, keeping her voice low. 'We're just going for a walk. Nothing to worry about.'

She opened the door and stepped over the threshold on to the path, reaching out her hand to catch hold of Milo's rope guide-line.

She could still hear the crying. It seemed to be coming from the long spit of rocks at the edge of the sand on the Port Quentin side of the cove . . . I can walk down there, she thought to herself. Milo's rope-walk goes most of the way. But I can't climb the rocks, it's too dangerous without eyes to see with . . . And if I can't get up on to the rocks, I probably can't reach the thing that's crying . . . Still, I'll have to try.

She began to walk steadily down the beach, holding the rope with one hand, tapping her stick forward with the other, while faithful old Bo'sun padded beside her, wondering what had got into his young mistress's head this time . . . The crying seemed to get louder and more desperate as she walked towards it, and Cressy was puzzled by the almost human sound of that lost, despairing voice. Could it really be a baby? Surely not — alone on the rocks in the middle of the night? Visions of shipwrecks and drowning mothers and floating infants came into her mind . . . But it didn't seem quite right, — didn't *sound* quite right . . . Those tiny lungs (she was sure they must be tiny) had a stranger, wilder quality about their urgent calling, — something more liquid and untrammelled, and at the same time fiercer than a baby's voice.

She had almost reached the rocks, having let go of the last notch of Milo's rope, when her foot caught a hidden stone deep in the sand, and she pitched over it headlong, landing flat on her stomach with the breath knocked out of her.

Bo'sun came forward at once, and helpfully tried to lick her face, but someone else was before him, with more practical aid. 'Are you hurt?' said Milo's voice. 'Take hold of my arm . . . ' and he waited for her to grasp his offered arm before he put the other one round her and heaved her up.

'What are you doing out here in the middle of the night?' Cressy asked, somewhat breathlessly.

'I might ask you the same question!' retorted Milo, helping to brush the damp sand off her jeans and making sure she was really unhurt and undismayed.

'I heard someone crying,' she said. 'Didn't I?' For all at once she realised that the crying had stopped for a moment. Had she imagined it?'

265

'Yes, you did,' said Milo reassuringly. 'It's all right. It's only a baby seal . . . Washed up on to the rocks, and crying for its mother.'

'Will she come?'

'I don't think so — not now. I've been waiting most of the night to see if she would turn up . . . But no other seals seem to be about.'

'Most of the night?' said Cressy. 'You must be tired out!'

Milo laughed. 'I don't mind being awake . . . It's a beautiful night.' He glanced at Cressy's pale face under the bright moon, and thought she was beautiful, too, — the wheaten-gold hair almost silver in the moonlight, the sea-green sightless eyes huge and dark, drowned in black shadow, and the planes of her face lit with glancing washes of silver and shade as the reflections of the moonlight on the water touched her . . . A mermaid or a sea-nymph, Cressy seemed to be, on this still, pure, moonwashed night . . .

'Is it a beautiful night?' Cressy said wistfully. 'Describe, please!'

Milo took a deep breath. 'Moonlight and magic,' he said. 'A night for spells and music . . . Did you bring your flute?'

'No.'

'A pity. You could have played to the

seal. The you'd have looked more like a sea-nymph than ever.'

'I said *describe* — not waffle!'

Milo laughed, a little shakily. 'All right . . . But mere words aren't good enough for a night like this . . . ' He took another shaky breath and tried again. 'A black and silver night . . . Brilliant moonlight on the sea, — even a silver path stretching away towards the horizon . . . You used to think you could walk along it once, — remember?'

'Yes, and I tried and fell in, and you had to pull me out!'

'Well, it looks even more alluring tonight — but don't try it again, will you?' He laughed a little in the dark, and felt on safer ground with laughter and childhood memories between them. 'The rocks are very black, — especially Lion Rock and Gull Rock. They stand out like sentinels, all hunched and dark and strong . . . The sand is so pale it is almost white, and the waves — quite small ones tonight in spite of the high tide — are kind of translucent so that each one as it breaks is touched with silver, and even the foam at the edge has a silver rim . . . and each line of the swell is silver as it rises . . . Truly a night for magic,' he repeated, his voice curiously rapt and strange.

But the baby seal cried again then, and now Cressy could recognise the loneliness and fear in the young voice, — the terror of being left alone in a totally unknown world. 'What ought we to do for it?' she asked.

Milo seemed to hesitate, and then to take a decision. 'Bring it in, I think. The mother has probably abandoned it anyway, — but we are always asked to wait a bit in case she returns . . . Only, this is not their normal hauling-out rock, — nowhere near where they usually congregate or breed. I've never seen them on these rocks, so close in, before . . . ' He paused to listen again to that desperate little voice, as if judging how frantic it's need was and how best to deal with it. 'The parents are quite tough with the youngsters, you know. They launch them into the sea when they think they are ready, — and then just go off and leave them to it . . . Sometimes they get swamped by the big breakers and just drown . . . but more often they get carried away down the coast and get lost — like this one.'

'Poor thing,' said Cressy. 'It sounds so lonely!'

'Hungry, more like,' said Milo shrewdly.

'Have you got anything to feed it with?'

Once again Milo seemed to hesitate a little. 'Yes — some powdered liquid feed the seal people left me last time they came . . . You mix it with water, almost like a baby's bottle mixture . . . But we ought to get it down to the Seal Sanctuary at Gweek as soon as we can. They will know best what to do for it.'

'Go and fetch it, Milo,' said Cressy, understanding why he had waited so long before taking action. 'No-one is coming to rescue it but you!'

Milo sighed. 'I think you're right,' he said, and began to climb up the dark, slippery rocks. 'Stay there!' he called, as he went. 'Don't try to follow . . . I'll be back soon.'

Patiently, Cressy did as she was told, and Bo'sun stayed with her, but with one ear cocked towards the receding sound of Milo's feet on the rocks. The baby seal cried again, even more forlornly, and then was silent. Maybe Milo had already reached it? . . . And Cressy waited, listening for him to return. The night was very still, — no sea-birds awake, and no shoreward wind . . . But the sea still moved in a gentle hush of breaking wave, receding water and rattle of pebbles, in a ceaseless, soothing rhythmic pattern, and Cressy could almost imagine herself to be rocking on the swell like the sleeping gulls drifting over the silken surface, safe in the arms of the sea . . .

'Stop dreaming,' said Milo's voice close to her, 'and take this frightened baby from me before I fall off the rock!'

Cressy looked up, smiling, the moonlight full on her face, and held out her arms. Milo took a sharp breath, and almost dropped the seal, — but he didn't, or did he leap off the rock straight into Cressy's upstretched arms. But he wanted to — oh, how he wanted to! — and the moonlight and the silver night and the ache inside him all conspired to make him unexpectedly gruff as he handed over the little seal into the safe sanctuary of Cressy's embrace.

'Hold it tight!' he said. 'It may wriggle. They're slippery creatures.' And he sprang down from the rock and landed beside her.

Cressy felt the lissom, sinewy little furry body wriggle in her arms, but not to escape, simply to settle down more snugly into the blessed comfort and warmth of human contact. It didn't seem at all afraid.

'They are friendly animals usually,' said Milo, his voice gentle again and without its sudden note of stress. 'They're like the otters — they can get quite fond of humans!' He watched Cressy cradling the smooth, alert little head against her arm like a mother with a human baby, and thought he would never in his life forget the sight of her face, moonlit and tender, bent over the abandoned seal-pup in loving concern. 'But all the same,' he added, still gently, 'I'd better take it from you, in case it trips you up again . . . '

'I can hold it in one arm, if you guide me,' Cressy said, and Milo could hear the wistfulness in her voice, and had not the heart to insist on taking the foundling from her.

So he took her other hand in his, and together, slowly and quietly, they took the baby seal up the moonlit sands to Milo's little sanctuary behind his mother's cottage, and Bo'sun followed after them, his shadow — like their linked ones — dark on the silver shore.

★ ★ ★

In the end, they stayed up for the rest of the night with the abandoned seal pup. Milo managed to get her (he deduced that it was a 'her') to suck some of the Seal People's mixture of krill, plankton and vitamins in a baby's bottle with a soft teat, and Cressy holding the ravenous baby while Milo experimented. He hoped it was the right consistency — it had been for the other seal pup that he had rescued earlier. But he would be glad when they could get her to the Seal Sanctuary to be looked after by the experts. After some of this emergency food had gone down, the little seal simply curled up where she was and went to sleep, after a few appreciative burps.

'Won't she get too dry?' asked Cressy, feeling the glossy coat with anxious fingers.

'Not for a while,' Milo told her. 'They are used to hauling out on to the rocks, after all. And the pups are bred on land and stay in the breeding grounds for some time before they get pushed into the sea.'

He looked at Cressy still nursing the little pup in her arms, and smiled at her worried face, — and then hastened to reassure her. 'Don't worry. She'll tell us soon enough if she's unhappy!'

Cressy laughed, hearing the smile in Milo's gentle voice. Certainly the pup knew how to let her wants be known! 'What shall we call her?' she wondered.

'Moonshine, I should think!' laughed Milo.

'Moonshine it is!' agreed Cressy, delighted. 'Especially if all that desperate crying was mostly an act!'

'No,' said Milo honestly. 'It wasn't an act. She was just hungry and lonely and frightened . . . It was pure instinct — and it had the desired effect!'

They laughed comfortably together, and

left little Moonshine to sleep off her hunger and fright, while they sat on peacefully side by side, with old Bo'sun also asleep, but with one eye open and his nose resting on his paws. He knew, thankfully, that his people had settled down and it was time to rest, — but he wasn't going to miss anything.

They talked quietly together, with long pauses in between while their night-thoughts took shape or drifted out of focus and dissolved into nothing . . . They were in no hurry. Time seemed to stand still in the little shed — there was no sense of urgency — no need to grasp each living minute, or fill the silence with words and doubts and fears for the future . . . The world could turn in its own good time, and everything would be resolved and simple if they let things take their natural course.

Cressy told Milo about her father's concern about her educational future . . . and how they had agreed to leave it all for the rest of the summer . . . She also admitted that she had felt obliged to tell him about the 'flash of blue' in Hetty's scented garden . . . 'And I said I was afraid to make too much of it, — but I'd tell him if it happened again.'

'And — it hasn't, so far?' Milo kept his voice slow and gentle, without anxiety, — but in truth his whole being wanted to hear her say 'Yes, it has happened again . . . '

But she did not. Instead, she reached out and took his hand. 'It will come when it will,' she said tranquilly. 'I can wait.'

Milo did not pursue it. He let the silence wash over them, and put his own hopes as steadily aside as he knew Cressy did. The moonlight poured on through the open shed door, and the night wind was still. The little seal-pup snored, and so did old Bo'sun. But Milo and Cressy were awake, and at peace.

At length, when dawn was edging the sky with pale primrose in the east, and Milo was just trying to persuade Cressy to leave the pup to him and go back to the Wrecker's Cottage for some rest, they heard Stephen's voice outside. 'Cressy? Is that you?' He sounded puzzled and anxious.

'Come in, Dad,' she called back, instantly aware that she must present the situation to him with the true innocence it deserved. 'We're playing nursemaid to a seal-pup.'

Stephen stooped his head and came in through the shed door. And what he saw made him pause and draw breath in wonder — just as Milo had done when Cressy held out her arms to him for the seal-pup, her face bright with moonlight, and her whole fragile beauty revealed to him in one blinding moment of truth. Now, Stephen saw

Cressy cradling the small, sleeping seal-pup, and looking down at it with a smile of extraordinary maturity and tenderness. It was like a sudden leap in time to Cressy the woman, Cressy the mother . . . And she looked so serene and secure in her new adulthood that he was almost afraid to speak and break the spell.

'I heard it crying,' she said. 'I couldn't leave it. So I went out to find it . . . But Milo was there before me.' She looked up and smiled in Stephen's direction. 'And then we decided to watch over her till morning . . . She's so little, and so lost! . . . We've called her Moonshine.'

'We might need your help to get her over to the Seal Sanctuary,' put in Milo, also aware that he must include Stephen in this escapade to make things easier for Cressy.

'Where is that exactly?' asked Stephen, admiring the baby seal with appreciative eyes.

'At Gweek . . . On the estuary on the other side of this tongue of land . . . not far away.'

'I could use my car,' suggested Stephen doubtfully. 'But you'd have to carry the seal up the cliff.'

'The jeep would be better,' Milo admitted. 'If you come with us, Mum won't mind us using it.'

Stephen laughed. 'Then I suggest we have

an early breakfast, — and you can ask her on the way.'

So Cressy laid down the sleepy pup and Milo wrapped her in a damp sack and covered her head so that she could go on sleeping and not be frightened. The quiet intimacy of their night-watch was gone now, but the two young people did not seem to mind. The magic still burned on in their minds, and they had no need of further words.

Before long, they were rattling along in the jeep with little Moonshine in Cressy's arms again, and making all speed to the Seal Sanctuary at Gweek to get her the help she needed.

'I can't keep up with all your rescues,' said Stephen to Milo, feeling that the young people somehow needed his approval, 'but I do admire your dedication!'

Milo changed gear, and grinned. 'Most people think I'm entirely daft.'

'Well, so you are!' said Cressy. 'That's why I love you!'

And no-one said any more.

★ ★ ★

Gramp-the-Champ came back from another fishing trip looking tired and rather discouraged.

Milo was on the quayside to help tie up. He had made a quiet pact with himself that if he couldn't go out on *Crystal Rose* without upsetting his mother, he could at least be there to help with the unloading of the catch, and give his grandfather what practical support he had in his power. Word soon got round that the fishing fleet was coming in, and Milo had many friends in the little port with mobile phones . . . He was well-informed, and if anything had been really wrong with Gramp, he would soon have known. Everyone in Port Quentin knew Gramp-the-Champ, and many of them loved and revered the good old fisherman who had always been their champion. And the sons of the crewmen who still went out with him were as loyal as their fathers . . . Yes, Milo was well-informed.

But this time, it was Milo himself who said anxiously: 'Is anything wrong, Gramp? You look a bit rough?'

Gramp shook his grizzled head. 'No. It was a rough trip.'

'Weatherwise?'

The old man shrugged. 'No worse than usual. But the Spanish trawlers were.'

'Were what? Worse than usual?'

'They're scooping the bottom off the ocean!' Gramp said. 'Scraping it bare. The sea floor will be a wilderness in a few years. Their net-mesh is much too small.'

'But there are regulations now, aren't there?'

'Tell that to the Spanish!' snapped Gramp. Then he sighed, as always trying to be reasonable and fair. 'It's not only the Spanish ... It's these 'unknown strangers' flying British flags of convenience, and buying up franchises. No-one can stop them, — and it's very hard to check every boat for illegal nets or quota-dodging.'

Milo nodded. 'And your own catch?'

'Smaller than it should be, — a lot of rubbish ... But then, if we get a good one and we're over the quota, we're supposed to throw it back!'

Milo snorted in derision. 'These bureaucrats in the ministry! They haven't a clue! ... What's the good of throwing it back when the fish are dead anyway? It's a total waste!'

'I know,' said Gramp wearily. 'And the trouble is, Milo, my lad, I'm not so brave as I was! These huge factory ships are too much for me to tackle! We can't drive them away. We can only sit by and watch them plunder the sea ... '

'And maybe report them?'

It was Gramp's turn to snort. 'Report

them? By the time the report gets through to anyone worthwhile, and anyone gets sent to inspect them, — the boats are a hundred miles away!'

He and his crew were slamming boxes of fish down on the quay by now, and he threw down one more loaded crate of gleaming flatfish with an extra thump of rage. 'I shouldn't get angry!' he told Milo, only slightly apologetic. 'But it makes my blood boil!'

'Here, here!' grumbled a couple of his crew, and gave their skipper a sideways grin of close support.

They finished the unloading and weighing, and set off the catch in the fish van to Newlyn fish market, and totted up the likely earnings to be divided among the crew. 'Meet you for a drink, Gramp?' they called, as they drifted off towards the Fisherman's Arms.

'Maybe,' said Gramp. 'Later,' and he winked at Milo and added quietly: 'I need a breather first!'

Milo walked back with him to his own cottage by the quayside, and went in to make him a cup of tea while the old man stripped off his fishy clothes and had a shower.

'You ought to take it easy for a day or

two,' Milo said, handing him his tea. 'You look knackered!'

Gramp sighed moodily. 'I'm strong enough still, Milo . . . It's just frustration . . . I can see our livelihood disappearing day by day, — and I can't do anything about it! . . . It's not only me, — it affects us all!'

Milo nodded agreement. 'I know. And God knows you've done enough in your time to fight it . . . But isn't it time to let someone else do the fighting?'

Gramp looked at him grimly. 'Who, for instance?'

And Milo knew there was no answer to that. Gramp had always been the leader, — the fishermen's champion, no less. His mates in the little fishing community were all loyal and supportive, — and loved him for his belligerent stance, but they were not leaders by nature. They were used to leaving it to him.

'I suppose I could try tackling the ministry,' he said sadly, 'and become a talker instead of a doer. But I hate committees!'

Milo laughed. 'You ought to try it, Gramp. You'd scare them all to death!'

'That'd be the day!' grinned Gramp, sipping his tea. Then he shrugged his perpetual warfare aside, and asked about other things.

'How is Cressy getting along?'

'Fighting her corner, — like you!'

Gramp grinned. 'She's a spunky little lass, that one!'

Milo agreed. Then he told Gramp about the 'flash of blue' in Hetty's garden, — thinking that if Stephen had been told it was all right for Gramp to know, — and he might bring some of his patient wisdom to bear on the subject.

'Only the once?' Gramp asked.

'Yes. Just the once. I asked . . . ' He hesitated, and added slowly: 'I didn't like to — to sound too eager about it.'

'No,' agreed Gramp. 'Best wait and see . . . It'll probably happen again.'

'Do you think so?' Now, away from Cressy, Milo did sound eager.

'I said *probably*,' Gramp told him severely. 'But I do think so, yes.'

Milo sighed, and then went on to tell Gramp about setting the other animals free, and the rescue of Moonshine, the baby seal. 'Cressy was very good with her,' he said. 'Cradled her in her arms like a mother. In fact she looked . . . somehow very grown-up and maternal.' His voice had changed and grown softer, and Gramp did not miss the note of tender recollection in his grandson's young voice. 'I suppose . . . ' Milo went on, almost shyly, 'girls grow up earlier than boys, don't they?'

'Reckon they do,' agreed Gramp, smiling. 'And know what they want sooner, too.'

Milo was silent about that. He did not think Cressy could know what she wanted while she was still blind and restricted, — and if she thought she did, she would probably be wrong . . . and he would be even more wrong to take her at her word . . . He sighed to himself, unaware that his grandfather was watching him with a shrewd, sympathetic gaze.

'Things will resolve themselves,' said Gramp gently. (It was a favourite maxim of his). 'But sometimes, you know, Milo, I think you have to trust to your own instincts, and not be afraid of them.'

Milo looked at him sideways, and almost blushed, except that he was too brown and sunburnt for it to show. 'You know too much, Gramp,' he said. 'Stop reading my thoughts.'

The old man laughed and changed course a little. 'What about the flute recitals with Sue and Joe?'

'The first one is today,' said Milo. 'This afternoon. The garden is open for the first time this year . . . If the music goes down well, it'll be a once-a-week arrangement for the summer.'

Gramp approved of that. 'I hope it works. It'll give her days a bit of a pattern.'

Milo nodded. 'It *will* work,' he said. 'She's more relaxed now, — and she and Sue seem to understand one another.'

'I'd like to hear this,' Gramp admitted. 'Shall I come?'

'Why not?' Milo agreed. 'Stephen wants to as well, — and even Mum might make the effort. But I've asked them not to tell Cressy they'll be there, — not till afterwards. I think she needs to feel it's an everyday sort of ploy, — not a grand event.'

Gramp nodded. 'More professional . . . and less 'making allowances' or condescension from her friends.'

'Exactly,' Milo said, as always comforted by his grandfather's instant comprehension. 'She's still a bit prickly about all that. Not that she needs to be, when she can play like a flying angel!'

'No, but she's every right to be,' said Gramp sturdily. 'She's a gallant lass, — and I'll be there. But mum's the word till afterwards. In any case, I'll probably be helping Hetty with the trays.'

Milo glared at him. 'I thought you were

going to rest! . . . I can do that, Gramp.'

His grandfather grinned. 'So you can . . . She's getting on a bit, our Hetty, you know, and she finds the trays a bit heavy. Especially with all those scones and home-made clotted cream and such that she goes in for!'

Milo laughed. 'Will the musicians get some?'

'You bet, — afterwards. A slap-up spread! We can all celebrate then. Cressy won't mind us after it's all over!' He smiled again at his grandson's expression. 'Tell you what, if you do the trays, I'll keep the others away in the quietest corner. Agreed?'

'Done!' said Milo, and he left his grandfather to his (supposed) rest, and went away laughing.

★ ★ ★

Cressy actually put on a dress for the little recital, — at Sue's prompting. 'You'll be the focus of attention,' Sue told her, 'you and me both. Joe's better off, he's sitting down at his keyboard, but you and I have to look willowy and flexible, floating about with the music . . . You got anything floaty?'

'I — I don't know. I think so . . . ' Cressy said doubtfully. 'I'll get Dad to have a look . . . He's quite good with clothes.'

'I'll come over, if you like?' Sue volunteered, being careful to sound extremely casual and off-hand. 'Different criteria from a male point of view?'

'Yes, why not?' Cressy laughed. 'Come and see.'

So Sue came, — the first real friend Cressy had admitted to her private and difficult world of dressing and undressing in the dark and choosing colours and shapes she could not see.

They spent a happy, giggly time, with Sue holding up garments to Cressy's slight figure and describing them to her in hilarious detail. 'This one is long and slinky, — a ghastly pink, where *did* you get it? . . . And this — pale yellow, like your hair . . . No, it's too understated. Makes you disappear . . . But *this* one — yes, this is better . . . Sort of sea-green-blue and floaty, — really dreamy . . . It matches your eyes, — and they are still beautiful, you know, even if they aren't functioning quite right at present!' Casually, Sue handed out her special kind of back-handed comfort. 'Try it on, Cressy, and I'll tell you if it works.'

And it *did* work. It made Cressy look more like a water-nymph than ever, with her pale-gold hair and her slender body lightly sheathed in floating iridescent chiffon which spun out into wave-like drifts of blue-green silk when she moved

'Perfect!' said Sue. 'You look just like your music — out of this world!' She gave Cressy an approving hug, and added softly: 'You'll be a wow!' Then she asked a more serious question to do with their music-making, feeling her way while she and Cressy were alone together and could say what they liked. 'Are you quite happy with the way we do things, Cress? . . . I mean, I know you're classically trained, like me. We *could* stick to the Three-Bs and things we've learned by heart and so on?'

'No,' said Cressy. 'I'd rather experiment, like you . . . It's more fun . . . ' She turned an enquiring face in Sue's direction. 'But I could put in a set-piece or two, like Syrinx or the Poulenc Flute Sonata, if you want? . . . It's up to you.'

Sue considered. 'I think Syrinx would go down well . . . We'll include it if you're willing! . . . And maybe later when we've had time to rehearse a few bits of the real stuff, we can include them from time to time? What do you think?'

'Let them down lightly?'

'And ourselves, as well!' laughed Sue.

Cressy laughed, too. 'Sounds ideal . . . And

we can take off in between.'

'That's what I'd hoped!' agreed Sue, and gave Cressy another encouraging hug, — this time of relief as well as approval.

★ ★ ★

So there they were — the three of them, not on a platform (in case Cressy fell off in the heat of the moment) but in a little enclosed space on the paved terrace, with the tea tables spread out round them at a suitable distance.

The garden was full of people that day, — full of cheerful voices and the scent of Hetty's flowers. Word had gone round about the music and Cressy's flute-playing, and they were here to listen to this girl who was blind but could play her silver flute like an angel.

'Won't the others in the group mind being left out?' Cressy asked, uneasy about breaking into a close circle of friends.

'No,' said Joe, playing one soft chord on his keyboard to get people's attention. 'They often play together as a threesome — gigs round the local pubs — and Sue and I sometimes do a duo ... This fits in very well. Stop worrying!'

'I think you'd better start them off with

287

Syrinx,' suggested Sue. 'That'll get them really listening! Then I'll take us off with something they all know, and we can sort of drift away where we like from there. OK?'

'OK,' said Cressy, suppressing the flutter of terror in her stomach, and putting the flute to her lips. Then she began to play, — and it was easier than she expected, because Syrinx was about Pan and his Pan-pipes in a magical land of sunlight and flowers . . . and what better setting could she have than Hetty's scented garden? The ancient magic of Pan seemed to be alive in every heavy-headed rose that dropped crimson petals on the grass, and every fragrant breath of the summer wind that laid a veil of heady scent on every leaf and flower . . . Yes, Pan was there all right, with his ancient magic, and Cressy's fingers seemed almost to be his, and the silver flute became the voice of his spellbinding Pan-pipes as Debussy's music fell softly on the listening air . . .

There was a moment of quiet silence when she had finished, and then a small and gentle burst of applause, as if the listeners did not want to break the spell. And then Sue took them all away with her into 'Tomorrow shall be my dancing day', — lightly and sinuously inviting those subtle dancing rhythms with her violin, and Cressy followed her with the clear, pure voice of the flute dancing already, and making all kinds of shining arabesques and rings of joyous jetées and twirls around Sue's violin, while Joe kept the warmth and shimmer of sunshine in the continuous miasma of deep chording on his keyboard.

Was it intentional of Sue, Cressy wondered? Is it a promise, or a prophesy, or just simple, kindly encouragement? *Will* tomorrow be my dancing day? *Will I ever dance again?* . . . But then her thoughts whirled away in the dance, and she forgot to have doubts or misgivings. Music was a joy in itself, and today was a dancing day, too, — and she let her fingers take her where they would . . .

And presently Sue's violin changed the dancing mood to one of more distant exploration, there was another hint of '*Over the hills and far away,*' and then there were high mountains beyond the hills, and dazzling deep snows . . . But then, after the snows and waterfalls, there was a hint of '*Shenandoah*' and there were rivers and boats and long voyages . . . and estuaries of shining water, and small still pools in peat-dark streams where otters played . . . and Cressy thought then of Milo's voice as he bent over the injured otter, crooning to it softly, full of affectionate concern, as if it was a friend of his that he knew and recognised . . . and for a moment Cressy's fingers almost faltered, the image was so clear in her mind. She could *almost* see his face, though she had not really seen it since he was a boy of thirteen, four long years ago . . . But she knew what he would look like now, oh yes, she knew! . . . His voice told her, — warm and gentle and full of loving compassion for every living thing in his care . . .

But the music left the peat-pools and estuaries and moved on again, and this time Sue took them back to the sea, — for after all, almost everyone here listening in the scented garden, lived and worked by the sea or on the sea, and its wide blue arms were all around them . . .

Blue? thought Cressy. Might I catch another glimpse of blue from the sea? And she let the silver flute sing of mermaids and dolphins playing in the blue-green depths of the ocean, and baby seals crying in the night on the black rocks, and moonlight that Milo said made the night black and silver and full of magic . . . and she hadn't brought her flute then when he asked for it, but she could play it for him now and bring the moonlight back . . . And the magic was still there, for the asking, behind the moonlight, and Milo's voice sounding strangely shaken, and the feel of Moonshine, the baby seal, warm and confiding, as it curled up in her arms . . .

Am I too sad? she thought. Is the sea too sad? . . . It can be joyous, too, on a glittering, breezy, blowy day. (Is Sue really playing '*Blow the man down*'?) . . . and it can be calm and hushed and peaceful like it was that night . . . (Now Sue seems to have reached some sort of Celtic lullaby . . . rocking little Moonshine to sleep? . . . How could she know? . . .) And I nearly nodded off then as well, nursing Moonshine in Milo's shed, but I mustn't do it now! . . .

And then Sue was off again somewhere new, — and Cressy was scrambling to catch up. She was still trying to reach the overtones of Sue's new thought, and staring sightlessly straight ahead of her at the tall flowers of Hetty's nearby flowerbeds, when she suddenly found herself looking — yes, *looking* — at one very tall, very straight, very blue flower which was standing right in front of her — very proud and tall and very, very blue . . . *Blue*! she cried to herself, soundlessly, joyously, — *a blue flower*! . . . and I can see it! . . . Her flute did not falter. It soared and leapt and wove new patterns of blue light round Cressy's brain — round Hetty's garden — round

Sue's still-exploring violin . . . But then, before Cressy could falter, or put out a hand towards that clear vision of blue, it had gone again . . . There was nothing in front of her eyes now, nothing at all, — but the blue sang on in her mind, and in her flute . . . For it had happened again! And that meant . . . it meant that it might return!

Sue was so tuned to Cressy by this time that she had sensed that sudden revelation, that sudden surge of ecstatic, unexpected joy, and she had looked across at her, wondering if she was tired and they ought to stop. But Cressy was playing on like one possessed, and she was somewhere now on the tops of mountains with blue sky above her head, and her feet were running because she was free, and her heart was leaping like Boxer the hare when he was set free on the summer grass . . . and Milo, — Milo was with her, still holding her hand, still guiding her in case she fell, because he, too, was part of the blue . . . And if she went too high, he would never let her fall . . .

But Sue was winding down now, gently and consolingly bringing Cressy down from the heights, and the song became soft and quiet and seemed to resolve into one she knew, — a classical song by Brahms she had listened to in the long night-watches . . . 'I

lie and dream among the waving grass . . . '
Cressy's flute took up the tune with sudden authority. She knew this song . . . '*And fair white clouds float gently on the blue . . . '* (Yes, I knew there was blue in it!) . . . The silver voice of her flute soared up, her mind remembered . . . '*Serene and pure in those eternal spaces . . . '* it sang, and gently repeated it on a dying fall . . .

I feel serene, thought Cressy, in the strange silence that ensued, and I've seen blue again . . . and if Milo is still here, I can find my way back . . . And Milo *was* still there. He had seen Cressy almost stumble with the pain of return, and he came up, quite simply and naturally, and took her hand in his and led her away.

★ ★ ★

'What made you do the Brahms?' asked Cressy, happily munching one of Hetty's scones-and-cream.

'I don't know,' said Sue dreamily. It seemed to fit . . . 'I knew it from college . . . Someone used to sing it.' She turned to exchange a glance with Joe, her twin brother. 'A friend of Joe's — he had a lovely voice . . . ' She turned back to Cressy. 'But you knew it, too.'

'Yes.' Cressy's voice was as dreamy as Sue's. 'Late night radio.'

'Classic F.M.?'

Cressy smiled. 'Sometimes — or Radio Three . . . '

'It's a lovely song,' put in Joe. 'When Alec sang it, we used to go all woozy at the edges!'

'When Cressy played it, we did, too!' laughed Sue.

'It was a lovely way to come down,' murmured Cressy.

'I didn't know how else to *get* you down!' retorted Sue, still laughing. 'I thought you were going to take off altogether!'

Amid the general laughter, Cressy said suddenly: 'Where's Hetty?'

'I'm here,' said Hetty's warm voice behind her. 'Making a pig of myself with my own cream tea! What can I do for you, Cressy?'

'You've done plenty!' said Cressy, turning round and smiling in her direction. 'But I wanted to ask you something.'

'Yes?'

'Is there — from where we were playing, is there a very tall blue flower somewhere nearby?'

There was a stunned silence. Not everyone understood the implications of what she was saying, but Milo did, — and Stephen did, and so did Gramp, sitting beside Hetty at the end of the table.

'Why, yes,' said Hetty, puzzled. 'A delphinium. Very deep blue. Why?'

'I — I just thought . . . ' She hesitated. But after all, they were all friends here, and she could not keep it to herself for ever. Only, don't let them say too much! she prayed. Let them take it sensibly, and not go over the top . . . It may not mean anything. 'I just thought,' she murmured, 'that I — I caught a glimpse of the colour . . . It was so blue!'

The silence was prolonged. But finally, Gramp was the one who knew how to put things in practical perspective. 'That's good news, Cressy, isn't it? . . . Even a small glimpse is a bonus. Especially one of Hetty's flowers.'

Cressy said steadily: 'It's gone now. I don't want to — I don't want anyone to expect too much . . . But — ' she turned to smile in Hetty's direction again, 'it was a *lovely* blue while it lasted!' Then, suddenly feeling a little tired and sad, she reached out for Milo's hand.

He did not fail her. 'Shall we walk down to the quay and listen to the gulls squabbling? . . . Mum can pick us up from there.'

Cressy rose gratefully, and made stumbling

attempts at thanks to Sue and Joe, and to Hetty who had arranged it all . . . But she was almost past lucid conversation now, and she allowed Milo to take her away from them all without further protest.

'You climbed too high,' said Milo softly. 'Relax, now. You're safely down to earth again, with me.'

Cressy was silent. There was no need for words.

★ ★ ★

But all the same, there was need of words, — and possibly of action, too, and Cressy knew that decisions would have to be taken. The only trouble was that it was all so nebulous, so uncertain . . . Impossible to believe anything, to hope anything, to plan anything . . . It was still waiting time, — but with these sudden momentary glimpses, it was becoming increasingly hard to remain tranquil and patient . . . It had been almost easier when nothing was happening and there seemed to be no hope at all . . . And now Stephen, her anxious father, would be asking questions and making plans, and she did not know what to say to him.

Stephen, however, was wise — and cautious. He did not want to fill Cressy's days with false hopes either. So he began gently enough: 'Cressy, I know it was only momentary, and you don't want to make too much of it, but this time I think we'd better tell the specialist, don't you?'

'Yes,' she said, reluctantly.

'And make an appointment for you to come up and see him?'

'Yes,' she said again. 'But — but Dad, don't hope too much.'

Stephen's voice was shaken. 'You can say that to *me*?'

Cressy sighed. 'You know that first doctor at the hospital? Euan Morris? . . . He told me that hope could be a terrible thing to live with . . . I think I'm beginning to understand him now.'

Her father's face was riven. He understood Euan Morris, — all too well. But he did not say so.

'It was almost easier,' Cressy admitted painfully, 'when it was *all* dark — and there was nothing to hope for.'

'I know,' agreed Stephen sadly. But he was thinking, not for the first time, how adult and calm Cressy had become about it all, and how amazingly serene and happy she had seemed to be, despite her limitations . . . And young Milo, he knew, had a lot to do with it.

'. . . Milo,' she was saying.

Stephen started, pulling his mind back to the present. 'What?'

'I owe such a lot to Milo,' she said, and her voice was strangely troubled, as if by a new thought. 'The thing is, I — I don't think I could handle this without him . . . '

She did not go on, but Stephen was not slow to see the implications behind the shy young voice. And he knew at once that he must be reckless enough to mortgage the whole of their future, if that was the reassurance she needed now. 'Well, you won't have to, will you?' he said, and waited to see the relief and gladness flow into her expressive face.

'Won't I?'

'No.' He was quite firm. 'If that is what you need most — you shall have it. So far as it is in my power.' He paused, and then added softly: 'But he'll be away at college soon, won't he?'

'Yes,' sighed Cressy, but the serenity was clear in her voice. 'He will. But he'll be back!'

Stephen smiled at her certainty, but he made no comment. Instead, he returned to practical matters. 'Well, I was going to tell you anyway, — I've been asked to go up to London again tomorrow, to meet an editor.

It's another book illustration job, and I could do with the commission.'

'Of course!' Cressy was always generous about his work.

'So I think I'd better go, — and I'll talk to your specialist too, and fix a date for you. Will that be all right?'

'Yes,' said Cressy, a little breathlessly. 'So long as I know I'm coming back — whatever happens!'

Stephen put a reassuring arm round her shoulders and hugged her hard. 'You're coming back!' he said.

Part Four

Hazardous Ventures

Once again, Catherine offered to drive Stephen up to the cliff-top to fetch his own car, and once again, Milo turned up on the doorstep just as Stephen was leaving. But this time he said to Cressy, as they were strolling peacefully down to the beach: 'I shall have to leave you on your own a bit later, — when Mum gets back. I'm going down to the school to get my A-level results.'

'Oh Milo, — how exciting!' She gave his hand an enthusiastic squeeze. 'I hope they'll be what you want.'

'I hope so, too,' said Milo.

But they both of them knew that what he wanted was a loaded question, — and it might take him away from her and the place he loved, perhaps for ever. The morning seemed to be fraught with imponderables, and Cressy could not bear it. She stopped still, and turned her face towards Milo. 'I've just made Dad promise that I can come back,' she said, 'whatever happens, — because I told him I need you.'

'You did?' Light seemed to flood into Milo's smile. Cressy could not see it, but

303

she could feel his sudden joy.

'And when Dad reminded me that you'd be going away, I said yes, but he'll be back.' She hesitated a little, and then dared to ask the final question 'You will, won't you?'

'Of course,' said Milo. 'Every spare moment! I'll always be here if you need me!' There was such joy in his voice that Cressy could not mistake it.

She laughed, and reached out a hand to touch his smile. 'That's all right, then,' she said, as if everything in the world had been settled for ever. 'Let's go and listen to the sea.'

So they strolled on, hand-in-hand, with all kinds of promises and pacts assured between them, though nothing more was said. And later in the morning, when Catherine was back, and Milo set off to catch the bus down to his old school, Cressy was quite content to walk alone on the beach, with Bo'sun beside her, while she contemplated an uncertain future without fear.

In truth, she was tired this morning, — having spent a rather sleepless night. What with the success of the little recital in Hetty's garden, and its attendant 'high' that was difficult to come back from, — and the sudden extraordinary glimpse of Hetty's blue delphinium, the night had been full of questions and anxieties. As usual, Cressy had tried to calm her fears by listening to music. She had already confessed to Sue how much she relied on her little radio in the still night-watches, but she realised that music had come to mean much more to her since her blindness.

Even before the revelation at the first little concert on the Hard when she had discovered a new freedom in improvisation, music had always been part of her life, from the earliest days of school music and flute lessons, and concert-going with Sally and Stephen, — but now it seemed to take on a new dimension in her darkened, listening world. Now she heard the great voices of Beethoven and Bach and Brahms, the dreamy landscapes of Vaughan Williams, the wild, fierce seascapes of Bax and Britten, the dark forests and icy wildernesses of Sibelius, and the heartbreaking anguish of wars and broken dreams of Shostakovich, — and they all seemed to have new meaning, to take her out on strange voyages, into strange countries and unknown regions of unimagined beauty and triumph, and sorrow and pity . . . a world she had never understood before.

Sometimes, even in the daytime, she just sat in her room alone, with the radio weaving its own spells, and the door to the sea outside open but unused. And sometimes she took her own small walkman with her and tapped her way down to the beach and to Milo's boat, which she knew would be pulled up high above the tide-line and made fast securely to the nearest stanchion beside the old slipway . . . Sometimes she would just sit on the sand and let the music wash over her in drifting waves like the sea, and sometimes, when she needed extra reassurance, she would climb into Milo's boat and sit there and dream, with the music still casting spells in her ears, and the darkness of her blindness forgotten . . .

It was only when Milo was away that she did this, and only then, when she was truly alone, did she try to come to terms with the real fact of her blindness, and this new uncertainty that came with the sudden flashes of blue. For the most part, she admitted to herself, her life was one big bluff, — one continuous attempt to seem brave and cheerful, and to cover up her despair. For there were still moments of black despair when she dared to contemplate a long, dark future in a lost world she would never see again, and a loved and loving mother she would never see again . . . never, — whatever happened to her sight.

She had never let these moods encroach on

Stephen. Her father, she knew, had enough dark griefs of his own to contend with. She did not speak of them to Milo either, — but she was sure he knew. And that was why she chose to sit in his boat and fight it out alone, and let the music and the sun and the sound of the sea banish the darkness from her mind, and let her dream in peace.

And this morning, with new things resolved between them and new promises given, Cressy's sleepless night and tired mind were catching up on her, and she felt drained but curiously content as she walked on the beach with Bo'sun padding beside her, — so when she came suddenly on Milo's boat, she decided to climb in and sit in the sun, and let the music lull her and disperse all her dark dreams.

It did seem to her that she stumbled on Milo's boat rather unexpectedly, but she was not — could not be — any judge of distance, and she assumed she must have walked further up the beach towards the high tide-line than usual. She knew Milo always beached the *Gannet* in the same place, and it was a sanctuary she had come to rely on.

For a time she sat and listened to Brahms (but not the same dreamy song of yesterday's recital). And then she resolutely got out her flute, getting her fingers ever more accustomed to working on their own without any help from her eyes. She had discovered quite early on with Sue and Joe and the group that her fingers were quite clever on their own, — and in fact her eyes had never looked at them very much once she had got hold of the notes, being much too busy reading the music and translating it into orders for her fingers to obey. Now they danced to another tune, — one inside her head or in her memory, or in her listening ear. It was a different approach — a different way of playing — but it worked . . . and oh! what a relief and a joy it was to find that her fingers could soar and prance and sing without any eyes to help them . . . She tried them out for a while, and then she grew tired, put her earphones on again, and lay down in the sun-filled boat to dream . . . and then to sleep . . . And Bo'sun lay down outside the *Gannet* on the sun-warmed sand and dreamed as well . . .

It was only when she heard the dog barking that she woke to a gentle rocking movement, and knew that the tide had come in and taken Milo's little *Gannet* out to sea.

* * *

Bo'sun had know the *Gannet* was not in the right place. But he could not tell Cressy so. He had known, somehow, that she ought not to have climbed into it today, and he knew now that she ought not to be in it alone and drifting out to sea. How could he look after her out there? . . . He had stopped barking by now, and after a tentative attempt to walk into the surf, he changed his mind and raced furiously away across the rocks down the long spit of land that enclosed Crocker's Cove and separated it from Port Quentin's safe harbour round the corner.

He ran and ran, across boulder and rock and fallen shale, across small chasms and rock pools and small inlets of sea where the spray sprang up in sudden plumes, on and on, tail flying, paws slipping and sliding on the shiny wet rocks, but never pausing, never flagging, until he came to the end of the last dwindling spur of rock, — a long way out beyond the cove into the open sea. Here he paused for only the briefest of moments, and then plunged unhesitatingly into the deep green ocean swell and began to swim.

Cressy was out there. It was his duty to take care of her. So he had to reach her somehow, and the only way now was to swim. So he swam and swam, and the tide went on running, taking Cressy further and further from him, and taking the gallant dog further and further from land . . . But Bo'sun went on swimming.

★ ★ ★

Catherine had known Cressy was on the beach alone. From time to time she had come to her door to have a look, and seen her down there, walking patiently along with her white stick tapping the way, and Bo'sun trotting beside her. Milo had told his mother he was going down to the school to get his results, and asked her to keep an eye on Cressy, though she didn't really need much of an eye these days, she was very independent. He did not tell Catherine, though, not thinking it relevant or important, that he had left the *Gannet* in Port Quentin earlier, and had arranged with his friend Jorky Beckinsale to bring her round and beach her for him, ready for the next trip with Cressy and Stephen.

Stephen had gone off in good time to catch the Penzance train for another visit to the studio where all his work came from, and Catherine knew it was important for his livelihood and was only too willing to help when he smiled in his kind, gentle way and said: 'I know Cressy will be all right with you and Milo.' . . . But was she? Catherine had been busy baking that morning. She was getting quite keen on providing a good, interesting meal for those friendly suppers. She was even beginning to look forward to them, and though she would not admit it even to herself, Stephen had more than a little to do with her softening mood . . . But now she had been busy over the Aga long enough, and had better take another look at Cressy on the beach.

Only, she wasn't on the beach. Nor was Bo'sun. Nor the *Gannet*. And, come to think of it, she had heard Bo'sun barking furiously at something not long ago . . . Probably chasing a seagull.

She went out on to the path and stood looking down across the beach, shading her eyes against the sun. No-one there. Nothing. Not even gulls. Would Cressy venture on to the rocks? Surely not . . . Her eyes swept across the beach again, over the rocks and down to the edge of the sea. The tide was going out fast . . . The sea was calm today, smooth as silk and clear of mist. Nothing in the sea either . . . and Cressy surely would not try to paddle or swim on her own? No. An empty beach. An empty sea . . . and not even Bo'sun barking . . .

And then she saw them. A tiny, bobbing shell that was the *Gannet*, and one small, upright figure sitting in it . . . and, a long way behind her, still close to the jutting arm of rock at the edge of the cove, one tiny wet gold head, still swimming strongly, still struggling with desperate determination to reach Cressy through the outgoing tide . . .

Catherine took one horrified look, and ran back into the cottage to the phone. Gramp, she thought. Gramp first . . . If only he is in port, and not out on *Kittiwake* or *Crystal Rose* She knew his mobile phone number. Oh, let him be there! (She did not stop to reflect that for all her rages against Gramp and the sea, it was Gramp she turned to in emergency). Oh! Let him be there! . . . Otherwise it would have to be the lifeboat or the coastguard and Search-and-Rescue.

Frantically, she dialled the number, and Gramp's deep voice soon answered. 'Gramp? Cressy's drifting out to sea in Milo's *Gannet* on her own.'

'Oh, my God,' said Gramp. 'I'll take *Kittiwake*.'

'And Bo'sun — ' Catherine was nearly crying with anxiety, 'your Bo'sun is trying to swim out to her.'

Oh God, thought Gramp again, and it was almost a prayer. The poor old dog. He'll never survive. But aloud he only said: 'Which direction?'

'Off the point — straight out to sea,' said Catherine. 'The tide's running. Hurry, Gramp!' Then she added breathlessly: 'Should I alert the lifeboat or the coastguard?'

'Not yet,' said Gramp. 'I'll do that from *Kittiwake* on her radio if need be. Don't panic, Catherine. I'll reach them!' and he was gone.

He was just casting off *Kittiwake* with the engine running, when Milo came along the quay.

'Where are you off to?'

'Cressy's adrift in the *Gannet*,' said Gramp shortly, and went on casting off. Milo leapt to help him, and sprang on board after him as the last rope was loosened. 'What are you doing?' barked Gramp.

'Coming with you,' said Milo. 'You'll need an extra pair of hands.'

'But Catherine — '

'To hell with all that!' said Milo, (not really meaning it, but this was an emergency.) 'Let's get going!'

'Bo'sun's out after her,' added Gramp, in a worried voice. But he did not say any more.

Together they manoeuvred *Kittiwake* through the narrow harbour entrance and set out to sea to rescue Cressy.

★ ★ ★

For *Kittiwake* the distance was not great, and the sea was mild and easy. But for Bo'sun it was a hard, exhausting swim. He had no idea if he was winning or losing in the tide-race. He just kept on swimming and hoping, even though the ache in his legs kept on getting worse, and his old heart pounding in his chest seemed to be doing its best to choke him . . . Still he kept on swimming, and finally he came almost within reach of the drifting boat, but by now he was too tired to go any further, let alone try to clamber aboard. With a last despairing splash of his front paws he made a hopeless attempt to push himself forward, gave a small, faint yelp to tell Cressy that he had at least tried, and began to sink beneath the waves.

But Cressy heard him. That's Bo'sun, she told herself. *Bo'sun?* Can it be? . . . He must have swum out after me. The poor old dog. It's much too far for him . . . What can I do? She thought, quite sanely and practically, I mustn't lean out of the boat too far or it will turn over, or I will fall in . . . That won't help Bo'sun . . . I can put out an oar, though . . . (She had already felt for the oars, and also discovered that the outboard motor and the petrol can were not on board, — but what could she do with either when she could not see to steer?) But an oar, now? One oar over the side, and Bo'sun might have the sense to cling on till she could get him in over the gunwale. After all, the dog was no fool, and coming all this way after her, *swimming* after her! . . . She couldn't let him drown.

'Hang on, Bo'sun,' she said. 'I'm coming . . . ' Only, she knew she mustn't be 'coming.' She had to stay put, keeping the little boat steady, and if — if she could get Bo'sun close enough to haul him in, she must be careful to lean backwards to take the weight. *Backwards*! she told herself. Not forwards. Oh Bo'sun, do catch on! (*Someone will come, she said. Milo will come!*

She felt for the oars, and got her hands round one hand-grip, then lowered it rather awkwardly over the side into the water. She could feel the current tugging at it, and then she heard a spluttering gasp, and a heavier weight came on its end. (*Don't panic! she told herself. Pull!*)

'Well done!' she called over the side. 'Hold on, Bo'sun, hold on . . . ' and she tried, cautiously, to pull the weighted oar towards her. But it was almost impossible. The sea kept pulling it sideways and any extra weight seemed to set the little *Gannet* careening wildly sideways to the swell. It was not a good idea. But still she tried again, and this time she turned the oar sideways to the boat and risked grasping it hand by hand lower down, relinquishing its proper hand-grip, — risking losing it altogether if a sudden swell took it out of her hands. But it didn't, and presently one groping hand felt something wet and shaggy with a thin, sodden band of leather round it, lifting and falling helplessly in the little waves round the *Gannet*'s prow. Bo'sun's collar!

Greatly daring, she caught hold of it in one hand, and wondered whether to risk letting the oar go altogether. But that might make it swing round and wrench the poor dog out of her hand . . . No, better hold on and see if she could lift the dog out of the water and into the boat by herself. But she couldn't. Try as she might, she couldn't find the strength to get the sodden animal high enough to topple him over the gunwale. And the more she tried, the more *Gannet* rocked wildly and tilted dangerously seawards, and she knew she mustn't let it go any further, or the boat would go over, and they would both drown.

'Hold on,' she muttered, through clenched teeth. 'Hold on, Bo'sun ... we'll try again ... ' and she clung on to his collar, trying at least to keep his head above the water.

'Hold on,' said a voice close to her — Milo's voice, wonderfully close. 'Hold on, Cressy, — we're coming!'

They had come up behind the little *Gannet*, in order to stop her drifting any further from them, and now they debated what to do next. Gramp could get *Kittiwake* pretty close to the bobbing craft, but he was afraid of running her down altogether, so he held off from totally close contact. It was no good throwing Cressy a line, — she could not see it, and anyway, if she let go of that sodden collar now, it looked as if the exhausted dog would sink like a stone.

'We'd better put down a ladder,' said Gramp.

'I'll swim across,' said Milo.

Gramp looked worried. Shades of his son, Kitto's gallant attempt at rescue still haunted him. If anything happened to Milo, too — he would never forgive himself, — and as for Catherine ...

'It's all right,' said Milo, knowing his thoughts. 'The sea's mild as milk, and you know I'm a strong swimmer.'

'Yes, I know, but — '

'It's not a force nine, like then,' Milo said gently. 'Come on, we're wasting time,' and he flung the rope ladder over the side and began to climb down it.

Gramp could do no more than hold *Kittiwake* idling against the swell, and wait for results. But Milo let himself go from the bottom rung of the ladder and struck out strongly across the little space to where the *Gannet* bobbed helplessly in the swell, while Cressy clung with all her strength to Bo'sun's collar.

'Sit still, Cressy,' said Milo from the water. 'Just keep holding on to Bo'sun and sit still. I'll do the rest.' He got his hands under the old dog and lifted the heavy, sodden body in his arms. I'll put him in *Gannet* first, he thought, and hold her steady . . . Then I'll get them both across to *Kittiwake* . . . 'Now, be careful, Cressy,' he said. 'The weight may tilt *Gannet*. Lean away when I lift him in.'

Cressy had already worked that one out, and she acted instinctively to the feel of Bo'sun's heavy body coming over the side. The dog hardly moved, but when he was deposited on the floor of little *Gannet*, he turned his wet head and coughed, and a stream of Atlantic ocean poured out of his mouth.

'That's it,' said Milo. 'Well done . . . Steady as she goes!' and he put one hand on the gunwale of little *Gannet* and began to kick-swim her close to the rope ladder dangling from *Kittiwake*'s starboard side.

'Cressy, can you manage to climb up a rope ladder, if I guide you on to it?'

'Yes,' said Cressy, making no fuss. 'But Bo'sun — '

'I'll see to Bo'sun.' He looked down for a moment at the half-drowned dog and added gently: 'It'll be better for him not to have to move again . . . '

'Yes,' agreed Cressy, still using as few words as possible, and then added succinctly: 'No outboard. You must have taken it home? You'll need a tow.' And she waited for his wet hand to guide her feet one by one over the side of *Gannet* and on to the bottom two rungs of the tarry rope ladder. By this time Milo had got *Gannet* securely tied to the side of Gramp's sturdy *Kittiwake*, so he could leave his own small boat swinging there while he guided Cressy up step by step until she was safely in Gramp's comforting grasp.

'I'll take *Gannet* astern,' he called up. 'We'll need a tow. Throw me a line,' and only then did he clamber into his own little boat and row her gently round to the stern of *Kittiwake*, where a tow-rope came whistling down to him from aloft.

Thus Gramp came home, with Cressy safe and sound on board the *Kittiwake*, and Milo cradling old Bo'sun's tired wet head in his lap as he kept little *Gannet* far back and on course well behind *Kittiwake*'s solid stern. It was a simple rescue, really.

There were quite a few people waiting about on the quay. Word had gone round, and Gramp-the-Champ and his exploits were a bit of a legend anyway. Gramp smiled and waved to tell everyone that all was well, and he told Cressy to wave, too, so that they could see for themselves that she was all right. About Bo'sun he was not so sure, and his heart ached a little at the thought. He loved that old dog, and though he could not fault Bo'sun's devoted action in swimming out after Cressy, he just hoped it would not have finished him off in the end.

But Milo was waving, too, from the stern of little *Gannet*, and nudging her in competently out of the way of the bigger trawlers in the harbour. And if Milo was waving, then the dog must be all right, after all.

Gramp's heart lifted a little and the ache retreated, — until he saw Catherine on the quay. And it was a Catherine he scarcely knew and did not wish to see.

She came storming across the quay just as Milo got out to tie up the *Gannet*, and just as Gramp came down from the *Kittiwake* with Cressy behind him, to have a look at his tired old dog. 'What do you think you're playing at?' she yelled at all of them, her real anxiety turning to flaring anger as soon as she saw that the danger was past. Then she turned on Milo. 'How could you?' Her voice rose alarmingly, almost to a scream. 'How could you be so feckless and irresponsible! How could you leave the *Gannet untied* halfway down the beach!'

'Now, just a minute — ' began Gramp.

But she would not let him speak, turning on him more furiously than ever. 'And you're just as bad! Worse, in fact. Encouraging them to risk life and limb in that silly little dinghy. Why can't you ever grow up, you men? How many times do I have to tell you that the sea is dangerous?'

Gramp's tall, solid frame straightened a little as he looked at his daughter-in-law's face, — sharp and bitter as winter blackthorn. 'We know that, Catherine,' he said with slow dignity. 'None better. But you are wrong. You can't shut the sea out of your life. Nor can Milo. He can only learn to respect it, and trust in his own judgement, — as we all have to do.'

'Judgement!' she shrieked. '*Trust*! When he nearly drowned Cressy?'

'He didn't!' said Cressy flatly. 'It wasn't Milo who left the *Gannet* half-way down the beach, with no holding anchor, and the outboard motor and the petrol can left *outside* the boat somewhere on the sand or on the old slipway. It wasn't Milo. You *know* it wasn't. He went into school today to get his exam results. He told you, remember? He even warned you to keep an eye on me. I heard him!'

That stopped Catherine in her tracks for a moment, but she still had not done with Gramp, and the well of her grief and bitterness continued to pour out on his defenceless head. 'Milo never should have let anyone else take his boat, anyway. It's your fault, Gramp, — you encourage them. You let these kids be foolhardy and reckless! . . . Adventure, you call it. But I call it death and destruction in the making, — and murder, too.'

There was a breathless, shattering pause, and then Gramp spoke wearily but still gently to this angry, wrongheaded young woman who would not be cajoled or comforted. 'There is always a chance of death and destruction to be found on the sea, Catherine,' he said slowly, 'and sometimes murder, too — though not very often these days . . . ' He sighed, and looked directly for a moment into his daughter-in-law's sloe-black burning eyes. 'But there is bounty too, you know. Generous living and silver harvests in the soft sea swells. You know it, just as I know it, — just as Kitto knew it. He knew it well, and loved it well, and understood its dangers. There was no murder in Kitto's life, or any other crewman's, that night, Catherine. It was the kind of risk he knew and took every day of his life, — and so do all his mates. I wish to God it *had* been me the sea took, but it was not. Don't deny Kitto the dignity of his own choice, — his own courage and conviction.'

There was silence again, but Catherine was not mollified, and Milo was too tired and sad to argue further.

But Cressy was not. 'My mother took the same choice,' she said, in a small, cold voice. 'And I don't blame her for it, — I honour her.' Then she turned her head to where she knew Milo would be and held out her hand to him very deliberately. 'And what about the living, Catherine? What about Milo? He must know the critical factors for his future by now. Have you asked him? Has even Gramp asked him?'

The old fisherman began to laugh. 'We were a trifle busy just then, young Cressy. I never thought of it, — and I'm sure Milo forgot it, too. But now, there, — we've at least got something we can all rejoice about besides Cressy's rescue. Haven't we, Milo?' And it was clear in his voice that he really did not know the answer.

'Er — well — yes, I suppose we have,' admitted the young, shy voice that was almost as deep as a man's.

'Go on,' urged Cressy, wagging his hand up and down, her lit face still turned in his direction. 'Tell them!'

'Three A's and a B,' he said. 'What I wanted. I can go anywhere.' (But he was not sure he wanted to go anywhere at all.)

'Do you want to go anywhere?' asked Catherine, unconsciously echoing his thoughts, with sarcasm biting into her half-proud, half-pleased voice. 'Beyond the sea, I mean?'

'*Beyond* the sea?' Milo said, in a strange, distant voice. 'Can one go so far?' Then he smiled with sudden kindness at his mother and said: 'No further than Exeter, Mum. And, in case you've forgotten, that's inland!'

They all laughed then, a little shakily, all too aware that the perilous structure of their lives had been saved yet again.

'Come on,' said Cressy, busy mending

fences, 'this calls for a celebration. I'm alive. Bo'sun's alive. And Milo's got a future. Have we got any champagne?'

'Cider, I can manage,' said Gramp, wondering what else he'd got on board *Crystal Rose*. There was no room for such frills on *Kittiwake*.

'Cider will do fine,' agreed Milo. 'More in keeping with our status!'

'And nicer,' affirmed Cressy. 'Can I have first shout? I want to give a toast.'

Cheerfully, old Gramp-the-Champ fetched his last bottle of vintage Devon cider from the galley of *Crystal Rose*, and poured out a glass of the best and put it in Cressy's hand.

'*Beginnings!*' said Cressy, her voice as clear and bright as the sea-green eyes that could not see. 'I'm sorry I put everyone at such risk, but it's all over now, and this is something new to rejoice about! So it's *beginnings*, Catherine, not endings. Can't you see?' (And really that was something only she could say to Catherine, and Catherine could not reply.) So Cressy held her glass up to where she thought the light ought to be, thinking to herself: Although I've been on the sea today, there was no blue in it this time . . . Will it ever come back?

And one by one the others followed her

lead, — even Catherine, and one by one they said: '*Beginnings!*' while pledging silent allegiance to the endings, too.

The little crowd on the quay who had watched the rescue boat come in, and watched the ensuing row with bated breath, (though they all knew Catherine Trevelyan's rages were usually more bark than bite) now perceived that all was well and glasses were being raised in a toast, so they gave a spontaneous cheer and began to clap their hands in approval. Then, seeing the crisis was over, and cider seemed to be the order of the day, they made their several ways towards the Fisherman's Arms for reinforcements.

Gramp did not insist on going with Catherine and Milo to see Cressy safely home. He thought it might be better to keep out of the way, considering Catherine's present mood, — even though he was directly responsible for Cressy's safe home-coming. But Milo did insist on carrying Bo'sun home for his grandfather, with Cressy anxiously following, still worried about the exhausted dog.

Gently, Milo laid him down on the floor near Gramp's wood stove, and stayed to get the fire lit for them, even though he was still in his wet clothes Cressy sat on the floor and took the old dog's head in her hands. Truly, the poor old boy did feel terribly floppy, and he was still panting furiously to get his breath back, so much so that she was afraid for him.

'Will he die?' she asked Gramp fearfully, and rested her hand comfortingly on the tired, silken head.

'Nay,' said Gramp sturdily. 'Not this time ... Some day, no doubt, poor old boy, he'll go one step too far — or one swim too far! ... But he's made of good stern stuff, is Bo'sun. He'll pull round, you'll see ... Won't he, Milo?' After all, Milo was the one who knew about animals. He would be able to judge his condition best.

'Yes,' said Milo softly. 'Given a long rest, and some tender loving care from Gramp himself, — he'll do!'

'You'd better go home and get a long rest yourself!' retorted Gramp, smiling. 'And get out of those wet clothes.'

Milo laughed. 'I'm all right. But Cressy could do with a rest. She was out there quite long enough on her own!' He put out a hand and pulled Cressy to her feet. 'Come on, stop worrying about Bo'sun. We'd better get home before Mum explodes again!'

'I'll give that Jorky Beckinsale a talking to!' growled Gramp. 'I don't know what possessed him!'

'He was probably in a hurry,' said Milo tolerantly, 'and he doesn't know the beach in the Cove. Don't be too hard on him!'

'Hard?' snorted Gramp, laughing a little. 'Just let your mother get near him, and see what 'hard' means!'

They were all laughing when Catherine banged on the door to say she had brought the jeep round and it was high time she got Cressy home. She wouldn't come in to Gramp's cottage, even now.

Gramp took a last look at Cressy and decided that she did not seem too shocked or exhausted by her experience. She seemed calm enough, and Milo had a steadying hand on her arm.

She'll do! thought Gramp, echoing Milo's words about Bo'sun. She's a plucky little lass, — and she'd do very well for Milo, if that's the way the wind's going to blow.

And Cressy, as if aware of his thoughts, suddenly reached out and put her arms round the old man, hugging him hard. 'Thanks, Gramp-the-Champ, I owe you a life.'

'Humph!' grunted Gramp. 'Better make it good, then!' And he hugged her back in mutual affection.

But Catherine at the door was a different matter. She was still stiff and angry, in spite of Cressy's gallant attempt at reconciliation. Her head was as proudly held as ever and she still walked like a queen, — but it was an angry queen with little forgiveness about her.

Sighing, Gramp saw Cressy and Milo into the jeep, and then turned back to watch over Bo'sun while he panted out his weariness and slept himself back to life . . . Gramp did not try to speak to Catherine again. There was no more he could say.

But Milo called softly after him: 'Bless you, Gramp. You did us proud today!' and stared his mother out of countenance with defiant loyalty.

Catherine made no comment, but let in the gear and drove away.

★ ★ ★

By the time Stephen came walking down the cliff path, carrying his working portfolio, and looking a trifle too smart from his London meetings, things had simmered down a bit at Catherine's cottage, though the atmosphere was still fraught, and a whole lot of anxious explanations spilled out as soon as he arrived.

'It was my fault!' cried Catherine, (something she had refused to admit in front of Gramp). 'I knew Milo was going down to the school for his results. He told me to keep an eye on Cressy. I did look out several times, but she's so independent these days. She always uses the rope walk down to the beach, and Bo'sun was with her . . . It never occurred to me that she'd get into Milo's boat.'

'But I often sit in his boat,' contradicted Cressy. 'It's warm and sunny and out of the wind. I can sit there and listen to the sea.' She was getting rather tired of Catherine. 'But it didn't occur to me either that the *Gannet* would have been left half-way down the beach by Jorky.' She turned her blank eyes towards her father. 'I had no means of telling where exactly it stood in relation to the tide-line.'

'You should never have climbed into it in the first place,' snapped Catherine.

'Oh, wait a minute,' protested Stephen, bewildered by all the heat generated by this pointless argument. 'Cressy's all right, isn't she? There's no harm done.'

'No, but there might have been — and other people's lives were put at risk, too.'

'Gramp's, you mean,' said Milo, with intent.

'Your Gramp is as feckless as all the rest of you!' exploded Catherine, exasperated. And the argument began all over again.

Cressy looked suddenly so defeated and driven that Milo reached out and took her hand firmly in his. 'I think I'll take Cressy for a walk,' he said. 'This argument is getting us nowhere.' And he led Cressy out of the door on to the safe path down to the sea, and did not look back.

Catherine and Stephen looked after them in some perplexity, and after a moment's reflection, Stephen said unguardedly: 'He's right, isn't he? Everyone is safe. What are you worrying about?'

'You don't understand!' burst out Catherine, suddenly furious again. 'People *drown* in the sea. Cressy nearly drowned. And Kitto *did* drown — in just such another stupid accident!'

'No,' Stephen corrected her gently. 'From all I've heard, that was *not* a stupid accident. Kitto actually saved a life.'

'Yes, and what happened to him? A young, lovely, active man destroyed to no purpose!' She had turned on Stephen, frantic with rage, and was beating hysterically at him with her fists, as if he was actually threatening her, — as indeed his kind, cool logic was. 'It's such a waste!' she yelled, almost weeping. 'Such a wicked, cruel waste!'

'Yes,' said Stephen heavily. And did not say any more.

But Catherine understood him at once, horrified at the insensitivity of her words, when Stephen — kind, gentle Stephen — had just lost his beloved wife, Sally, who was also young and beautiful and full of life, like Kitto. 'Oh, my God, Stephen, what have I said?' Her hands did not drop to her sides, they clung to him instead, clutching him in helpless grief. 'It's just as bad for you, — worse, because there's Cressy, too.'

Stephen stood looking at her, not knowing how to answer. 'Yes,' he said again, slowly, 'there's Cressy, too.' But his glance strayed through the open door to follow the two young people walking on the shore, and then he seemed driven to amend the sadness in his voice. 'But Cressy is more of a triumph than a tragedy, isn't she?'

For some reason, this crumpled Catherine's fierce defences utterly, and she suddenly found herself sobbing in his arms. 'It's all such a *waste*,' she repeated again. 'Such a terrible, awful waste.'

'No, Catherine, listen to me. It's not quite like that. Gramp has tried to tell you this before, I know, only you wouldn't listen. Your Kitto was like my Sally. He *chose* to take those risks himself. He wasn't driven to take them by Gramp or by his fellow crewmen, or anyone else, or even by his own conscience. He just chose to risk his life for the sake of another, — and so did Sally. She *chose*, Catherine, between Cressy's life and her own, quite deliberately. It was a split-second decision, but she knew what she was doing. And so did Kitto. We can't — we *mustn't* take that decision from them. We have to honour it.'

'*Honour* it?' she whispered. 'That's what Cressy said about her mother. But how can I? How can you? What is there to honour about death?'

'Oh, quite a lot,' said Stephen, smiling. 'But I think Cressy would say *honouring life* would be better!'

Catherine stared up at him, totally over-thrown by his words. It was as if the whole brittle edifice of her towering pride and hurt was crumbling into dust, disintegrating round her in a falling heap of broken certainties, — and Stephen's face, young and sad and unexpectedly glowing with renewed and ardent purpose as he spoke of honouring life, seemed to banish every nightmare terror from her mind.

'Life?' she whispered.

But it was too late now for words. The lonely months of loss and pain were suddenly changed. The sound of the sea was in their ears, roaring in anger, singing in wind-blown joy, sighing in forgiveness, softly lapping in gentle consolation, and then sweeping in with a dark and glorious tide.

★ ★ ★

Milo and Cressy, walking on the shore, paused, listening to the eternal voice of the sea.

'Will they be all right?' asked Milo.

He is always a bit too anxious, Cressy thought, — too easily distressed by the hurts of others. Life will always be difficult for Milo, he has too much heart . . . But I love him for it, and anyway, I am tougher than he is, so it will work out for us somehow. But aloud she only said: 'Yes . . . the tide is coming in.' She smiled towards the sound of Milo's voice, and then turned her head away from him towards the sound of the waves breaking gently on the rocks. 'Tides are slow . . . ' she murmured, hearing the pebbles rattle as each new small wave broke and retreated. 'But they always come in when the time is right.'

They didn't say any more. They understood one another too well for words to be necessary. So they wandered on, hand-in-hand, in perfect content, along the sea-wet sands.

But for Gramp, — Gramp-the-Champ — it was a different matter. For him, the tide was running out, and he knew it. It wasn't only the endless bitterness between himself and his daughter-in-law. That unforgiving rift was hard to bear, but he understood its reason. He knew the pain behind it. After all, he should. Kitto was his only son, — always his right-hand, and his left as well. Always the affectionate, hard-working, loyal son, the one he could always rely on. And, beyond that, he was the one who understood the old man's faith, his long-sight vision of the mighty strength and power of the deep, wild ocean that he served. Only Kitto had known how a man's heart ached at the beauty of a cold dawn across a limitless turmoil of moving water, — how his spirits lifted to the sunrise, exulted in the tearing winds, laughed with the sea gulls and played hide-and-seek with the joyful dolphins. And only Kitto knew how his father fought the storms, dodged the waves, coaxed his boat over hidden rocks or snagged nets, sailed into the wind and ran before the squalls, — or how his father's brave and loyal heart grieved over a lost seaman, wept silently and secretly for the wives and children, went out in all weathers with the lifeboat crew to seek and save and fight their way through storm and tempest to landfall and safety . . . Only Kitto had understood the need — the compulsion — the certainty that the sea was his love and his hate, his mistress and his goddess, his enemy and his friend, — and all his powers must be used to serve her, and save his men if he could, — to serve and save . . . And now young, bright-eyed Kitto — as brave or braver than his father — was gone . . . And not even broken-hearted, angry Catherine felt a deeper loss than he did. But he could not tell her so.

But it wasn't only Kitto who was gone. The work was gone. The fishing was gone, — or going. Each year the quotas got tougher, — the competition got fiercer, the foreign boats got bolder . . . And Gramp-the-Champ got older. No longer could he sail out ahead of his little fleet, spear-heading a solid wedge of angry fishermen on churning trawlers, aiming to intimidate or maim or ram or drive the marauders back where they came from, fighting as bravely as Drake himself to keep the invaders away . . . That was only a dream now, and though the famous nickname Gramp-the-Champ had stuck, he wasn't a champion any longer, and he knew it. Even his boat — the *Crystal*

336

Rose, the crowning glory and most treasured possession of his life — was getting old now, mortgaged to the hilt, and likely to be de-commissioned soon. What would he do then?

His little inshore fishing boat — the *Kittiwake* — was good enough for crabbing and lobsters, and sometimes mackerel and local sole, (and good enough for rescuing Cressy!). But it was the deep sea that he loved, and the deep sea fishing that was his master-craft, and without it his life would have no purpose. He was tempted sometimes — as other trawlermen besides him — to take *Crystal Rose* out alone into the wild receiving ocean and scuttle her. Let her sink without trace and lie at rest cradled by the deep sea swell, with him beside her . . . It would be so easy, — and there would be the insurance for Catherine. Better than the de-commissioning compensation, — if he got away with it. And if Catherine would stop glowering and accept it . . . But of course he probably wouldn't get away with it, and going down with your boat is harder to achieve than you'd think . . . Old habits of survival die hard . . . And he loved *Crystal Rose*. He didn't think he could do it. Or could he?

To tell the truth, Gramp didn't really feel old. He didn't really feel used up. He was like Bo'sun. There was plenty of life in the old dog yet, — and a sudden wave of anger came over him at the thought of being written off as a has-been by his mates . . . He didn't really hold with anger, — he was always telling Catherine so. Or he used to be when they were actually on speaking terms. And even Stephen — Cressy's father — needed telling the same thing now and then, poor devil, and he had reason enough for anger . . . Losing the ones you loved was always hard. But anger never solved anything — never brought you peace. You were left as fierce and unrepentant as ever. Just like now.

Yes, just like now. Somehow, this latest spat with Catherine over Cressy's rescue was just too much, — just more than he could take. There was no way he could reconcile that stubborn heart of hers, no way he could help her or be any use. He even came between her and Milo, — for Milo was like his father, and loved the sea with the same deep passion. But with Gramp out of the way, he might settle down ashore and be a comfort to his mother. Mightn't he? . . . With Gramp out of the way, he might have a chance . . .

Yes, it was time to go. After all he had sent the old dog back to Cressy as soon as he had recovered from his long swim . . . He was Gramp's only tie now. There was nothing else to keep him here . . . Yes, it was time to go.

Without really making a conscious decision, Gramp found himself starting up *Crystal Rose* and nosing her out of the harbour, crewless and provisionless, and almost purposeless, except that he wanted to get to sea, he wanted to get away, — away from all these conflicting loyalties and angers and griefs to a place where there was only himself and the turbulent sea to contend with . . . where he could sail on and on into the sea-spray and mounting wave-heads, into the swell, into the dark . . . He chugged quietly out of the harbour, past the last jetty wall, and out into the grey, squally bay. No-one saw him go. No-one questioned him. He slid out like a ghost to face the sea.

He hadn't really thought about the weather. In fact he had really broken the first rule of the experienced trawlerman, — ignored the weather forecast, and gone out blindly on the tide before the wind, without considering the implications or the dangers, — possessed with nothing except this fierce compulsion to get away — to get away fast and never come back. He stood squarely in the wheelhouse, set his course for the far horizon leading to the blue

Atlantic and the sea-lanes to America, and settled down quite happily to let the voyage take its natural course.

But of course, the weather wasn't going to be ignored. Fool that he was, how did he think he was going to get away with being so feckless? He hadn't paid any heed to those mounting cloudbanks or those suddenly-increasing snappy squalls and odd little catspaws of rain and wind. He knew the signs — he knew them well — but he paid them no attention, and he didn't care a damn.

The sky grew darker, the wind rose. promising to develop into a full gale when they rounded the point and faced out into the real ocean. Gramp laughed to himself, and continued on his grim and steady course.

There was not much shipping about. The wind was rising too fast, and the glass had fallen too suddenly. They had taken the warning signs seriously and either stayed in port or sought shelter along the coast to ride out the coming storm in safety. But there was a group of foreign trawlers out to the south-east, — Spanish, he guessed, the greedy devils, with their smart factory ships and all-devouring trawl nets scraping the sea-bed. They'll fall foul of one of those old wrecks and snag their nets if they go too far down that bit of the coast, he thought. Serve 'em right! . . . Gramp knew a lot about where the old wrecks were. There were charts in the wheelhouse full of dire warnings, and he had memorised them long ago, — and there were others not charted that he knew about too . . . He'd been fishing these waters long enough to know the dangers, — and what a snagged trawl-net could do to his boat . . . Well, it was their look-out, he thought. If they don't know, they'll soon find out!

He did not heed them, but ploughed grimly on, neither taking evasive action, nor attempting to approach them. There was a time, he thought angrily, when he would have approached them, all flags flying, with his own small fleet strung out behind him, defiance in every line of their small, belligerent craft. And, often as not, the Spaniards, who were craven-hearted sailors when it came to the crunch, would back off and pursue their fishing a little further afield . . . But this time, he took no notice of them, his mind still occupied with his own angry rebellion, and his automatic sailor's attention fixed on the hazards of the weather and the oncoming storm. He had badly miscalculated that wind. It was already a force eight, and growing stronger.

He did not know, of course, how the *Crystal Rose* looked to the Spanish boats as she ploughed steadily onwards, intent on her own grim purposes. Nor did he remember (or perhaps even know) that he was already a legend to the marauding Spanish pirates. They knew *Crystal Rose*, and they expected the rest of the little Cornish fleet to be close behind him, bent on trouble, as usual. Confrontation they did not want, especially in this weather. True, the smaller craft were no match for their larger, tougher boats. But they were apt to be a thorough nuisance with their fierce, bulldog tactics — not even afraid to risk collision or ramming (though they never had actually made such dangerous contact) — the crazy English, coming out of the darkening sea-swell at them in their tight little wedge of corporate power that refused to scatter . . . This time there was no following wedge that the Spanish could see, — though it might be lying in wait while *Crystal Rose* reconnoitred . . . But the Spaniards decided to take no chances. They didn't want a fight today. The weather was enough to deal with, without an angry little pack of English sea-dogs that was barking mad. So the Spanish fleet observed *Crystal Rose*'s undeviating course, and took evasive action, veering away further south and east, pulling their trawl-nets with them, and leaving the open Atlantic swell and the tearing force nine gale to little *Crystal Rose*, alone in the dark sea.

Victory! thought Gramp vaguely, victory for once! But he did not really heed it. He was on a voyage, his purpose fixed, and he wasn't turning back.

★ ★ ★

It was while Cressy was on the beach alone, waiting for Milo to come back from feeding the hedgehogs and his latest patient — a great crested grebe from the otter pool, that she noticed Bo'sun was no longer beside her.

'Bo'sun?' she called, and called again more sharply. But there was no answer, and no warm, silky head came thrusting up to reach her outstretched hand. Puzzled, she turned back to the rope-walk she had just left, and began to climb the path again back to the cottage, and then along the extended rope path to Milo's house.

She had not gone far, however, before Milo came out, hearing her call for Bo'sun. 'What is it?' he said.

'Bo'sun's gone.' She stood still, looking in Milo's direction, but not seeing his face.

Would he feel as she did? A frisson of fear seemed to touch her. Bo'sun would only leave her for one reason. Something must be wrong with Gramp.

'I'll get on the mobile,' said Milo, instantly understanding.

But there was no reply from Gramp's phone, — either his normal house one nor his mobile which he took with him everywhere. Milo knew enough people in Port Quentin to get some kind of news from someone, — but he rang the harbour-master. There was a bit of a pause, and then a deep voice came back to him, saying: 'Sorry, Milo. Can't reach him. He's gone out on *Crystal Rose*.'

'*On his own?*' Milo's voice was filled with dread.

'Apparently, — yes. Don't know what he's up to.' The voice seemed to sense Milo's anxiety, and added kindly: 'Don't worry. He's probably gone round to Newlyn for some spares or something.'

'Yes,' said Milo doubtfully. 'Perhaps ... Thanks, anyway. Tell him — if he comes in, tell him to give me a buzz.'

'Will do,' said the voice, and briskly rang off.

'What can we do?' asked Cressy, equally anxious.

'Nothing,' said Milo. 'He's his own master. We can't stop him . . . But at least I've told Jim Hawley. If Gramp doesn't come back, he'll get Search-and-Rescue on to it.'

'It was the row with Catherine,' said Cressy. 'It was sort of the last straw.'

'I know,' agreed Milo, and his voice was grim. 'If anything happens to Gramp, Mum will have a lot to answer for.' It didn't make him any happier to say it, — and maybe it was too soon to jump to conclusions. Gramp might be on a perfectly ordinary legitimate errand with *Crystal Rose* . . . But somehow, like Cressy, he could not rid himself of the feeling that something was wrong.

'Let's go up to the top of the cliff,' said Cressy. 'I'll be all right if I can hold on to you . . . Then at least you can look down at the harbour and see him coming in.'

'We might have a long wait,' said Milo.

'Does that matter? Knowing that Gramp is safe is more important.'

Milo had to agree with her. So they walked the steep way up the cliff together, with Cressy making a creditable job of keeping on her feet, with Milo's hand to cling to. But when they reached the top and Milo looked down at the harbour, there was no sign of *Crystal Rose*. Her familiar berth was empty.

★ ★ ★

The first bad squall hit *Crystal Rose* without warning, flattening a deck awning, and sending something sharp and heavy (probably a winch-pin) through one side of the wheelhouse roof. Gramp ducked and laughed. Water was cascading across from every side. The waves were growing mountainous and black with venom, hurling towards *Crystal Rose* with every evil intent. But the gallant little trawler answered to her name, and rose happily to every challenge, leaping and bucking, soaring and sinking, rising again and careening merrily into the next trough and up, up, up again to the dizzying height of the next wild surge, with her propellors screaming for something to bite on as she came up out of the water and then sank thankfully down again into the next deep trough.

Gramp kept her heading into the swell, into the wind, riding out the storm, exulting in every quiver and shock of her sturdy frame. He was a little drunk with excitement by now, he thought, but he didn't care. Let the sea take him. Let *Crystal Rose* have her head, let the wild waves batter and smash, let the swell push, the spray fly, the deep, deep undertow of the mighty ocean pull, but

Crystal Rose would rise above it.

'Come on!' he shouted, laughing again. 'Come on, my beauty! Let her rip. Let her ride free! Let her rise, rise, rise!'

But this time the seventh wave struck sideways with a clap like thunder, and the wheelhouse came down with a smashing of splintered wood and glass, and all his fancy new instruments on their flashy new panel, all his ariels and up-to-the-minute VHF radio controls and direction finders came down amid the debris in a heap of tangled wires and broken terminals.

'No communication, then,' he said. 'Just you and me, *Rose*. Come on, my dear! We're on our own now!'

But they weren't on their own. For suddenly, behind the roar of the wind and the crash of the waves, Gramp heard another sound — the urgent barking of a dog.

Bo'sun? he thought. It *can't* be. He never comes out on *Crystal Rose*. He knows he mustn't. And since the Cressy episode he's been too weak and tired to move much. Besides, he *knows* he's got to stay with Cressy . . . But that sound? He couldn't mistake it . . . And, come to think of it, the old dog had been a bit clingy since his long swim, — a bit too loving, a bit too aware of the precarious hold he had

347

on the ones he loved . . . Like me, thought Gramp, falling into a daydream for a teeming second of flagging attention . . . But the dog barked again. It was no dream. Somewhere on this pitching, dancing, wallowing trawler, a faithful, brave old dog had crept aboard, knowing somehow, as dogs do, that his master was on a voyage of no return, and making quite sure that he was not left behind.

'Bo'sun!' shouted Gramp. 'You damn-fool dog! Where the hell are you?' He staggered drunkenly along the deck and peered down into the swashing open fish hold. Sure enough, the rough gold coat and anxious amber eyes were there, crouched behind a pile of empty crates, almost invisible in the flying spume, almost submerged by the water slopping about all round him, and the turgid crests of broken waves that kept falling on his defenceless head.

'Come out of there!' shouted Gramp, louder than ever. 'I've a good mind to leave you there to drown! What the hell do you think you're doing?'

But he knew what Bo'sun was doing. If Gramp was mad as a hatter and determined to die, then Bo'sun was going with him. It wasn't any harder for a dog to die than a man, and it would be worse to be left behind . . . So the old dog reasoned, if he reasoned at all. And Gramp could read him like a book. Well then, he thought. That's the three of us now. *Crystal Rose* and Bo'sun and me. We'll all go down together. Nothing is changed.

But it *was* changed. Somehow he knew it was changed. He couldn't let his old dog die out of blind, misplaced devotion. He couldn't let his own mad mood of anger snuff out the life of a faithful retainer. It simply wouldn't do.

Groaning and cursing, he clambered down to the swirling depths of the hold and grasped Bo'sun by the collar. At least you can have a life-jacket, he thought, and I suppose I shall have to have one, too, because, you see, we're not going to die after all. You've put paid to that! . . . And painfully he climbed back on deck, got a wet life-jacket on to the old dog's back, and tied his collar to a bit of rope on one of the remaining supports of the broken wheelhouse. (At least he won't get washed overboard!) Then he seized another floating life-jacket and fixed himself up. At least we'll float, he said. And there's a life-raft somewhere. If *Crystal Rose* goes, we can hang on.

But suddenly he didn't want *Crystal Rose* to go. He wasn't going to let her go. And he

349

wasn't going to let old Bo'sun go, either. To hell with the weather — to hell with everyone and love and anger and all . . . He was going to bring *Crystal Rose* home if it was the last thing he did, — and old Bo'sun with her, safe and sound. Of course he was. What was he thinking of to have planned otherwise?

He would ride out the storm somehow, running before the wind if it seemed the safest course with those mountainous waves, — and then, when the wind dropped and the tide turned, he would make for home. Only keep her afloat till then, and it would be all right . . . Yes, then he could make for home . . . The wheel itself was still intact, so he lashed it, firmly facing into the worst of the weather, knowing it was his best course. Bits of broken planking flew off at tangents, something hit him on the head and he felt a small rush of sticky blood run down one ear, and another flying bit of debris caught him on his left shoulder, spinning him round and landing him flat on the deck in a pouring flood of water close to Bo'sun's wet flanks.

'Sorry, old boy,' he muttered. 'Stay put. It's safer . . . ' He laid a hand on the sodden head for a moment. 'If she founders, I'll cut you free,' he said. 'Don't worry. I won't leave you behind . . . '

But they didn't founder. Gamely, lurching

and plunging, *Crystal Rose* ploughed on. And gamely Gramp nursed her and coaxed her through every lethal trough and every sidelong surge that threatened to capsize her and send her to the bottom. He seemed to be a man possessed now in another way, no longer mad or reckless, but cunning and crafty, anticipating every gust of force nine wind, every swirling current and sucking eddy, every treacherous change of swell and mounting, towering wave. He seemed to know without thinking just where the next dangerous pull would come from, where the shifting gravity of his boat would be unbalanced next, where that sucking whirlpool of sullen wave-trough would tug hardest on her beleaguered hull.

'Come on!' he cried to her again. 'Come on, my darling! We need you! Old Bo'sun needs you. Rise and shine, my beauty! We're going home!'

He was still a bit mad, of course, still mad and exultant. But it was a warmer madness now. The cold anger had gone. Only the love of his dog and his boat remained, and the strange deep-sea love that somehow sustained him and made him know that his implacable enemy and his life-long friend would not, this time, let him down. The sea this time, like Gramp himself, had changed her tune. She knew he was on his way home, and she was letting him go. And as he thought this, feeling the change under his heaving boat, a small bird dropped down from the storm-laden sky and perched on the edge of the broken wheelhouse. The storm petrel was back.

'Are you with us, bird?' said Gramp, aloud. 'Funny time to choose. It's none too safe a perch just now!'

But the bird did not seem to mind. She clung on with her tiny feet, and hunched her back against the wind, swaying unperturbed by the movement of the boat.

It was at this point that the shattered radio on the deck suddenly let out a faint but clearly audible crackle, and a voice said distinctly: '*Snagged . . . turning over . . . mayday . . .* ' and then faded into another series of indistinguishable crackles.

Gramp didn't know what to do. He had no instruments left to plot anyone's course, — and he couldn't send on the VHF in its present state . . . Or could he? . . . He got down on his knees and crawled towards the smashed radio and scattered pieces of ariel. Maybe if I pushed a bit of ariel up somewhere, I could send *something*, he thought. At least alert someone . . . But I can't help those people, — I don't know where they are . . . As if in answer, the radio crackled again, and a voice said more clearly and in Spanish '*volcando . . . zozobando . . . emergencia . . . urgente . . .* ' and again the English cry for help '*mayday . . . mayday . . .* ' Then there was a crackling attempt at a position being given, but it kept fading, and finally ceased altogether.

It's those Spanish trawlers, they've turned a boat over, he translated to himself. Snagged it on something . . . I thought they were getting too near to those old wrecks . . . Well, I can try to send, but I can't help them. He fumbled around with the ariels and the knobs on the shattered radio, and turned something that gave a faint click of life, but the water kept cascading down on him and he wasn't sure what he was doing. '*Crystal Rose* out of Port Quentin . . . ' he said, a couple of times. 'Instruments smashed, no communication . . . Spanish trawler in trouble . . . Cannot assist . . . No navigation aids . . . ' He attempted to repeat the position the fading voice had given, but he wasn't in the least sure he had got it right, or that anyone had heard him . . .

'Done my best,' he muttered aloud. 'If they sent up a flare, someone might see it . . . ' But the night was as black as ever, — and the tearing wind as strong.

There was nothing else he could do but

struggle on, fighting with the storm, and somehow trusting the sea and his own built-in survival instincts to take him home. The little storm petrel looked at him out of a beady eye, and hopped a little further into the shelter of the broken wheelhouse, nodding its head at him almost, he fancied, in approval. And Bo'sun looked up at him trustingly, while still more cascades of water poured over his head.

'It's all very well for you,' he told them both. 'I'm the one that's got to get you home! ... But I will, God help me! ... Don't worry, — I *will*!

★ ★ ★

Milo and Cressy sat for a long time on the headland, waiting hopefully for *Crystal Rose* to return. But she did not, and when the evening was closing in, and a burst of squally rain came down with the twilight, signalling the storm that was to come, they decided to make one more phone call to Jim Hawley to see if there was any news, and then go home.

But there was no news from the coast-guard's office, — no word from Gramp — no sighting of *Crystal Rose* — and no indication of any trouble or emergency, either . . . Gramp and his boat had simply vanished without a trace.

'We can only wait,' said Jim's voice, warm and reassuring. 'He'll call in if he's in trouble . . . But we'll keep listening out for him . . . Don't worry.'

At least Jim's on the alert, thought Milo. There's nothing else we can do. And he put his mind to the task of getting Cressy safely off the high cliff path and down to the cottage in safety before the light had completely gone.

'We'll have to tell Dad now,' said Cressy. 'And Catherine.'

Milo sighed. 'If she'll listen!'

'Surely — ?' began Cressy, and clung suddenly to Milo's hand as her foot slipped a little on the rain-wet rocky path.

'She won't *want* to think Gramp could be in trouble,' said Milo grimly. 'Especially when I point out that her tantrum has probably driven him to do something silly.'

'Do we *need* to point it out?' Cressy asked. 'Won't she *know* what she's done?'

'Probably,' agreed Milo, and shrugged a little uneasily. But it isn't easy to shrug when you've got a very precious girl by the hand and you are trying to steer her down a path that is far too steep for comfort.

'And anyway,' went on Cressy, trying to

355

sound reasonable and comforting, 'Gramp wouldn't really do anything silly, would he?'

Milo was slow to answer. But at length he said: 'I don't know . . . I think he might . . . He was very upset. I could feel the anger in him . . . '

'But he didn't say anything.'

'No,' said Milo. 'He wouldn't. He would just act.'

They were both silent then, still filled with foreboding, and at length they came down on to the safe, easy path by the cottages, and went to find Stephen and tell him the news before tackling Catherine.

Stephen was still working at his desk, but the light was fading now, and artificial light changed the colours so he was glad to stop. But not glad to hear what they had to say.

'Missing?' he asked sharply. 'Gramp?'

'And *Crystal Rose*,' said Milo.

'And the dog,' put in Cressy.

'*Bo'sun*, too? . . . Since when?'

'No-one seems to have seen him go,' said Milo. 'But since the morning, anyway.'

'What have you done so far?' Stephen asked, and listened intently while Milo explained about Jim Hawley, the harbour-master, and his other friends who had searched round for him and found neither

Gramp nor the dog, nor any sign of his boat.

'We'd better tell Catherine,' Stephen said, and then looked into Milo's reluctant face. 'Milo?'

'Yes,' the boy said heavily. 'We'd better . . . '

'What is it?' Stephen asked, feeling the uncertainty and dread in Milo's deep, uneasy voice.

'I'm afraid . . . I mean, I think the row over Cressy's rescue might have upset him.'

Stephen understood that. But he wasn't going to let it destroy his belief in Gramp's good common sense. 'He'd never let *that* make him take risks with his boat — or his dog — would he?'

'I don't know . . . ' said Milo again. And he sounded so troubled that Cressy took his hand again and said: 'Let's go and tell Catherine. She'll have to know, anyway, — and she may know more about what he's up to than we do.'

But Catherine didn't know, and was horrified to hear that Gramp was missing, — and all too well aware that this whole new crisis might be due to her sharp tongue and unremitting anger . . . And it was a new and softened Catherine who now spoke. 'I shouldn't have been so hard on him,' she said. 'Poor old Gramp . . . Especially when he had just gone out and *rescued* Cressy! It was most unfair!' She sighed, and then went on, unable to resist her perpetual argument against the sea. 'But you see what he's like? Even now, he takes risks — and goes off to sea by himself! What can you do with him?'

'Get him back safely,' said Milo shortly. And Catherine, looking at her son with new respect, was suddenly silent.

★ ★ ★

The night was still black as pitch, and the storm did not relent, though Gramp felt somehow that the pull of the sea was a little less fierce . . . It was a long, hard haul, though, and he never let up. He didn't dare. He still had to watch for every hazard, every hidden snag or unexpected danger . . . He still had to gauge the force of each wind-gust and its wayward, capricious direction, still had to judge the height of the next wave, the lurch of the next crooked swell, the wicked, beguiling smoothness of that flat, treacherous plain between the towering wave-crests . . . Patiently, doggedly, he plunged on, sometimes cursing, sometimes singing to his boat, sometimes crooning comfortingly to his dog, sometimes cheerfully addressing the little travel-weary bird sitting on his deck, — and sometimes returning to curses when the seas got rougher.

Bo'sun never flinched, never whimpered, never wasted another breath on a protesting bark. He sat still and waited, amber eyes wide and fixed on Gramp's streaming face, entirely certain that he was where he wanted to be, — and safe, and loved, and forgiven — and going home.

Gramp was very tired by now. He didn't know what the time was, his watch had long since been smashed in the general maelstrom, and the sky was still blind-dark and he could find no streak of dawn in it. He had no idea how long he had been sailing his bucking trawler single-handed through the seething, sucking swell. He wondered vaguely if he should have tried to put the trawl-nets down either side just below the surface to act as stabilizers, but he knew he couldn't do it alone. The release button in the wheelhouse was gone, and the clever hydraulics with it, and without his crew it would be impossible to shoot both nets at once, and a one-sided trawl waiting for him to rush across and put down the second would simply turn the boat over . . . Like that Spanish trawler, God help it! . . . And briefly he worried about those Spanish seamen, desperately calling for a help that could not come . . . No, he thought. I can't help them. And I can't even help *Crystal Rose* much . . . Two tame under-surface anchors would have helped, but one would be lethal . . . We must just carry on without.

In any case, he thought, surprised, I believe the shape of the swell is changing — the wind is as strong as ever, but it's blowing straighter, and the tide . . . ? Yes, the tide is on the turn, I can feel it . . . Even after all this beating into the wind, and driving poor old *Crystal Rose* further and further out to sea, I can still feel the tide under my feet, — and it's on the turn. It's ready to carry us home . . .

The next huge wave that came over the bows hit him fair and square between the shoulders and he went down again, almost too tired to resist. But Bo'sun was beside him, nudging at him, pushing a black wet nose against his face, offering an encouraging lick or two of hopeful support, and he found himself scrambling to his feet again, clinging to the guard-rail, lurching back to his shattered wheelhouse, fighting yet again with the surging swell to keep *Crystal Rose* afloat . . . But it was changing, — yes, it was changing, the swinging sky was turning, and yes, there *was* a gleam of light on the horizon . . . the waves were still breaking over his head, but somehow pushing him less fiercely, no longer pounding him into pulp in a swirling whirlpool of power . . . And the tide, he thought, the tide . . . ? Can I really feel it? . . . Can it have turned? . . . Is it ready to carry us home, or am I dreaming . . . ?

He fell again a couple of times, and once *Crystal Rose* heeled over so far in a sudden, sucking swell that he thought she was gone, but she righted herself somehow, and went gallantly ploughing on into the next sea-mountain. Maybe I should send up a rocket, he thought. But what for? It's not a mayday. I'm not sinking. I'm damned if I'll ask for help, — I don't need it. Carry on. Let's carry on. The dog is alive — he wouldn't survive if we abandoned ship, anyway, the life-raft wouldn't hold him, he'd fall out . . . Anyway, I won't. I *won't* abandon ship. I won't abandon *anything*, or *anyone*. We're going home.

But then he suddenly thought of those Spanish seamen again, — enemies, yes, who stole his fish and drove him off his own fishing grounds, but men, too, — human beings — adrift in an angry sea . . . I could let off a rocket for them, he thought. They might be near enough to see it, and send up one in return? . . . How do I know where

361

they are? . . . But I could try.

The first rocket fizzled and went out. The second misfired and fell into the sea. His hands were almost too cold to light anything, anyway, but he tried again. And the third one went up in a shower of sparks. There was no reply from the dark sea — no flicker of hopeful light — nothing moving on the stormy surface except the surging wave-crests. I've only got one more, he thought. But I'll try . . . And the last rocket went up bravely, unquenched by the driving rain. His tired eyes, still streaming with sea-spray, searched the horizon, — and there, quite close on his starboard side, was a faint, pale flicker of light. They're there! he thought. Somewhere in the murk and spume, they're there . . . And I shall have to change course to look for them, — I can't just pass them by . . .

Painfully, he swung *Crystal Rose* round towards the flickering light. It was very faint, — sometimes he could see it, and sometimes it was gone . . . He drove on towards it, but cut his speed a little. Better not get caught up in whatever had snagged their boat. Where were they? Why didn't they make more light?

And then, as *Crystal Rose* slid over the next wave-crest, he saw them . . . Not an upturned trawler, half held under by a snagged trawl-net, — not a boat at all, no sign of a boat anywhere — but three tiny hunched figures on a bobbing, half-swamped life-raft, and one of them holding nothing bigger than a flaring cigarette lighter in his hand . . . And even as Gramp watched, the tiny light went out, doused by the next big sea.

If I dare get near enough, I could throw them a line, he thought. And put the rope ladder over. I can't do more. I've got to keep *Crystal Rose* afloat, — and try not to mow them down . . . But I can't see them in all this murk. Can they see me, I wonder? . . . God help them, I can't let them drown.

The generators were still working on *Crystal Rose*, and there was some light spilling out of the galley, but the wheelhouse lights had gone, and so had the riding lights in the trawl-rig that came down with the tangle of broken ariels. There was not much for the Spaniards to go on, but probably just enough for them to try to catch a line . . . But there was nothing at all for him to go on, — and how could he throw a line when he couldn't see the target?

Why don't they put up a flare, he wondered? And then dismissed it. They would have done by now, he realised, if they had any . . . Either they've run out, or the wretched things are waterlogged and useless . . . Or they left in such a hurry that they forgot them . . . There was lightning playing across the sky to the south-east, following the storm, but it was too far away to be any use.

I shall just have to guess, he thought, — hope and guess. God knows, I've often had to do that! . . . But as he thought it, an extra close lightning flash did illuminate a strip of sea in sudden brilliance, and he caught sight of his target for a brief, startling moment. There! he thought. Not too far to throw a line. Not too close for safety, either. Keep the position in my eye. I can try! . . .

Twice he threw a line, but the wind carried it away. He did not dare bring *Crystal Rose* any closer, but he thought the most active of the three figures was trying to paddle the raft nearer with his hands . . . Try again, he thought. Never say die. Try again! And he threw again, blindly into the wind, and this time the line pulled taut. Someone had caught it.

The rest wasn't difficult — though painfully slow. Two of the Spanish seamen were so drenched and cold — and so shocked and frightened — that they could do little to help themselves. The third — braver and stronger — urged them close to the ladder, heaved their sodden bodies on to it one by one, and climbed up after them, pushing them forward and upward, and swearing at them in voluble Spanish at every step. Once, one of them let go — too tired to hold on — and nearly fell past them, but he was caught and pushed back, amid an even louder volley of curses, and finally was thrown down in a half-drowned heap on the streaming deck. The second one was not much better, but the third one was at least on his feet.

'Below!' shouted Gramp. 'Get below. Drier. Make some tea. TEA! . . . HOT! GO ON. GET BELOW!'

He couldn't leave the wheel now, especially as he was turning *Crystal Rose* again for home — wherever home was . . . The only thing he could do was send the traumatised Spaniards below out of the way, and hope they would survive somehow till he got them home.

Bo'sun once again tried to lick his human companions into life, but they didn't respond as well as Gramp had. And the bird, which was still there, simply sat and looked at them, and put her tiny head on one side as if considering the matter . . . Gramp wondered, for a moment, whether he ought to send

Bo'sun down to the comparative warmth and dryness of the galley with the Spanish seamen, but one look at that alert, devoted face made him know the dog would not go willingly, and he had no time to spare to carry him down by force. No, better let him stay . . . It was his choice, after all, to be with Gramp, wet and cold or no . . . But for the seamen it was different — and they looked near to perishing with exposure already.

'Get on with you!' said Gramp to the most alert of the three. 'Go on! I'll get you home if I can . . . GET DOWN BELOW!'

And the shivering Spaniard seized his companions and bundled them down into the warmth and comparative safety of the galley . . . I can't go down after them, Gramp told himself, for a moment thinking longingly of warmth and soft bunks and cups of steaming tea. They'll have to fend for themselves. And he returned sternly to the task of turning *Crystal Rose* into the tide (yes, it *was* the tide) and let her find her way home . . . If the sun would come up, he thought, even for a gleam, I could plot a course . . . But it was still dark, and that pale gleam on the horizon had gone again, and the sky was still full of cloud, — and little *Crystal Rose*, alone in the wide ocean, was half-shrouded in driving rain . . . He would have to trust in instinct again, and hope for the best.

At this point two things happened at once. The most active Spaniard appeared, clutching a steaming mug of tea which he thrust into Gramp's cold hands. '*Gracias*,' he said, smiling a wide, weary smile. '*Muchos gracias . . .* ' and disappeared again down to the galley. And overhead, out of the swirling mist of rain and spume, came the comforting throb of a Nimrod, — Gramp knew a Nimrod when he heard it — out on a Search-and-Rescue reconnaissance from Culdrose. It was playing a powerful searchlight on the sea, but its beam did not reach *Crystal Rose*. Gramp waved vaguely upwards, and held up three fingers for the three Spanish fishermen, but he knew it was too dark and stormy for any such gesture of bravado to be recognised . . . I don't know how I found them, anyway, he said to himself, almost crossly. What were they doing out there? How could I have had the luck to come so close?

He glared rather suspiciously at the storm bird, over the top of his mug of tea, (and oh! how blessed that hot tea was!) and said aloud: 'I have a suspicion it's all your fault, bird. And I shall have something to say to you when we get home!' Then he laid a hand on Bo'sun's wet head and added:

'And to you too, my friend! You wicked stowaway!' But though his voice was gruff, Bo'sun did not mind, and gallantly wagged his tail.

★ ★ ★

'We've picked up a signal,' said Jim Hawley. 'Weak, but just audible.'

'Yes?' Stephen's voice was sharp.

Jim smiled at them all — the four anxious people crowded into his little office — and said kindly: 'I think it's all right. He's lost his ariels and his instruments, but he's still afloat . . . and he gave us a fix for the stricken Spanish trawler . . . I don't quite know how he managed that, but there's a Nimrod on its way to have a look.'

'In this weather?' asked Milo.

'It might be able to do a drop,' said Jim, 'or at least pinpoint the trouble spot . . . The helicopters can't get out there till daylight and the wind drops, anyway . . . But it sounds as if Gramp at least is still in charge!'

Cressy said strangely: 'He'll come home. The worst is over now.'

Milo looked at her, and it was on the tip of his tongue to ask: How do you know? . . . But he didn't. The certainty was clear in Cressy's face, and who was he to question it?

'He's still quite a long way out,' said Jim, 'judging by the fix we could get on his signal, which wasn't very precise . . . It was too faint for accuracy . . . If I were you, I'd go home and get some sleep. He won't be in till morning.'

It was then that the second signal came through. Gramp had found time to try his radio again, drenched and broken as it was. '*Crystal Rose*. Picked up three Spanish. No sign of boat. On way home . . . ' and then silence.

Jim's earphones positively hummed with relief as he dutifully wrote down the message and handed it to Milo. 'There you are, lad. The Champ's done it again! Go home now and sleep sound!' His voice was deep and slow, as Cornish voices are, and full of quiet reassurance. He knew how Milo loved Gramp-the-Champ.

Milo turned to Cressy and took her hand. 'Yes, you are right,' he said.

'The worst is over. Let's go home.'

Beside them, Stephen looked at Catherine and saw real tears in her eyes, and a decided tremble in her softened mouth. Following Milo and Cressy, he took her hand in his, and went out into the wet,

dark night. It was going to be all right.
Yes, they could wait till morning. Gramp
was coming home

★ ★ ★

He was in truth going steadily homeward
now, — though he was almost too tired to
notice, and almost too blind with sea-salt
and drying blood on his face to see where
he was going at all. But he went on, and
presently he noticed vaguely that the swell
was dropping, and the sound of *Crystal
Rose* ploughing steadily through the water
was smoother and more tranquil. The wind
was dropping, too, — he could hear the
curling hiss of the wave-tops as they came
slapping over the gunwales . . . Home, he
drowsed, and gripped the wheel harder with
his cold wet hands. Going home . . .

And presently he noticed that the sky was
lightening, and (at last) there was a glimpse
of blood-red sunrise far out to the east. The
east! he said exultantly. Then I am right
on course! . . . And as his eyes came back
towards what he hoped was his destination,
he glimpsed a thin line of coast behind a
swirling grey veil of mist, and it seemed to
him a welcome, familiar shape that he knew
. . . Home?

He drove on towards it doggedly, light-headed with exhaustion, but the word 'doggéd' came into his mind and made him giggle helplessly.

'Bo'sun,' he said, 'we're doggéd, did you know? We're going to make it, my boy . . . Though you've no business to be looking so pleased with yourself. You shouldn't be here at all.'

But Bo'sun *was* looking pleased about something. He was sitting up more alertly, and his tail was beginning to thump a welcome on the deck. And when Gramp looked round to see what the bird was doing, the little storm petrel had gone. Funny, he thought, I didn't see her go. But she's seen me safely home, and she knows we're near landfall . . . so she's gone back to the ocean. Thanks for your company, bird!

Then he noticed that several boats seemed to be coming out to meet him, and small whoops and screeches came from several hooters and sirens, like faint greetings across the diminishing swell. What are they doing? he thought. Why are they out here? I'm not bringing home any catch — only three half-drowned Spaniards and a wayward dog . . . I haven't seen off any marauders. I haven't won any war.

But he had won a war, — a small,

terrifying war of his own. He had gone out in a black rage of despair, — and he was coming home on an altogether different tide-race, — with a dog to keep him company, a dog who had somehow managed to make him change course with one reproachful fit of barking, — and three men's lives saved because of it ... Funny, he thought, their hooters sound like barks, short sharp barks — of reproach? ... or approval? Are they telling us they're glad we're coming home? Or yelling at me for being so stupid and reckless? Which, I wonder? ... But he found he didn't really care. He was too tired to care.

'Bo'sun,' he said aloud, 'I do believe they're applauding! But it's you they ought to hoot at! Did you know?'

Bo'sun did not know, but his tail kept on thumping, and his face really seemed to have a kind of smile.

So *Crystal Rose* came on, and Gramp was too tired to see the little boats line up, — the boats of his friends, in-shore fishers and trawlers, dinghies and crabbers, and even flashy speedboats, like a guard of honour, saluting him with their short sharp barks, and escorting him safely in through the harbour gap, and past the long jetties to the harbour wall and a familiar resting place. He didn't see the line of faces along the harbour wall, or hear their faint voices cheering. He didn't understand what all the fuss was about.

But as he brought battered old *Crystal Rose* gently into her berth, and stooped down to untie the rope from Bo'sun's collar, he suddenly found himself weeping happily into the broken shards of his shattered wheelhouse. She's made it, he said. We've made it! I've got her home. We're home!

And he passed out cold on the deck.

Part Five

'Behold! The Sea Itself'

There was a price to pay, of course, and Gramp paid it without complaint. After all, he reasoned, it was his own fault that he had gone out in a force nine and got himself thoroughly drenched and exhausted.

The three Spanish trawlermen were treated for hypothermia and shock, and one broken arm, and sent home as soon as they were fit to move, to report on the loss of their trawler and (sadly) the rest of their crew. But Gramp lay in a hospital bed, supposedly recovering from a mild heart attack and a touch of bronchial pneumonia, and fretted about his dog and his battered boat, *Crystal Rose*. Bo'sun needed care and attention after that stormy voyage. So did *Crystal Rose* ... And he couldn't attend to either of them. It was all rather frustrating, and it made him cross.

Milo, coming in to see him with Cressy, found the old man feverish and impatient, longing to get home. He looked somehow quenched and diminished by the high hospital bed and the neat white pillows behind his grizzled head, — and it was not the sort of hero's return that Milo felt he ought to have had.

'How are you doing, Gramp?' he asked, knowing it was a silly question. Gramp was not doing too well, and hating every minute of it.

'Lot of fuss about nothing,' grumbled Gramp tiredly. 'Time I came home. Things to do.' He looked hopefully at Milo. 'Can you get me out of here?'

'In a day or two,' said Milo, hoping it was true. 'Your mates want to have a party. They say you've earned it!'

Gramp grunted irritably. 'Can't see why. Took a lot of silly risks. Ashamed of myself really.'

'No, Gramp,' contradicted Cressy suddenly, speaking from close beside his bed, though she could not see his weary, frustrated expression. 'There are some risks that have to be taken, aren't there? You always told us so.'

'Did I?' sighed Gramp, and held out his hand to grasp Cressy's young one. 'I was younger then!'

'Good grief!' exploded Milo, laughing. 'You're still young enough to bring *Crystal Rose* home through a hurricane, and mount a major rescue all by yourself as well! What more do you want?'

'*I want to come home*,' said Gramp. And there was such longing and sadness in his voice that Milo was frightened. He was afraid that if they didn't get the old man out of there soon, he would give up and die.

They went to see the doctors, — and took Stephen and Catherine with them to strengthen their argument. But the doctor in charge said seriously that Milo's grandfather was not yet well enough to go home. He needed rest and care.

'He could get rest and care at home,' said Milo obstinately.

'I could come over — ' began Catherine, and Milo looked at her in surprise. But neither Stephen nor Cressy seemed surprised at all. Catherine was thawing, — and Stephen did not forget the tears in her eyes that night in the harbour-master's office when the signal came through.

'Go and see him,' he said to her suddenly. 'Go and tell him what you've just said.'

'What, now?' Catherine sounded doubtful, — almost scared.

'Yes, now,' Stephen said, his voice gentle but insistent.

If she says she'll come over to care for him, thought Milo, Gramp will probably opt to stay in hospital! But though he smiled a little grimly, and caught a glimpse of the

379

same thought on Cressy's face, he did not say anything. Better let things take their course, — especially if it would help Gramp.

'We'll wait for you downstairs,' he said, and thanked the doctor politely for what he privately thought was probably the wrong decision, and then took Cressy by the hand again and led her away.

Stephen went with Catherine to the door into Gramp's ward, but he did not go in. He just smiled encouragement at a rather flustered Catherine, and waited quietly outside.

Catherine knew very well what she ought to say to Gramp, but she didn't know how to say it. How do you atone for four years of unremitting bitterness and reproach? . . . She almost tiptoed up to the bed, but when she saw him lying there, looking somehow so frail and tired and discouraged, she simply sat down beside him and took his gnarled old hand in hers. She was not a demonstrative woman at the best of times, and it was hard to find a way to tell him what she felt.

But Gramp was no fool. One glance had shown him the change in Catherine, — and he was much too wise and kind to let her make a fool of herself over him. 'Well, Catherine,' he said briskly, 'it seems I need patching up, — and so does *Crystal Rose*.

But you're right, you know, — I've only myself to blame!'

Catherine looked at him, and it was touch-and-go whether she would laugh or cry. There was so much to say — so much to apologise for — so much to be forgiven ... But in the end, tearfully and happily, she began to laugh. 'Oh Gramp! You old fraud! You knew I was talking over the top of my head all the time!'

'Yes,' admitted Gramp, a stern twinkle in his eye. 'But hurts have to come out somehow ... With me it was taking risks! With you it was blowing your top! ... What's the difference?'

And Catherine understood then that everything was all right between them — everything was forgiven and accepted and made good ... There was no need for any more words at all.

She bent down then and kissed her father-in-law, still laughing a little, and said: 'I shall never believe a word you say any more! ... And here have I just been telling the doctor I'd come over and keep an eye on you, if they'd let you go home!'

'That'll be the day!' said Gramp, chuckling. But laughing turned into a fit of coughing, and Catherine looked at him anxiously.

'You have a good rest,' she told him

severely. 'I'll come again tomorrow, and so will Milo.'

'Get along with you!' spluttered Gramp. 'You sound too good to be true!'

★ ★ ★

But all the same, they were all worried about Gramp, and they were worried about old Bo'sun, too. At first, with the excitement of coming home and seeing Milo and Cressy, the dog had been all wags and smiles. But when they took Gramp away in the ambulance, along with the sodden Spanish seamen, he had looked after the retreating vehicles very anxiously, and had even made a feeble attempt to follow them until Milo had put his arms round the wet, weary dog and lifted him bodily into the jeep and taken him home. Since then, the old dog had submitted to being cosseted and made a fuss of, and had laid rather limply and dejectedly on the floor of Cressy's room, wrapped cosily in blankets, — but though he still tried to wag his gratitude at their concern, his eyes kept turning towards the door where he hoped Gramp would walk through any minute now . . .

'It won't do,' said Milo, who knew how animals could pine and die when the one they loved was not there. 'He's fretting, and Gramp's fretting. We've got to do something about it.'

Cressy was sitting on the floor beside Bo'sun, stroking the tired golden head, and she lifted a concerned and anxious face towards the sound of Milo's voice. 'Yes, we have. And soon.'

Milo agreed that it ought to be soon, — but he detected an added urgency in Cressy's voice which puzzled him. 'Why *soon?*'

'Because I — I've got to go to London with Dad to see the specialist. And I can't go — I simply *can't* go with Gramp and Bo'sun like this.'

Milo took hold of Cressy's hand and pulled her to her feet. 'Why didn't you tell me?'

'Oh . . . because we were all so worried about Gramp . . . It didn't seem the right time.'

'*Cressy!*' Milo's voice had deepened suddenly. 'When could it ever be the wrong time to tell me anything?'

Cressy laughed, but she was a little shaken by his sudden gravity. She hesitated, looking down blindly to where the old dog still lay at her feet. 'Is he all right? . . . Let's walk along the shore. There are things to say.'

'Yes,' agreed Milo. 'There are for me, too.' And he led her out of the door and down the rope walk to the empty shore. Once there, with the soft sand under their feet and the sound of the sea close to Cressy's ears, they began to stroll slowly along together.

'What's on your mind?' asked Milo, when the silence had gone on long enough.

Cressy stopped walking, and turned her face earnestly towards him. 'You know I made Dad agree to come back here, no matter what the verdict, because I — '

'Because you need me,' said Milo firmly. 'Yes?'

'But, Milo, I don't want you to feel — trapped.'

'*Trapped?*' His voice was blank with disbelief.

'No, listen, Milo. *Please.* It's all very well . . . But there may be no real change in my eyes. It may be going to go on for ever.'

'So?' Milo sounded clipped and stern.

'So . . . I — I just wanted to let you off the hook,' Cressy said helplessly.

Milo began to laugh. 'But that was just what I was going to say.'

'Was it?' She reached out a hand to touch his face. 'Are you smiling?'

'Yes,' he told her. 'But I am serious, Cressy.'

'So am I,' she said, getting in first. 'And so I want you to promise me, Milo Trevelyan, that if you ever get tired of me, you'll tell me so.'

Milo took her by the shoulders and shook her. 'Don't be so silly!'

'No, Milo — *promise!*'

He sighed. 'All right — but you must do the same.'

Cressy began to laugh then, too. 'Who's being silly now?'

Milo shook her again, (but still gently.) 'I'm serious, Cressy . . . Try to understand. You're so young . . . All sorts of things may happen to you, and you'll meet all sorts of different people — especially if your sight comes back. You could go anywhere — all over the world! How can I — hold you back?'

'You couldn't hold me back if you tried, Milo,' she said, with supreme confidence. 'You are part of my life, and you can only increase it.' She drew a long, slow breath. 'Let's get it straight. I can't be coy or shy with you about things that really matter . . .' She took another shaky breath and dared to go on. 'You see, I shall always love you — and even if I did fall in love with someone else, I should still love you, too. And I should *tell* you. Is that enough?'

'More than enough,' said Milo, shaken. 'But — are you sure — if your sight returns, are you sure you'll want to come back here?'

'Of course I'm sure,' said Cressy, exasperated. 'Haven't you understood a word I've been saying? I want to be here — with you — as long as you want me to be here. And if you have to go away, I'll wait till you come back — just as you would wait for me. All right?'

'Oh Cressy!' groaned Milo. 'What am I to do with you!'

'Love me — just a *little*,' she said, smiling. 'It won't hurt!'

And Milo, unable to resist that flower-like upturned face, had to admit that it didn't hurt at all.

★ ★ ★

But loving Cressy didn't solve the problem of Gramp and Bo'sun, — however much it lit up Milo's day, and he knew they had to do something positive soon.

'The District Nurse!' he said. 'Alice Broadbent. She'll help. Let's get Stephen and Catherine. They can persuade her, — and she can persuade the hospital.'

So he and Cressy went in search of

Stephen. But when they got back to the cottage, Bo'sun had gone.

'He's probably gone to look for Gramp,' said Cressy.

'I expect we'll find him in Gramp's front garden,' Stephen added reassuringly, hearing the note of panic in Cressy's voice. 'Let's get Catherine and take the jeep.'

But when they got to Gramp's cottage in Port Quentin, there was no sign of Bo'sun.

'Could he . . . do you think he could try to find the hospital?' asked Cressy. 'Would he *know* where Gramp was?'

'He might,' said Milo, who knew you should never underestimate an animal's instincts.

'Let's get Alice Broadbent,' said Catherine practically, caught up in the urgency of the moment. 'If she's free, she'll come with us. I know she will . . . and maybe we'll find Bo'sun on the way.'

Allie Broadbent, the District Nurse, was free, — and she understood very well what was wrong with Gramp, and with Bo'sun, too. She knew them both well. 'He'd be better at home,' she agreed at once. 'Gramp's not the sort of man who can bear to lie about for too long. We can keep an eye on him, Catherine, you and I — and probably Hetty Longhurst will be glad to lend a hand. She's very fond of old Gramp.' She smiled cheerfully at Milo. 'you're right. He'll be much happier near his friends and his boats.'

'And the sea,' murmured Cressy, knowing somehow that this was the most important thing of all.

'Come on then,' said Allie. 'I'm game. We'll talk to the doctor together. I'll take my car as well, and follow you.'

Then they piled into the jeep again, and Allie followed them in her neat little Peugeot, and drove off along the coast road towards the town. And sure enough, before they had gone more than a mile, they saw ahead of them an old, tired dog padding along on sore, aching feet, looking neither to right nor left, — a fixed and urgent purpose in every line of his pointing head.

They stopped the jeep, and Allie pulled up behind them. Milo ran ahead to scoop Bo'sun up in his arms, but even then the dog tried to resist for a moment.

'It's all right,' Milo said to him. 'It's all right, old boy. We're going to fetch him home. Don't worry, we'll find him for you, — and bring him home!' and he put the weary dog in the back of the jeep, with Cressy (at her own insistence) beside him for reassurance. Then they went on in convoy to

388

the difficult interview with the doctor at the hospital.

But Allie Broadbent was a tower of strength. She was a rosy-cheeked, friendly soul, with an easy manner, but she could be extremely firm and strong when required. And she understood her charges in Port Quentin, and knew very well what they needed most.

'He will do better at home,' she insisted firmly to the doctor. 'Men like Gramp are like fish out of water in here. They start gasping for air, — and die on you without warning.' She smiled cheerfully at the doctor. 'You wouldn't want that, would you?' Her smile was beguiling, but there was steel behind it, and the doctor knew it. 'He can finish the course of antibiotics perfectly well at home,' she pointed out, 'and I can go in each day to keep an eye on him. That will do, won't it?'

'And we can all take turns and see that he rests,' put in Catherine, surprising even herself.

Allie saw the doctor, — who was really only doing his duty and what he thought was best for his patient — begin to protest, and added swiftly: 'He's threatening to discharge himself anyway. It would be better coming from you.'

'Well, — ' said the doctor doubtfully. But Allie knew she had won. (And she also knew that the hospital was always short of beds and glad to see a patient ready to go.)

'He'd better go with you, Allie,' said Stephen practically. 'I don't think he should come in the jeep, it's much too bumpy and draughty!'

'And we'd better let Bo'sun see that Gramp is actually coming home,' added Milo. 'Otherwise, he'll have a fit if he sees Gramp being driven off somewhere else!'

'He can come with us,' said Allie, laughing. 'My car is used to all kinds of passengers!'

So it was arranged, — and Gramp's face was so filled with relief and new energy when Milo told him that he had truly 'got him out of here' that even the conscientious doctor could see that it was the right thing to do.

The jeep party — consisting of Milo and Cressy with Stephen and Catherine, got back to Port Quentin first. Catherine went into the cottage to start up the old wood-burning stove, and Milo just had time to rush round the Hard and the harbour wall to tell Gramp's friends that he was coming home.

So when Gramp and Bo'sun arrived, with Allie in charge, there was a sizeable crowd of waving and cheering people lined up outside Gramp's front gate. 'Welcome home, Gramp-the-Champ!' they called. 'Welcome home!' 'Glad to see you back!' 'Now we can have a party!' . . . 'Welcome home!'

'That's better!' said Milo to Cressy. 'That's more like a hero's welcome! He'll be all right now.'

★ ★ ★

And then it was time for Cressy's trip up to London. Milo went up with them all in Catherine's jeep to offer what last minute support he could to Cressy, but she seemed calm and serene, and undismayed by whatever news she might have to face. As always, he was amazed and touched by her fortitude, and wondered if he could have faced the future with such steady courage and lack of fuss. He watched her go with doubt and fear and hope warring within him, and a desperate prayer almost coming out aloud as he begged: *Please God, let it be all right . . . Let her see again . . .* But he did not say anything except: 'I'll be here when you get back!'

And Cressy did not say anything either, — just hugged him hard and got into Stephen's car and allowed herself to be driven away. But when she had gone, Milo stood for a long time alone, looking after them, and wandered off along the cliff top by himself, leaving Catherine to take the jeep back on her own . . . There was too much to think about, too much to hope for — to pray for . . . He could not bear other people's company just now.

He came back down on to the shore at a different point on the rocks, and made his way slowly across the wet sands to where the sturdy little *Gannet* was back in her proper place. Automatically, he checked to see that the ropes were secure, and the drag-anchor firmly in the sand well above the tide-line. No chance now of a dangerous mistake . . . and no Cressy here either to take any unexpected risks . . . It all looked very normal and ordinary, — a placid scene with no alarming overtones.

He was just turning away, still feeling disturbed and anxious, when he suddenly noticed the bird perched on the *Gannet*'s blunt bows. The storm petrel was back! (Or was it the same one?) . . . At any rate, it was a storm petrel, and it sat there quite calmly, looking at him out of a beady eye.

'Is that you?' he said. 'Gramp said you were with him on the way home . . . ' He stood still for a moment, taking one huge, deep breath and summoning all his powers for one last prayer of hope. 'If you know how, bird, help my Cressy now! . . . I know you're a bird of omen, — but is it good or bad?'

The bird did not answer, but it bobbed its head and took a firmer grasp on the edge of *Gannet*'s bows with its tiny webbed feet. It did not seem in the least afraid.

And Milo went away and left it there, with no real lightening of the anxiety in his heart. But on his way back across the beach to the cottage, he suddenly changed his mind and decided to go over and see how Gramp was getting on. He had taken Cressy over to say a temporary goodbye to him and Bo'sun the evening before, but he hadn't been back there today yet, and he liked to keep a quiet watch on how his grandfather was doing, — and how Bo'sun was, too, for the old dog — like his master — still seemed very frail and tired after all his adventures.

He could cast a glance at the otters' pool as he went by, he told himself, for he had just released the male otter back into his own natural habitat, now that his injured leg had been declared mended by the friendly vet. So he took the back way along the inland cart-track that wound round to Port Quentin, and did his best to concentrate on the needs of his various animal friends, and stop fretting about Cressy and the ordeals and decisions ahead of her.

He stopped for a few moments by the pool, waiting hopefully for them to come out, and after a while they did appear, — father and mother joyfully together again, and the two kittens playing happily round them in and out of the water, across the gleaming wet boulders and under the waterfall. And at one point the male even stood up straight and looked across at Milo as if he was glad to see him, and Milo remembered that the vet had told him the animal had got very tame and friendly in captivity . . . 'Well, hello!' he said, smiling a little. 'You're all right then!' and he went on quietly past them, not wanting to disturb their cheerful play.

He was just rounding the last bend leading to the Port Quentin road when he almost stumbled on a golden-brown, motionless heap of fur lying across the track. 'Bo'sun?' he said, horrified. '*Bo'sun*? What are you doing out here?'

The old dog did not move, but when Milo stooped over him, the amber eyes opened and looked up at him, and the plumy tail made a feeble attempt at a welcoming wag. But the look in Bo'sun's eyes, Milo recognised, was one of helpless puzzlement. He didn't know quite where he was, or understand why his heavy limbs would no longer obey him. He had been going somewhere, trying to find someone, following someone in duty bound, as he knew he should . . . but he couldn't remember now who it was he was looking for, — or why he could not reach them.

But Milo knew. It was Cressy the old dog was trying to reach. And, being Milo, he understood the pulling loyalties that had driven Bo'sun to this last extremity. Now that Gramp was safe at home and getting better, Bo'sun reasoned in his doggy mind, maybe now he ought to be looking after Cressy again, as he had been told to do? . . . When Gramp was in danger, or taken away from him to a place he didn't know, he knew where he had to be — with Gramp, and no-one else. But now, Cressy had come to say 'goodbye' and was going away somewhere . . . He understood that word 'goodbye', and the threat of parting that went with it, and he did not like it . . . But what was he supposed to do? . . . In his tired and confused mind, he decided he had better go and look for Cressy and make sure she was all right. Then perhaps, his duty done, he could go back to Gramp and snooze by the fire . . . But he hadn't got there. He hadn't found Cressy. And now he could not even get up and go back to Gramp. He didn't know what to do now . . . He had somehow failed them all, and he didn't know where to go next.

But Milo knew. Back to Gramp he must go — and quickly. For if old Bo'sun was going to die, he had better do it at home, with the one he loved best beside him.

'You poor old boy,' he said, and lifted the heavy, weary body in his arms. 'Still trying to obey orders! . . . What a faithful dog you are!' and he hurried away, with as much speed as he dared, to bring Bo'sun back to Gramp before it was too late.

Gramp warned me, he thought, that too many new duties and responsibilities might be too much for him . . . He said the dog might be confused and torn with conflicting loyalties . . . Oh Bo'sun, what have we done to you?

But Bo'sun just lay in his arms and looked up at him, entirely tranquil and confident now that he knew Milo was taking him home to Gramp. His world would be whole and complete again soon, and he didn't care about anything else. Milo was taking him home to Gramp. That was all that mattered now.

When they reached the familiar corner, Gramp was already out in his garden, peering anxiously up and down the road, looking for his wandering dog. But as soon as he saw

Milo and his burden, he turned swiftly and went back to hold his own front door wide to let them go past him, and said no word until Milo had laid Bo'sun down on the warm wool rug by the fire.

Only then did Gramp say sadly: 'Where did you find him?'

'On the track to the Cove,' said Milo. 'I think he was going to look for Cressy.'

Gramp nodded slowly. 'Yes. He would be. I was safe, — but she was going away.'

Milo put a gentle hand on his grandfather's arm. 'He was doing his duty, Gramp, — as always. As you taught him. I never knew such a faithful old dog. But I'm afraid we asked too much of him.'

'Yes,' agreed Gramp. 'We all did. But he didn't grudge a single moment of it. Even on *Crystal Rose* he never even whimpered!' He sat down heavily in his chair, and leaned forward so that his hand could rest on the old dog's tired head. 'What can we do for him?' he asked, for Milo of all people knew best what could be done for a sick animal.

'Not much,' said Milo, aware that it was no good keeping the truth from Gramp. 'But I'll go and fetch my friend Alan, the vet, to see him. Can you hold on here alone?'

'Yes,' said Gramp. Where else should he and Bo'sun be but alone together, as they had so often been in the long years of loving companionship they had known?

'Keep your hand on him,' said Milo softly. 'He'll like to feel you there . . . I won't be long.' And he hurried off again, with long, swift strides, to find his friend the vet. It wouldn't be much use, he thought, for it was clear to him that Bo'sun's days were numbered, — but at least it might reassure Gramp that everything had been done that could be.

Alan the vet, when he came, was of the same opinion as Milo, and said so as gently and kindly as possible. He knew Gramp well — who didn't in Port Quentin? — and he knew the long years of devotion that lay between Gramp and his dog. 'His old heart is giving out,' he said. 'He's had a good long life, Gramp, and he's with you. That's what matters now . . . How old is he, exactly?'

'Fourteen,' said Gramp. He sighed, and his hand moved gently on the golden head and fondled the drooping ears. 'Yes . . . we've had some good years together. Things have been a bit fraught for him just lately, though. It's all been a bit too much for him.'

'I think it would have happened anyway,' said Alan sensibly, and still very kindly. 'That heart of his was already failing . . . He had come to the end of his natural span. You mustn't blame yourself.'

Gramp did not answer that. But he roused himself and asked, more practically: 'Is there anything we can do for him?'

Alan shook his head. 'He's not in pain now. I could give him a heart stimulant, but I don't think it would help much, — and it might even . . . hasten the end.' He smiled encouragingly at Gramp, and added gently: 'I think he'll just drift off to sleep, — and probably that's the best way.' He looked at Milo, and asked hopefully: 'You'll stay with him?'

'If Gramp wants me,' said Milo, uncertain whether his grandfather would really rather be left alone with his dog till the end.

'Yes, stay, Milo, will you?' said Gramp, coming out of a dark dream of his own. 'You understand Bo'sun as well as I do — and I could do with your company.'

The vet nodded, satisfied at least that Gramp would get some comfort, for he was going to need it. 'I don't think he'll last the night,' he said, but I'll come again tomorrow if you need me.' And he went off quietly, saddened, as always, by a patient he could not save, and an owner who would be grief-stricken by the loss of his old friend.

'Well,' said Gramp to Milo, trying to

summon up his old brisk way of dealing with emergencies, and signally failing. 'We've had many a night-watch, you and I, one way or another, what with your animals and my boats, — but this will be a long one . . . How about some tea?'

'I'll get it,' said Milo. 'Don't leave him. He still knows you're there.'

So he made tea — several times in the night — and they sat together, watching over their faithful companion. Bo'sun did not move very much, but his eyes were fixed on Gramp's face, and from time to time he managed another faint wag of his tail. His breathing grew quicker and shallower, and sometimes it seemed to hesitate and stop altogether, before plunging on again, like a faulty engine struggling to keep going. It hurt Gramp profoundly to hear that laboured breathing, but he could do little to help him, — only keep his hand close by, caressing the tired head as the long, slow moments ticked by.

But towards morning, with Gramp's hand still resting on his head, Bo'sun gave a great long sigh, as if relinquishing at last his frail hold on the world he knew, and turned his weary head close into Gramp's loving hand and fell asleep.

There was a long silence in the cottage,

and then Gramp said in a bleak, sad voice: 'He's gone.'

'Yes,' said Milo. 'To run about like a two-year-old in those Gladden Fields we're always hearing about.'

Gramp laughed a little. 'You're a good boy, Milo. I'm glad you were with me.'

'You mustn't grieve too much,' said Milo. 'He did what he wanted to do, every time. And he had what he wanted in the end — to be with you. He's all right now.'

Gramp nodded, swallowing tears, — and his hand still lingered on the quiet golden head. 'All right now . . . ' he repeated softly. 'God speed, Bo'sun — to those Gladden Fields!'

★ ★ ★

They buried him at the bottom of Gramp's garden, where the ground sloped down in sight of the sea, and the sea-birds sailed overhead, saluting him and calling to him in their far-away voices. And Hetty came with an armload of flowers, and some special plants to grow on his new green grave, — and the blacksmith who had made her wrought-iron gates sent Gramp a little plaque in an iron frame which said simply: *Bo'sun, faithful friend*,' — and they planted that too, at the head of his grave.

But when everything was done that could be, and things had settled down again, and Gramp was trying to get used to being alone, — Milo knew he must talk to his grandfather about the future, for it seemed to him that unless Gramp-the-Champ had some future to look forward to, he would fail to get well again, and decide — in his clear-sighted, ruthless way — to give up and follow his dog to those distant Gladden Fields . . . and that he must not do! . . . There had been enough tragedy, enough death and destruction in both his family and Cressy's, and it was time now to consider the living, — and to keep them all living, if Milo had his way!

So Milo decided to talk. And it had to be now, while Cressy was away with Stephen, and Catherine was busy cooking the lunch she was going to bring over to Gramp later on. 'Gramp,' he said, plunging straight in because he was rather frightened, 'I want to ask you something.'

'Yes?' Gramp looked at him suspiciously, hearing the note of urgency in his voice. 'What is it?'

'What are you planning to do — when you are better?'

Gramp stared at his grandson. 'Go back

402

to sea, I suppose. Why?'

'Two reasons, Gramp,' said Milo, marshalling his facts. 'One is, you've already had one heart attack, and the doctors have told you to take it easy for a bit . . . and the other is, you will be needed here.'

His grandfather looked surprised. '*Needed?* Who by?'

'By Cressy,' said Milo firmly. 'And Catherine.' He smiled at Gramp's astonished face, and added gently: 'Didn't you know? . . . They *both* need you, Gramp, — Cressy because you are wiser and older than Stephen or me, and can steer her through all kinds of stresses and strains, whether she gets her sight back or not, — and my mother, Catherine, because she needs someone to look after . . . She may think she is taking care of you, Gramp, but in fact you can take care of yourself perfectly well, you know that! Only, she *needs* to feel needed!'

Gramp laughed. 'You've got it all worked out very pat!'

Milo shook his head at him seriously. 'Gramp. I'm going away to university in the autumn. I shall be back, of course, and there are long vacations, but — but I can't be here all the time . . . and Cressy has decided she wants to stay down here, regardless of what happens to her eyes . . . And I — I'm worried about her being here without me, unless she's got you to turn to. And — and my mother, too, especially now that things are all right between you. She'll need you more than ever when I'm away . . . ' His voice failed him a little, — he was afraid he had said too much — or perhaps too little?

Gramp was silent, considering a lot of things in his mind, and admitting to himself that Milo was very clever, and knew exactly what he was doing. 'Shackles?' he said.

Milo grinned, and then gave a long rueful sigh. 'There are always shackles with people you care about.'

'You and Cressy — ?' began Gramp.

'Oh yes,' Milo told him. 'Why else do you think I'm binding you in the same chains?'

'I suppose . . . ' said Gramp carefully, 'I should be honoured . . . ?'

Milo let out a sudden shout of laughter. 'Oh Gramp! I might've known you wouldn't fail me!'

Gramp pretended to be cross. 'It's asking a lot, you know — though I must admit *Crystal Rose* is going to need a long re-fit . . . ' He glared at Milo.

'So are you!' retorted Milo, still laughing.

Gramp gave up sounding cross and shrugged nonchalantly. 'Oh well, I can always go crabbing!'

To his shame, Milo suddenly found tears in his eyes. He had expected a fight with Gramp about staying ashore. He had wanted most desperately to find a way to keep the old man safe and well and happy, and also to safeguard the other two people he loved, and instead of a fight, Gramp had instantly understood him, and instantly responded to his need. What a wise, generous old man he was!

'No chains in crabbing, Gramp,' he said, smiling through tear-dark eyes. 'Not even a trawl-net to catch you out! You'll be free as air!'

'But close in-shore,' said Gramp, — and it was a pledge, not a complaint.

They looked at each other and grinned happily. Nothing else needed to be said. But Gramp always liked to have the last word. 'As a matter of fact,' he admitted with a mischievous grin, 'it's rather nice to be needed!'

★ ★ ★

In London, Cressy's specialist was very kind and very thorough, and Cressy went through all the tests and scans again with stoical calm. Stephen, watching her, was amazed — as always — by her steady lack of fuss. But after all had been done that could be done, the verdict was very little different than before.

'I can detect a little more sensitivity to light,' said the kind voice. 'But *very* little . . . I don't think I can promise anything . . . But the two brief flashes of blue may indicate that something is happening, — that the healing process is working . . . ' He sighed. 'But I can't be sure. I wish I could be more positive.'

Cressy sighed, too. 'Never mind,' she said sadly. 'I can wait.'

Wait and see. That was what they always said, she thought. (And I wish they could be more positive, too!) Well, I *will* wait. And *see*?

'It could happen quite suddenly,' the specialist added. 'Especially after a head injury. I have known cases which — ' But he broke off and added in a quiet and grieving voice, 'but I don't want to raise your hopes too soon.'

Too soon? thought Cressy. What is *too soon*? But she did not protest or argue. What was the use? With touching and unconscious dignity, she got to her feet and reached for her stick. 'Well,' she said steadily, 'we'll just have to wait a bit longer, won't we?' And she turned and made for the door with Stephen beside her.

She went then, as she had promised, to see her first doctor friend at the hospital, young doctor Euan Morris, and told him all about the specialist's verdict, and the flashes of blue that she had seen in Cornwall. 'As a matter of fact, it seemed to make it harder, not easier,' she told him. 'I mean, before it had been *all* dark, and now — I didn't know what to think . . . ' She turned her head in his direction and smiled. 'You told me once that hope could be a terrible thing to live with, — and I begin to understand you now.'

'But you are still being patient,' contradicted Euan, letting the smile show in his voice. 'Everything you have said so far tells me that you are. And what's more, I detect a certain . . . confidence in you now, as if you've got some sort of support or comfort down there in Cornwall. Have you?'

'Oh, how clever you are!' glowed Cressy. 'Yes, I have! I'm terribly lucky . . . And he will support me and comfort me always, — whatever happens.'

Euan Morris looked at Cressy's radiant face and smiled more openly, somehow enormously reassured by her evident happiness.

'You are indeed lucky,' he said. 'But so, I think, is your young man. Is he young?'

'Oh yes,' Cressy laughed. 'Young and

probably good-looking, though I can't see him now. But I could when he was twelve, and he was handsome even then! . . . And he's wizard with animals, — well, with all injured and frightened creatures, really, including me . . . and his grandfather, Gramp, is just like him, only older!'

Dr. Euan laughed. 'You sound as if you've struck gold. I'm so glad, Cressy. And will they be there when you get back?'

'Yes!' she almost sang her answer. 'He'll be there . . . They'll be there. We've made a sort of — kind of pact to be there for each other . . . and I'm sure it will last!'

She sounded so supremely confident and happy that Euan's kind heart ached a little for her. It was wonderful to be so young and so certain of another human being's infallibility! But he did not say so. Let her be happy while she could. There might yet be a long way to go before her darkness lifted — if it ever did.

But aloud he only said: 'Thank you for coming to see me, Cressy, and for telling me all this. Do you know, I think you are the one who is dispensing hope to me!'

Cressy laughed. 'Am I? Then that must be a good thing! I should think doctors need hope more than anyone!'

That is certainly true, thought Dr. Euan.

And oh, how I hope this child does get her heart's desire — whether it is her sight or her young love by the sea.

Cressy got up to go then, and Dr. Euan gave her an extra warm hug round the shoulders as she left, saying: 'Come again, won't you? Good news or bad, I'll always be glad to see you.'

'I will,' Cressy said gaily. 'But I think it will be good news, anyway, — one way or another!'

And she went out to find Stephen who was waiting patiently for her in the hall.

The last person she went to see before she went home to Cornwall was Florrie of the deplorable carpet slippers and the important bird table. She found her, as usual, sitting on one of her own shabby chairs, watching the world go by, and when she saw Cressy coming, she let out a cheerful whoop of delight.

'So it's you, is it? How are things then, Cressy? Still got your stick, I see.' Thus, perfunctorily, she dismissed all talk of blindness and hope or no hope. 'Did you hear any more of that bird?'

Cressy turned her head, almost as if she wanted to look at Florrie's face. She seemed uncannily aware of the events surrounding Cressy's new life.

'Yes, I did,' she said. 'It's funny you should ask, because I was coming to tell you.' And she did tell her, all that Gramp and Milo had related to her about the little storm petrel, and added at the end: 'And Gramp said she was back there on his boat, *Crystal Rose*, in the middle of the storm, and she seemed to see him home safely almost into port, and then she was gone.'

'Hmph,' said Florrie. 'More to that bird than meets the eye. Is she a good omen, do you think, or a bad one?'

'Oh, good!' said Cressy, still bubbling with inner radiance. 'You've no idea how my life has changed since I went back to Crocker's Cove . . . and met Milo and Gramp again.'

'I can see it's changed you,' said Florrie. 'You look a hundred per cent happier, and lots more confident. What have they done to you down there?'

'Just . . . let me find my own way,' said Cressy, and then, daring all things to kind old Florrie, 'and — and loved me a little.'

'Is that Milo or Gramp?' asked Florrie shrewdly.

Cressy laughed. 'Both, I hope . . . At any rate, I love *them* both . . . and I think my father, Stephen, is getting quite fond of Catherine, though she's still a bit prickly.'

'Sounds like a hedgehog,' snorted Florrie.

But Cressy laughed again. 'Oh no, that's Milo's prerogative, hedgehogs!' Then she grew serious for a moment. 'Florrie, — am I really too young to know what love is?'

'No,' said Florrie roundly. 'You are not. I don't think one ever is too young, — or too old! . . . But you may not know *all* about it yet, you know! There's lots to learn!'

'Oh, I know,' said Cressy humbly. 'And I'll go on learning till the day I die. But — but — but I am right to hold on to what I've got now, aren't I?'

'So long as he wants to be held on to as well, — ' Florrie said sagely, 'I should think you are. Have you asked him?'

'Yes, I have.'

'And what did he say?'

'He said that was just what he was going to ask me!'

They both chuckled together, and then Florrie said: 'It sounds to me as if you've got a good one there, Cressy. Yes, hold on to him, I say!'

And when Cressy got up to go, old Florrie put her arms round her and gave her a smacking kiss. 'I know now that things will work out for you,' she said happily. 'But let me know if the bird comes back!'

'I will,' said Cressy, and almost danced away up the path she knew so well. And though Stephen was waiting for her at the top, he did not go down to meet her. He let her come to him, free and unguided. This was one place where she did not need guidance. But he also knew she was not yet ready — might never be ready — to return to the house where he and Sally and she had once been so happy. No, Crocker's Cove and the comforting sea was best for Cressy now. And Milo, of course . . . Especially now that the verdict on her eyes was still the same.

* * *

Milo was waiting at the bottom of the cliff path when they came back. Cressy had told him not to come up, she would rather walk down to him, with Stephen beside her. Blind or seeing, she wanted to come down the cliff under her own steam, independent and self-reliant, as ever.

But when Milo saw her coming, and the white stick was still tapping its way in front of her, he felt his heart clench with pity and sorrow. It was no good. The visit to London had made no difference. Cressy's eyes were still sightless, and the long, slow waiting game would still have to go on. He watched her steady, gallant progress, step after careful step on the rough cliff path, head held high, her slight form poised and taut, refusing to be afraid, to give way to too much caution. And Stephen, her father, holding her other hand, and guarding her against every unseen hazard . . . And the ache inside Milo grew to such an intensity of pain that he could scarcely bear it.

How I love her, he thought. So brave and so enduring! I would die for her if it would help! . . . But he knew it wouldn't help at all. Cressy would laugh at him. What would I do without you? she would say. Dying is no good. We've got to live!

He was still half-dazed with disappointment, and trying to dispel the dazzle of tears in his eyes, when he saw Cressy stumble. It was only a momentary slip, — a false step on a stone that rolled under her foot, but she seemed to fall slightly sideways and hit her head a glancing blow on the rock-face that bordered the path. He saw her stagger a little and drop her stick, and put up one hand to her head, as if suddenly confused and out of balance. And he thought he saw, then, the flutter of wings from a small bird who seemed to have been disturbed by Cressy's sudden fall against the rock . . . The bird seemed to fly up, almost into her face, and then hover for a moment above her head before it flew away towards the sea. And then Stephen put an arm round Cressy's shoulders to steady her, and waited for her to recover her balance.

But Milo didn't wait to see any more. He simply leapt from the sand on to the bottom step of the cliff path, and raced up the rocky slope to reach her before she fell again. He arrived, breathless and anxious, but Cressy was standing quite still, head lifted, staring out above her head to where the flying bird had gone, as if transfixed by the view below her.

Transfixed? To Cressy, the slight blow on her head had meant very little, except a small, sharp pain behind her eyes which was quickly gone, and then a curious, widening sense of space and light which seemed to grow brighter and brighter behind the darkness of her sightless eyes . . . It seemed to be dissolving the opaque darkness into skeins of mist which curled and divided, and parted like veils, one behind the other, drifting further and further, widening and opening, layer after layer, so that the faint radiance filtering through the parting veils of grey mist became brighter and ever brighter, and suddenly burst into sight in a glory of marvellous light.

And there, below her, was the whole round bowl of Crocker's Cove, with the sea spread out before her in a curve of brilliant, dazzling, vivid gentian blue, and the huge, wide ocean beyond an even deeper blue, and the sky above her head equally clear and deep and equally, dazzlingly, summer-day blue. The whole new world before her eyes seemed to sing with blue . . .

'It's blue!' she cried. 'The sea is *blue*!' She flung up her arms, as if she would embrace the whole new world before her eyes. *'Behold, the sea itself!'* she cried, remembering Vaughan Williams and the Sea Symphony and Walt Whitman's words, and all that she had always loved about the sea.

Then she noticed that Milo was wearing a bright blue shirt, and so was her father, — and this so touched her that there were suddenly tears in her eyes. Both of them waiting and hoping that one day, some day, she would be able to see them . . . And she could! She could see the two people she loved most, — both of them wearing blue for her sake! And they looked as she knew they would look — as she remembered they had always looked — loving and smiling, and now at this moment full of incredulous joy . . .

She turned again to the view before her, and she could see the sea, and it was blue, and the sky was blue, and the world was

alive again before her eyes, singing with blue!
. . . A shining miracle of light and colour and
lovely living things.

'Dad!' she cried. 'Milo! I can see! . . . And
the whole wide world is *blue!*'

And below her, between air and water,
the first wild living creature she saw was a
small, swift bird, beating away on tireless
wings across the blue sea towards the deep
blue ocean and the limitless blue horizon
beyond.

THE END

We do hope that you have enjoyed reading this large print book.

Did you know that all of our titles are available for purchase?

We publish a wide range of high quality large print books including:
Romances, Mysteries, Classics
General Fiction
Non Fiction and Westerns

Special interest titles available in large print are:
The Little Oxford Dictionary
Music Book
Song Book
Hymn Book
Service Book

Also available from us courtesy of Oxford University Press:
Young Readers' Dictionary
(large print edition)
Young Readers' Thesaurus
(large print edition)

For further information or a free brochure, please contact us at:
Ulverscroft Large Print Books Ltd.,
The Green, Bradgate Road, Anstey,
Leicester, LE7 7FU, England.
Tel: (00 44) 0116 236 4325
Fax: (00 44) 0116 234 0205

TALES FROM THE ANIMAL HOSPITAL

David Grant

Vet David Grant has become a familiar face to millions of viewers of ANIMAL HOSPITAL. Based at the RSPCA Harmsworth hospital, where he is veterinary director, the television series has proved a huge success. Now David re-lives the stories of the animals featured in the programmes, as well as telling what happened to them after the cameras were switched off. He also takes the reader behind the scenes at this busy hospital as he describes his day, the kind of routine problems a vet faces and the emergencies that regularly come through the door.